Praise for Barbara D'Amato

"D'Amato keeps her characters and her readers constantly on their toes." —*Chicago Tribune*

"D'Amato is not only artful with historical setting, but also creates complex and believable human beings that live in the mind's eye. . . . Makes for almost compulsive reading." —*Chicago Sun-Times* on *Good Cop, Bad Cop*

"Along with her talent for dreaming up wild, whiz-bang climaxes, Ms. D'Amato has a talent for creating refreshingly complex characters." —*The Baltimore Sun*

"[D'Amato's] standards are high, as this gripping, streetwise novel clearly proves." —*Publishers Weekly* on *Good Cop, Bad Cop*

"D'Amato's stories are hard-hitting . . . . y, and wise." —*. . . . . oklist*

"All of D'Am . . . . e: a lightning-fast pl . . . . ped clues, and an ea . . . . *Help Me Please*

Praise for Jeanne M. Dams

"Ms. Dams serves up genre conventions with as much relish as if they had come fresh from the garden, and, despite her familiarity, Dorothy is a dear." —*The New York Times Book Review* on the Dorothy Martin series

"Dams brilliantly crafts a mystery that defies the usual category."
—*Chicago Sun-Times*

Praise for Mark Zubro

"Edgy, tense storytelling . . . heart-wrenchingly realistic. The reader can't rip through the pages fast enough."
—*San Francisco Bay Times* on
One Dead Drag Queen

"The plot moves at a fast enough pace to satisfy even the most impatient murder mystery fan. A delightful book that'll bring readers back, wanting other Zubro sleuthers."
—*Booklist* on
The Principal Cause of Death

FOOLPROOF

Barbara D'Amato
Jeanne M. Dams
and Mark Zubro

FORGE®

A TOM DOHERTY ASSOCIATES BOOK   NEW YORK

This is a work of fiction. All of the characters, organizations, and events portrayed in this novel are either products of the authors' imaginations or are used fictitiously.

FOOLPROOF

Copyright © 2009 by Barbara D'Amato, Jeanne M. Dams, and Mark Zubro

A Forge Book
Published by Tom Doherty Associates, LLC
175 Fifth Avenue
New York, NY 10010

www.tor-forge.com

Forge® is a registered trademark of Tom Doherty Associates, LLC.

ISBN 978-0-7653-6442-5

Forge books may be purchased for educational, business, or promotional use. For information on bulk purchases, please contact Macmillan Corporate and Premium Sales Department at 1-800-221-7945, extension 5442, or write special markets@macmillan.com.

First Edition: December 2009
First Mass Market Edition: November 2013

Printed in the United States of America

0 9 8 7 6 5 4 3 2 1

To *chocolatiers* everywhere, whose artistry keeps Mark, Jeanne, Barbara, Daniel, and Brenda happy and productive

ACKNOWLEDGMENTS

Our thanks to Susan Gleason, literary agent, whose advice improved the book.

And to James Schaefer, Paul D'Amato, and William Bachman, who gave us technical advice and help with computer questions.

The executive power shall be vested in a President of the United States of America. He shall hold his office during the term of four years . . .

CONSTITUTION OF THE UNITED STATES OF AMERICA, ARTICLE II, SECTION 1

The Tuesday next after the 1st Monday in November . . . is established as the day for the election . . .

UNITED STATES CODE, TITLE 2, CHAPTER 1, PARAGRAPH 7

FOOLPROOF

CHAPTER 1

"One decaf mochacchino with a sprinkle of cinnamon," Daniel said.

Brenda said, "That's pitiful. The only decent coffee is fully leaded espresso with just a dash of caramel. Total bliss. Trust me."

"I'm having decaf. Sorry."

"Decaf!" Brenda rolled her eyes. "You might as well open your mouth and let the moon shine in."

"Yeah, well."

Brenda shrugged and shook her head in mock despair. She and Daniel played this game all the time. They met here for coffee nearly every morning before going to work. He ordered something different each time, but never her caramel espresso.

Brenda turned toward the attractive young man

behind the counter and said, "And we'll get six large regulars for all the boring-coffee people in our office."

"It'll be a minute," said the man. "Name?"

"Grant," said Brenda, at the same moment Daniel said, "Henderson." They both giggled, as did the barista.

Daniel eyed the young man with interest. He was new on the job and a little slow getting the orders up, but very hot-looking, with short blond hair and well-muscled shoulders in his mocha brown Brew-Ha-Ha shirt. Daniel raised his eyebrows when he caught Brenda also ogling the young man. Today it looked like Brenda had won, as the young man gave her a smile of enormous sweetness. Brenda, however, was really out of the running. Her romance with Jeremy Caringella, one of the founders of their young Internet security company, was on the verge of getting very serious indeed. Daniel, who lived alone, wasn't much into casual pickups, either. It was just fun.

Before Brenda and Daniel could take the byplay much further, their coffee was ready, nestled in two elegant tan fiberboard holder-trays. Blond-and-Gorgeous had pushed the trays along the counter to the cashier, who was even now ringing up the order.

The Brew-Ha-Ha's outdoor banner read, The Best Coffee on this Block. The boast was in fact not modest, because this was coffee row, with five shops, two on this side of Duane Street and three on the other. Two were major brands. One of the others billed itself as The Best Coffee in New York, and another as World's Best.

It was Daniel's turn to pay. Then he and Brenda stepped outside.

Although it wasn't even nine a.m., the mid-September sun was warm. Brenda uttered a sigh of bliss and held her face up to the yellow light. She leaned back against the building and took a sip of her espresso.

Daniel said, "Come on, let's go."

"I grew up in New Hampshire, Danny. We had long winters. We learned to grab all the sun we could get."

"Sure. But we've got the boss's coffee here."

"It's gonna be cold for a long time, real soon."

"And so's the boss's coffee."

Daniel and Brenda were not nearly as subservient to the boss as Daniel implied. Both were considered top guns in CGI, a Manhattan firm specializing in corporate computer security, with large offices in the north tower of the World Trade Center. They were the youngest specialists in the office, but possibly the best.

Brenda took another sip out of her cardboard cup. "I need my caffeine before I can go anywhere."

"I've gotta meet with Timothy on the firewall program. It's buggy."

"A couple more minutes won't matter. Technically, nobody has to get to work before nine."

"Oh, for heaven's sake, Brenda. They've all been there since seven."

"Okay, okay!" She shoved her coffee back into the tray Daniel held, but his grip had relaxed and she nearly tipped the whole thing on him. "Gee, sorry," she said.

"No, my fault. I wasn't looking. I was watching that plane. Look, isn't it awfully low?"

"Oh, my god!"

Daniel immediately phoned the boss, Eric, in their offices in the north tower but reached his assistant, Melanie. They talked maybe two minutes before Eric came on the line and said the elevators weren't working, so they couldn't get down. "But we seem okay here."

"The building's supposed to be fireproof," Daniel said.

"Yeah. The fire department's on the way."

"I hear them already."

"Well . . . if the fire's confined to a couple of lower floors . . ." Eric said he wanted to call his wife to let her know he was okay. Then he'd ring Daniel back. Brenda had tried to phone Jeremy, who had probably been at the office for an hour or two already, but he didn't answer.

Daniel and Brenda ran to the World Trade Center, where WTC security people were gathering on the sidewalk. She and Daniel knew several of them.

"Are all the elevators really dead?" Daniel asked one of the guards from their building.

"Yep. Always are, in a fire."

"But . . . our friends are in there, and besides, we need to evacuate documents."

"You and everybody else," said the guard. His voice wasn't unkind, just weary.

By now firefighters were carrying packs into the building. "How come they get elevators?" Daniel asked.

"They don't. They're walking up the stairwells."

"Fifty floors?"

Brenda started to say, "Well, if they can—" but then she stepped back and pulled Daniel back too. Seeing the firemen carrying heavy loads on their backs, she and Daniel realized that blocking the path was worse than stupid. The two of them moved even farther away, craning their necks, trying to see their floor, the seventy-sixth. With a building that tall, above a certain point there was no way of telling which floor was which. But Eric was right that the fire and rolling smoke were coming from well below their floor. Thank god.

By then it was 9:03.

There was a growing roar, a shriek from the crowd. A plane was approaching from the west. A jumbo jet. Far too low. Déjà vu, but it couldn't really be happening a second time. The crash into the north tower had been a hideous accident, hadn't it?

The plane kept coming and coming, not swerving—unbelievably, not swerving to avoid the huge building in its path.

It lumbered in slow motion, but of course not really slow motion at all. And kept coming. And hit the south tower with such force that flames and fuel and pieces flew right through the huge structure and out the other side.

Eric phoned. "Did that noise . . . was that another plane?"

"Yes."

"And it hit the south tower?"

"Yeah, Eric, it did."

"I called home." His wife wasn't there. He'd left a message. They couldn't get down the stairs, but they were going to wait for the fire to burn itself out or be put out by firefighters.

"Where's Jeremy?" Brenda shouted over the bedlam.

"Right here."

Jeremy picked up Eric's phone as Daniel handed his to Brenda.

"Brenda! What do you see down there?"

She tried to keep the fear out of her voice. "The firemen are on their way up, love. Are you all right?"

"It's getting hot. The smoke is getting thick. We may try to go up a floor."

"Yes, do that!"

"I've got to give Eric back his phone now. He needs to call home."

"Where's your phone?"

"I don't know. We can't see much."

"All right." She paused. "I love you," she whispered.

"Me, too. I mean . . . Oh. Here's Eric. Bye."

Eric came back on.

Now Brenda and Daniel saw bodies falling from the north tower. Eric would not be able to see them, thank god. He was above the fire, and the smoke would cut off his view. Their offices were so high up that when Daniel and Brenda had looked out their windows, people walking on the streets had just looked like dots. But Eric and Jeremy might be able to see if people jumped from the south tower. They might even see the jumpers on the television news. Brenda hoped that nobody up there was watching television. Maybe the reporters had not picked up on the catastrophe yet, she thought.

Fat chance.

"Is there any fire on our floor?" Daniel asked Eric.

"No. Lots of smoke, though. I guess if it gets worse we can go to the roof. Helicopters could pick us up."

"That's right."

"We're under attack, aren't we?" Eric said flatly. "Two planes is no accident."

"I guess so. Did you see the other plane?" Daniel knew their offices faced the side of the south tower away from where the plane hit.

"No, but we see the flames coming out."

"Dan, from out there, how bad does the fire look?" Eric asked. His voice was steady, but like a steel wire, thin and tight.

"Bad on three floors," Daniel said. "No fire above that."

Brenda trembled. Daniel had tears in his eyes. After a pause, Eric said, "I've got to call my wife again."

"Sure," Daniel said.

Brenda and Daniel didn't want to watch and yet couldn't look away. Emergency personnel and fire trucks, fire chiefs' cars, pumpers—every kind of fire vehicle either one of them had ever seen—pushed into the streets and the plaza. Pumpers couldn't put water higher than a few floors. Brenda thought the ladders reached only as high as the fifth floor; none of the fire-fighters were even trying to deploy them. Hopeless, obviously.

Daniel and Brenda were forced back a block by the trucks and hoses, but stayed within sight of the buildings. Media vans pulled up but couldn't get close because of the clots of fire equipment. Surely there were sprinkler systems that would put out the fire. And of course it wouldn't spread up the stairs. There was nothing combustible, was there? Their friends would be all right if they just stayed put.

9:15 . . . 9:30. Sirens filled the air. Daniel and Brenda stood with their arms around each other's waists, clutching so hard it would have hurt if they'd been aware of anything but what was happening a block away. Leaving would feel like abandoning their friends. Staying made them feel totally helpless. They stayed.

Their cell phones didn't ring. Human forms now fell from both buildings. More emergency vans arrived, and Daniel and Brenda moved back another half block. They took up a position on Duane Street, which had a view of the World Trade Center.

9:59.

It was a hallucination. It was not believable. What made the building look so—

It had to be an illusion that the south tower was shrinking. Then Daniel said, "*Oh, god, no!*" and she knew it was no illusion. Slowly, and then in an acceleration of smoke, dust, and sound, the south tower collapsed. Within seconds, a steel-gray killer cloud rolled toward them.

Daniel grabbed Brenda by the hand and they ran. Down two blocks. Then two blocks east. Around an old graveyard and past a church. Finally, coughing and half blind from dust, they sagged down on the side of the church that was in the lee of the dust storm. Tears coursed down their cheeks, leaving trails in the grime. Neither of them noticed.

The day was suddenly dirty brown, but they saw, through the dense particulate haze, huge white snow-flakes spinning and sliding lazily in the fog.

"What is that white stuff?" Daniel said.

"I don't know . . . Yes, I do. It's paper. Thousands of sheets of paper."

Daniel's cell phone rang. He held the earpiece at right angles to his head, so that Brenda, placing her head against his, could hear too.

"Dan!" Eric's voice was shrill. "Dan! Can you see what's going on?"

Daniel glanced sideways at Brenda, then said, "Uh, sort of." There was no way Eric or the others at the top of the north tower could know how thick the smoke and dust were at ground level.

"Did it really . . . uh . . . Dan, did it really fall?"

"Yeah, Eric." He pulled the phone back. They both knew what Eric would ask. Brenda shook her head just slightly, and Dan, to be certain, covered the mouthpiece and whispered, "Play it down?"

Brenda nodded.

"Dan! Are you there?"

"I'm here, Eric."

"Does this mean our tower will fall, too?"

"No. I don't think so. The south tower was hit later and fell very soon. You must have been hit by a smaller plane." It hadn't really looked that way, but Daniel wanted to believe it.

"Really?"

"But if you can get down, you should."

"We can't get down! All the stairwells are full of smoke. We've closed all the doors to try to keep the smoke out."

"Then you've done the right things."

"Well," Eric said very softly, "I'm going to try my wife again. She's not in her office and she's not at home, and . . . now that I think of it, I guess I'll call my daughter. She's in kindergarten. Usually, they don't put through calls from home. But maybe in this case, do you think they would?"

"I'm sure of it, Eric."

Eric in his haste hung up without saying good-bye.

"Is Jeremy there?" Brenda asked, trying not to sob.

"No, Eric hung up."

Brenda didn't say anything. "We should get out of here," Daniel said.

"I don't think I can run anymore. Even sitting still, I'm out of breath." She coughed.

And they didn't really want to get farther away.

They didn't know what was happening to Manhattan, didn't know whether it was any safer anywhere else. Plus leaving their friends was too hard. So they were waiting.

A few minutes later—or an eternity—at 10:28, there was a roar that went on and on and on, and the sky turned black.

CHAPTER 2

Sarah Swettenham hesitated in the doorway of AllTech. Little known except among the computer companies that used its highly specialized software, AllTech was a large company located in the techy/light-manufacturing district west of Eighth Avenue. Ordinarily, leaving work was a letdown for Sarah, almost as if she were being forced to go home. She ought to enjoy time away, but in fact she didn't. Sarah felt more alive at her keyboard than anywhere else.

Not that she didn't have plenty of computing power at home. That was what she spent most of her salary on. New electronic gear. Faster modems, clickier keyboards, wireless mice, zip drives. When she couldn't find what she needed, she made it. She'd even built her own high-end motherboard.

But her job was real, a life. At home she didn't have much life at all. She might be writing code at both places, but the fact that she had nothing else to do was apparent only when she was at home. At work she got nothing but respect. Anything too difficult for other programmers landed on her desk. When there was a major project, or a supersecret one like the one she had recently finished, it was Sarah they picked to head it up. She would dole out pieces of it to her team, but masterminding it was her job—sometimes a worrisome job. But when she got back to her apartment building, she was just frumpy, dumpy Sarah, who lived upstairs on the second floor and never had any visitors.

Today was different. Today she was feeling energized, ready to forget her misgivings about that job. For a couple of weeks she'd been receiving e-mail at work from someone who signed himself "A Secret Friend." At first she thought his compliments had to do with her having finished her latest project right on time, though the messages didn't say so specifically. They said things like "You're so brilliant" or "They don't pay enough for the wonderful work you do."

The last three days, however, the e-mails had changed. Monday's message was "I see you every day. I like your style."

Tuesday's was "Your conservative dress style sets off your inner beauty."

Today's was "I want to meet you outside work. How about Parotti's at six tonight?"

With her heart thumping, Sarah answered, "Okay." That was all she typed, but it took her half an hour of staring at her screen before she got up the nerve to hit Send.

Of course, this hadn't left her any time to go home and get dressed in something better-looking. She wore Levi's and a shirt, a typical computer nerd outfit. Thank goodness it was one of her prettier shirts, a deep purple that she thought went well with her hair. At least it made her light mousy brown hair look a bit more golden.

Parotti's was supposed to be a fun place. She hadn't actually ever been inside, but she'd heard about it around the coffee machine. Overheard people talking about it to each other—not to her, of course.

At five minutes of six, Sarah left the office. This was much earlier than usual. Ordinarily she stayed on and worked well into the evening. What was there to go home for? Several other engineers often worked late too, and they'd say good-night to Sarah when they parted on the sidewalk. But they weren't really friends. Now, as she joined the crowd of early home-goers at the elevator, she noticed some sidelong glances cast in her direction. Her coworkers were wondering why she was leaving early. No one was quite rude enough to ask whether she actually had something to do after work, but she knew they were thinking it. She put a small smile on her face and stepped briskly into the elevator when it arrived.

She couldn't help scanning the men who got on with her. One of them might be her Secret Friend.

The building where AllTech was located was well west of the high-rent district. While the CEO's office suite and the upper-level management's and p.r. reps' offices were luxurious, the programmers' and engineers' cubicles were simply functional. Sarah's was bigger than most, because she supervised entire projects, but it was still functional, not fancy. The AllTech lobby on the main floor was marble and looked prosperous. The building, though, was basically an old garment-district warehouse. Twelve floors faced with brick, it occupied a quarter block. The square footage was what the company had wanted.

This location, west of anything trendy, presented Sarah with a five-block walk to Parotti's. No problem. Like most New Yorkers, she always walked when the distance was less than a couple of miles.

As she covered the five blocks, Sarah passed through three distinct neighborhoods. There was warehouse/manufacturing, then middle-class housing, then upper-class housing and trendy restaurants. The warehouse and middle-class housing areas were separated by a very narrow strip of tiny delis and meat markets or groceries, the latter displaying their wares on tables outside.

Parotti's was even more sophisticated than she had expected. She stopped, intimidated, in the entryway, then was swept toward the hostess by six or seven people who entered after her. The hostess had all the great things that Sarah didn't have: cheekbones, an hourglass body, legs that went on forever. And long ash-blond hair. She looked at Sarah with kindness, which was horrible, and said, "May I help you?"

"Uh, I'm waiting for somebody."

"Let me seat you at the bar."

The bar was polished zinc. The rows and rows of bottles behind were lit by neon tubes of pink and azure. Behind Sarah was a dining room that was entirely mirrored, including the ceiling. As a result, it looked a thousand feet deep. "Disorienting—in a good way," Sarah mumbled to herself, trying to keep a sense of emotional balance.

Beyond this room, she could see part of another room angled away behind the bar, a room that glowed red. Sarah wanted to get up and look inside, but her need to appear sophisticated prevented her from moving.

A bartender dressed in azure pants and a white billowy shirt appeared. "All alone?" he asked, as of course she was.

"I'm waiting for somebody." Since he kept standing there, she added, "I'll have a Chablis."

"Of course," he said with a small sneer, as if, naturally, she would have Chablis. Too late, she realized that Chablis was probably the ultimate in triteness. Unless maybe you gave the name of a specific vineyard. But she didn't know any. Oh hell!

Sarah had considered when she received the e-mail that maybe the invitation was a joke. Maybe her Secret Friend never intended to meet her. Maybe some people from work were in Parotti's right here and now, watching her wait, saying things like "As if a guy is going to take her out!" or "She sure fell for it!" She'd had a couple of horrible experiences in high school when some of the popular girls told her one of the popular guys wanted to ask her out. By college she had learned not to fall for that.

She peered between the bottles, trying to see in the mirror behind the bar whether any faces at the tables behind her looked familiar. No, not that she could tell, but the view was fragmented. Certainly she was not going to turn around.

Since there had been no name on the e-mail, there was no implication that the guy was especially hunky or even popular. It didn't claim to come from Andy Torrence, for instance, who looked like Brad

Pitt on his best day. Or from John Foulkes, who was rich.

It was seven after six. She had arrived right on time. That was probably a mistake. It showed she was too eager. It wasn't sophisticated to be on time, was it? What would have been sophisticated? Ten minutes late? Half an hour? Surely half an hour late would be too much.

Maybe the Secret Friend was planning to tease her by standing her up. Leave her here, waiting. How long should she wait before she looked like a fool?

The bartender came by with the white wine, slipping it in front of her as he passed. Obviously he was not interested in chatting her up.

Six-twelve. With tiny, tiny sips and lots of pauses, Sarah could make this wine last half an hour. Would that look ridiculous? Probably. She could drink it relatively slowly, taking up fifteen minutes, and then leave. That was the thing to do. It would look like she had just stopped in for a glass of wine before going home. The only people she had told she was meeting someone were the hostess and the bartender. No one else would know she'd been stood up.

What was she worrying about? She could go to any damn restaurant she pleased and order a glass of wine! She didn't have to prove anything to anybody. Anyway, nobody would be watching her. Don't get self-conscious, she told herself. Or paranoid. Nobody was keeping score. Nobody was paying any attention to her at all.

And that was just the trouble, wasn't it?

"Oh, for heaven's sake," she whispered to herself. "Get a grip." Then silently she gave herself an order to stop feeling sorry for herself. She was healthy, not exactly wealthy, and maybe not always wise, but smart enough to have a great job.

Six-twenty. One more swallow and the wine would be gone; then she'd pay the bill and escape.

"There you are!"

The tallish man appeared to be in his early thirties. His blond hair was quite long, and he wore schoolteacher-ish glasses. She was sure she had never seen him before.

"I'm really, really sorry, Sarah," he said. "I didn't mean to be late."

Not bad, Sarah thought. Not very muscular. Dark eyes. Dark eyes are good on a man. Never understood the appeal of light blue eyes. Nose too large. I'm not sure I like the earring. Dressed okay otherwise.

Then Sarah realized what she was doing by being mildly critical of him. She was protecting herself against future disappointment. Which was silly. Truly lame. He had approached her, hadn't he? By running down his appearance, she was warding off the knowledge that he was really very good-looking. Automatically, her first thought had been, too good-looking for me.

Actually, he's almost a hunk. A hunk who thinks I'm okay. Why shouldn't he? I'm smart; I'm good at what I do. She giggled. This is good. This is very good.

As she started to speak, he held up his hand. "I know we haven't met. I'm Todd Levenger, and I'm not from your department. I'm in Adhesives."

Sarah recognized Adhesives as part of the chemical research wing for assembly and design. "I've seen you in the hall and the lobby," he said. "I'm sorry I'm late. We had some solvent catch fire. Nothing serious, really."

He threw a ten-dollar bill on the bar. "Let's blow this pop stand. I know of a really good restaurant where they have really good white wine."

"Okay." Sarah laughed and stood up.

"And even better Chianti," Todd continued.

"An Italian restaurant, then?" Sarah asked.

"Ah. That's very good. Your deductive skills are almost the equal of your code-writing skills."

They hurried out of Parotti's, Sarah laughing, trying to keep up with Todd, who headed crosstown with long strides. The crowds were thicker as they got to Seventh Avenue. Everybody and his brother was heading home, Sarah thought.

They ran across Forty-seventh Street at Seventh Avenue just before the light changed. The TKTS booth was down the street. "The restaurant is beyond TKTS," Todd said, pointing, while downtown-bound traffic picked up speed and thundered past.

"Right about there," he added, as she looked and he pushed her into the oncoming traffic.

"Help!" he yelled. "That woman fell!"

A taxi hit Sarah square on the side, and she bounced off the bumper. The driver screeched on his brakes and swerved, crashing into a Jeep Cherokee to his left. The bus following the taxi struck Sarah in the small of the back, rolling her under its wheels while her legs and arms flopped bonelessly.

By now a Saturn had run into the taxi, and the whole of Seventh Avenue came to a halt. Two women and an elderly man rushed to help Sarah, who showed no signs of responding. A dozen people milled around, gaping at the accident. More arrived from the sidewalk.

Todd shook his head sadly and moved away. Nobody looked at him.

He went a couple of blocks farther, then into a subway entrance. In a restroom, he pulled a gray and white plastic bag with a running-shoe logo on it out of his pocket, then removed the wig of longish blond hair, under which was a very short haircut, barely enough hair to show that it was dark brown. He took off the glasses and stuffed them and the wig in the plastic bag.

Then he left the subway by a different staircase.

CHAPTER 3

Six blocks north of where Sarah Swettenham lay, Brenda Grant was talking with her last client of the day. He had insisted on an after–five thirty meeting "in order to finish my paperwork first."

"The problem is, your solutions cost money," said the man in the glen plaid suit. He looked pointedly around the well-appointed conference room, plainly implying that DB Security didn't need to worry about money.

Brenda didn't think the client had big money troubles either. "Mr. Claymore, you came to us. I've spent two days now inspecting your buses and talking with the drivers."

"Well, you've certainly done your part. I'm not saying that."

"You wanted an assessment of how safe your buses are." Brenda patted the report he had just read. His company, Safety Bus, was a small but exclusive firm that ferried preschool children to private nursery schools around Manhattan.

"We have a companion in every bus, besides the driver, and seat belts for every child—"

Sighing at the thought that he might go through the company's entire brochure, she interrupted. "That's very good. I am appalled that most school buses don't have seat belts. But they won't keep terrorists or kidnappers away. They won't stop a hijacking."

"Our drivers carry cell phones—"

"Mr. Claymore, your buses need a silent alarm, accessible to the driver, that would alert both your company and the police simultaneously. You need a deadman switch on every bus that cuts off the engine, shuts the doors, and activates an alarm if the driver is injured or killed. Or if he slumps past a certain point. It's all in the report."

Mr. Claymore all but wrung his hands at the thought of the cost.

"It's not that expensive, Mr. Claymore. You need faster door closers, for example. Things like that can be implemented quite quickly at reasonable prices. And you need that security more than most bus companies do. After all, you carry children of diplomats, CEOs, UN officials—"

"The finest families in New York trust their children to Safety Bus."

By the time Brenda walked Mr. Claymore through the quietly elegant lobby, he seemed to be getting used to the idea of spending money on security. He said, "Our next brochure might mention the steps we've taken. 'Your child's safety is our profoundest concern.' Something like that."

"Well, don't be too specific, Mr. Claymore. Terrorists read brochures too."

As Claymore left, wide-eyed but apparently resolute, Brenda exchanged a glance with the receptionist, Helen Gruner. "Meant to tell you. Nice hair," Helen said.

"I'm not sure it really works," said Brenda.

Helen shook her head, sighing patiently.

Brenda had decided the previous evening to go strawberry blonde. She changed her hair color the way Helen changed boyfriends, every week or so. Partly she liked the small energy rush from that glimpse of a stranger in the mirror. Partly she thought that if anyone was following her, maybe targeting her, this minor difference might give her three or four seconds' warning. A look of doubt in a person's eyes . . . ?

No, she wasn't paranoid. That was the kind of world it was, ever since 9/11.

CHAPTER 4

The front door slammed back against the wall. Daniel staggered in, pushing the door closed with his foot. In his hands he balanced two boxes, each a foot and a half square.

"Ho, ho, what's this?" Nate asked, coming out of the living room.

"You know how you say I never get you anything?"

"You don't."

"Never bring you flowers? Never buy you candy?"

"Well, there was that box of Raisinets at the Mets game."

"Now I've bought you something."

Nate inspected the boxes. They were glossy pasteboard, solid and crisp-sounding when he tapped one. They were dark blue, with a thin white line around the edges and the name of an expensive clothing store in raised white glossy letters.

"One for you, one for me," Daniel said.

"Angel food cakes?"

"You're no angel."

"Am too. Lightweight bowling balls?"

"Please!"

"Pet tarantulas in their own cages?"

"Open it. Put me out of my misery. Here. This one is yours."

Nate slit the shiny white sticker that held the box closed. He lifted out a white cowboy hat. "Stetson!" he exclaimed, reading the label on the inside band.

Meanwhile, Daniel had taken his out too. It was black. "Wool Stetsons," he said. "You know how you always say I'm built like a cowboy. Yours is called the Rancher and mine is the Silver Saddle. Why silver when it's black, I have no idea."

"So you see me as the good guy in the white hat and yourself as the bad guy in the black hat?"

Daniel gave him a devilish grin.

"I'm really, really touched," Nate said. He put his arms around Daniel. They bumped hats and laughed.

"Maybe we could wear these tomorrow night," Nate suggested. "The Giants are playing the Cowboys. Want to go? One of the guys at the station has a couple of tickets he's trying to get rid of, and we'd fit right in, looking like this."

"Right. Sitting on the Giants' side. We'd be lucky if getting booed was the worst thing that happened to us. Anyway, though, I can't. I leave first thing in the morning for Atlanta, and I won't be back for a couple of days at least."

"And by that time I'll be on duty." Nate took off

his hat. "I wish you didn't have to spend so much time away." He twirled the hat on one finger and didn't look at Daniel.

"Hey, me spend time away? You're gone for twenty-four hours straight every three days, week in, week out. Do I complain?"

"Yeah," said Nate. "All the time."

"Well, but you know it's just because I miss you. I'm not serious, not really. I know you have to do it. It's your job."

"Umm." Nate went back to twirling his hat.

"So what's really wrong? Hey, it isn't the hat, is it? You don't think it looks silly or something?"

Nate sighed and put the hat back on his head. "It's great. Nicest hat I've ever had. It's just . . . your sister called while you were out, and that nephew of yours is still missing. What if he shows up while you're gone?"

Daniel sighed in turn. "Why would he do that? Last time he was here, he acted like he was going to catch cooties from us or something. He's a grade A homophobe. If he'd known you were living here, he wouldn't have come. So now that he knows . . ."

"I'm not gonna bet on that." Nate looked morose. "He's a grade A little shit, is what he is. I can see him turning up anytime, if only to make trouble."

"He's back with his Wisconsin buddies by now."

"He said that was where he was going when he blew out of here, and that was weeks ago. And your sister says he's not there. We don't know if he left New York at all. He's been e-mailing you, hasn't he?"

"Hey!" Daniel was starting to get ticked. The evening wasn't going at all the way he'd planned. "You haven't been reading my e-mail, have you?"

"What do you think? Would I do a thing like that?

No, I can just tell when you've heard from him. You mope and get even touchier than usual. Listen, Daniel, I know he's your sister's kid and all, but he's a rebel and a gay basher and a lazy good-for-nothing. And the worst thing is he upsets you. I'm serious. I don't want him around."

"You're worried because he upsets me?" Daniel's snit evaporated. "Hey, that is so sweet. You're a hell of a guy, you know?"

"I know. And good-looking, too. Specially in this hat."

They reached out their hands to each other.

"No time for mushy stuff," said Nate, reluctantly pulling away. "Brenda is due in half an hour."

Daniel and Brenda played chess once a week, job demands permitting. Tonight's match was at Daniel's place. He wasn't playing as well as usual.

"I guess my mind was wandering," he said.

"Oh, snort! You've just lost fair and square, that's all."

Nate loomed over the board. Each chess evening ended with a dessert, and the dessert was always chocolate.

"I haven't quite lost yet," Daniel said.

"I've got you in a classic zugzwang."

"What's a zugzwang?" asked Nate. He thought chess was a waste of time, but was too polite, or too kind, to say so. He liked to see the friendship between these two. Daniel had few friends, and Brenda was good for him.

Daniel and Nate had met shortly after 9/11.

Daniel and Brenda had inherited a large part of the tech company they had been working for. Of the three partners who had founded and owned CGI, Simon Laird was survived by a wife, and Eric Helfers by a wife and children; Jeremy Caringella, Brenda's almost fiancé, was single with no living parents, no family whatsoever. If he and Brenda had become engaged, possibly he would have left his share of the company to her, but he had made a will a couple of years before and not changed it. At the age of thirty-four, who expects to die? His will left his sizable estate to the employees of the firm, to be divided equally, share and share alike, among management, secretaries, maintenance people, and computer engineers.

But there weren't any. No janitors or secretaries or programmers were left alive except Daniel and Brenda and two other employees, the only people who had survived that day, out of an office employing sixty-five. One of the two, a programmer named Oklu Kebede, had been out with the flu on 9/11. He called Brenda a week later, when the bridges and tunnels were reopened, and said he never wanted to see New York again. They had an address for him in Grand Rapids, Michigan, and the attorney had sent him the money, but no one had heard from him since. The other employee, Harlan Boucher, was a repair guy. He had been away from the office on 9/11 because his mother, much to his embarrassment at the time, was having a baby. "At the age of forty-two. Sheesh!" he had said. But after 9/11 he felt quite different about the new little life.

So Daniel, Brenda, Oklu Kebede, and Harlan Boucher had a huge estate to be divided among them.

Daniel and Brenda had been friends for years, but that didn't answer the question: what were they going to do with the rest of their lives?

"I've been thinking a lot. I know what we should do," Daniel had said. "We'll take the money, you and me and Harlan, and start our own company."

"Wait, I know what you're going to say."

"Yeah?"

"A security company with a hidden agenda: terrorism detection and prevention."

It had been a huge risk, starting a company. And more than the financial risk, they were aware that lots of people who had been good friends became enemies when they had to deal with the stresses of a business. They had built in as many defenses against that as they could, holding a just-the-two-of-them once a week and even alternating jobs. Brenda would be CEO for two years, and Daniel president. Then they would switch. So far, it had worked.

B renda studied the chessboard. "See, Nate, I haven't checkmated him yet. But he's trapped. Any move he makes now, he's mated. That's a zugzwang."

"Say, Daniel, I think I'll get you in a zugzwang, buddy," Nate said.

Miming high dudgeon, Daniel said, "How about that dessert?"

"How come you're such a great cook, Nate?" Brenda asked.

"All firemen can cook. It's a tradition."

"What are we having tonight?" She and Nate were engaged in a friendly competition—how much chocolate they could work into one single, reasonably legitimate dessert. Last week she had made chocolate mousse with bits of black-black bitter chocolate stirred in.

"Chocolate-frosted brownies with cocoa whipped cream."

"Oooh. Cocoa whipped cream. That's an elegant solution."

"Challenges. Always challenges," said Daniel.

A pleasant break, Brenda thought, from the never-ending tensions at work. She didn't say it aloud, but over their dessert she caught Dan's eye. She thought he was thinking the same thing.

CHAPTER 5

Thursday, October 16
New York City
Nineteen Days before the Presidential Election

Helen's desk looked ordinary from the public side. From Helen's side it was somewhat different. She had two monitors, a large and a small one. The large one, part of a system they were beta testing for a client, showed an infrared picture of the person who entered the door. If the IFRSUUTI—Infrared Face Recognition System Using Uncooled Thermal Imagery (which DB Security Consultants predictably pronounced "iffersooti")—recognized the face of the man or woman who had just entered, it froze the picture and displayed the name. If it did not, it ran a rudimentary body scan, intended to find any object that blocked the sensor's "view" of the thermal field of the body, an object like a knife, gun, Kevlar body armor, or a pack of explosives. Or unfortunately, a Snickers bar, a pack of playing cards, or a cell phone.

Brenda ducked briefly behind the desk, seeing her face as a blob on the screen in different shades of green, and the name Brenda Grant beneath it.

DB Security had little use for IFRSUUTI. There were thirty-eight employees in the New York office, including eight top people, and everyone knew everyone else. Clients occasionally came to the office, but almost none without an appointment and a thorough background check. People did not just walk in off the street.

DB had security systems, of course. That was, on one level, what the company was about. A lens mounted behind one of the many holes in the distressed finish of Helen's oak desk connected to an old but efficient video recorder. Motion sensitive, it switched on only when an object in its field moved. Also, a disaster dial in Helen's pen tray would automatically and silently turn on warning lights in all the offices if it heard a preselected combination of words. This month Helen was using the innocuous if ditzy-sounding phrase, "Oh, my, my, my!" She hadn't tested it yet, but she planned to combine it with an energetic patting of her cheek, as if hot, for verisimilitude.

Nobody unwanted was likely to get into the DB offices. But the IFRSUUTI, if redundant, was certainly interesting. So far they had found no bugs in it, although Brenda thought it was way more expensive than it needed to be. The gadget included an IR camera which was mounted three feet above Helen's head, next to a hanging plant. The basic invention had been used first in medical diagnosis. What it did was read the pattern of skin temperature—in this case, of the face. Each person's face pattern was based on where and how close to the surface the blood vessels ran, so the picture was hot over the carotids and cool at the forehead and end of the nose. The pattern was as unique as a fingerprint. The important part of the gadgetry was the recognition algorithm that actually identified the face from its arterial structure.

Brenda studied her face on the screen. The thing was much more accurate than she and Daniel had expected it to be. They had tried to fool it for a couple of weeks. Helen had an acquaintance she swore looked exactly like her. She brought her into the office one day, and Brenda was amazed at the resemblance. She had almost said, "Hi, Helen, did you cut your hair?" before she realized it wasn't Helen. But the IFRSUUTI wasn't fooled for an instant.

Now Helen pointed at Brenda's infrared picture and said, "Hmm. Your face is all steamed up. New boyfriend?"

Brenda ignored her. Helen knew perfectly well that a blush wouldn't affect IFRSUUTI. She also knew Brenda didn't have a romantic interest, but she kept pushing her to find one. Helen had been hired five years ago, and while she knew that Daniel and Brenda had worked for a company in the World Trade Center, she didn't realize that Brenda had been in love with one of the people who died. Other than Dan, few people had known about the relationship between Brenda and Jeremy. And Brenda wasn't going to talk about it. It was dead, it was past, and the memory was too painful. But Helen meant well. Brenda grinned and said, "Gosh, I've lost count."

Helen shook her head and went back to her work.

With an undergraduate major in physics and a master's in social statistics, she was much more tech-sophisticated than she acted. At forty-one she was a little older than most of the employees. She did serve as receptionist, but her real job was to head a three-person team specializing in vetting people. Their success was one of the skills for which DB was justly famous. Her second monitor, a conventional one, was the one she stared at most of the day, checking out people's resumés for clients. She found lots of lies and inconsistencies. Often they were nothing more sinister than a little padding by a person overeager to get the job. Sometimes they were perpetrated by garden-variety crooks. Sometimes, though, Helen and her team found pointers to potential terrorists who wanted to work their way into sensitive positions.

Brenda was still musing about the IFRSUUTI. "What if I had a life-size black-and-white print made of that?" she said to Helen now, pointing to her own face on the screen. "Then, say I printed it out on some semitransparent film so the hot spots would be more transparent than the cool ones . . ."

Helen waited patiently.

"Then I carried an infrared source—anything warm, like a red light bulb maybe—behind it. Would the machine think it was me?"

"Hey, try it. But you're not going to get into any well-staffed office with a sheet of film in front of your face."

"Well, a company might use it as a security device in unstaffed entryways. Like, have it ring an alarm if it doesn't recognize somebody and let the others in." She'd try it. In her experience the companies that developed these things did a superb job on the hardware and the software supporting it, but had a blind spot for simple human ideas for thwarting the technology. Most techies weren't people-oriented enough to predict what weird things ordinary people might do. One of Brenda's great strengths in her work was an ability to think outside the technical box.

What if she carried a sheet of warmed plastic—?

Wait a minute! Turn the question around. Suppose you were a known employee and didn't want to be recognized by the company IFRSUUTI. Suppose you were disguised enough to fool humans—longer hair, mustache, makeup, whatever—but not enough to fool the machine. If you held ice cubes to certain parts of your face for a minute or so before you walked in—

Helen said, "This is funny."

"What is?"

"Well, not funny exactly. Peculiar. Actually, it's sad."

"Don't make me beg."

"A woman called yesterday for an appointment with you. So I gave her six p.m. It's the one hour you haven't blocked out today."

"So?"

"She's dead. Hit by a taxi." Helen spread the paper out on the desk.

WOMAN KILLED BY BUS, TAXI

Sarah Marie Swettenham, 32, was struck and killed by a city bus and a taxicab Wednesday as she attempted to cross Broadway at 47th Street. An investigation into the accident is ongoing.

Observers told police that Ms. Swettenham stepped from the curb and into the path of traffic. No citations were issued at the scene.

Ms. Swettenham was employed as a computer engineer at AllTech Systems in the city, a manufacturer of computer software. She is survived by her parents and two cousins.

"She was a very popular employee," said Garth Kennick, vice president for human resources at AllTech.

"Sarah Swettenham!" Brenda said. "I knew her!"

"Of course you did. She said that when she made the appointment."

"I haven't seen her in years. We were in college together. Some of the same computer classes. But she wasn't a close friend."

"She just said she knew you from a while back, so she thought you'd see her. I told her your schedule was pretty full."

"Did she say why she wanted to see me?"

"No. Just that she wanted to ask your advice."

"That's odd. She never seemed to be the kind of person who needed advice. She was a little standoffish. Although maybe it was shyness. Did she say whether it was a professional question?"

"That was absolutely all she said. You want me to play back the call?" DB recorded every call that came in. And the date, time, and phone number, of course. You never knew.

"No. Maybe later. I've got a full day. I'd better get started."

Brenda spent a couple of hours telephoning four of their twelve satellite offices in turn, the ones located in time zones where it was still office hours. She started with the farthest away, the ones that would close for the evening soon. She would stay up very late Sunday night and call the ones on the other side of the world, where it would already be Monday. Despite e-mail and fax, she liked to chat in person with the office supervisors at least once every two weeks, finding out about issues that could turn into big problems later. She nibbled on a stale doughnut and sipped pretty good office coffee.

After the phone calls, Brenda dug into a pile of paperwork. By eleven she had half cleared her desk, in between three appointments, one of which was an interview with the CEO of a Fortune 500 company who wanted a complete evaluation of its protections against industrial espionage.

She found her mind kept going back to Sarah Swettenham.

There was something tantalizing about an old friend—even an old acquaintance—you hadn't seen in a while. You wondered what had become of them. Whether your perception of them at the time you knew them had been accurate. That must be the appeal of class reunions.

As she passed through the firm's lobby on her way to an early lunch appointment with a major client, she said to Helen, "Could you do a little backgrounding on Sarah Swettenham, Helen?"

"Heh, heh." Helen leaned back in her chair and waved a hand tipped with blush-pink enameled fingernails. "I did her already."

After lunch, Brenda started down the carpeted hall to her office, stretching her back as she walked. The large corner room was appropriate to her status as CEO, but she was often hit by a small shock when she entered it and realized she was now the boss.

The office itself was entirely functional, with oak parquet floors and no rugs, so she could wheel her desk chair all over it, back and forth to the banks of three keyboards, a fax, copiers, printers, and large monitors. Four large windows, two on the right wall as you entered the room and two directly ahead, gave a wide view of Manhattan.

To the north and east.

When Brenda and Daniel had first decided they were going to pursue anti-terrorist activities, they were smart enough to realize they needed additional skills. So they went through an arduous program of training in unarmed combat, among other esoteric disciplines. They learned at least a smattering of most of the languages they thought they might need, including Arabic. Daniel had gone on to secretive, armed combat instruction and exercises. Some of those experiences had been harrowing enough that Brenda had, at one point, wondered if they would ever be happy again.

But when the training was over, nearly seven years ago, and they felt confident of their ability to take on whatever came their way, they had started searching for office space. They looked at more than forty possibilities. A few days into the search, Brenda had realized Daniel kept coming up with various reasons for rejecting any offices with a southwest exposure. And she was doing the same. Southwest was where the World Trade Center had stood. Neither of them had said a word about why those office spaces weren't right. They just kept looking. A north view. An east view. Nothing that showed them lower Manhattan.

Sometimes when she looked out the window, she saw them anyway. The two immense towers crumbling, her world crumbling with them.

CHAPTER 6

Thursday, October 16
Nineteen Days before the Presidential Election

Daniel and Brenda met most days, at least briefly, to talk about the day's business. But Daniel had left that morning to go out of town on a job, so Brenda decided to catch up on the work piled on her desk. She sat down and zapped on her office television. TV watching wasn't an executive perk, nor was it a waste of time. Keeping current was part of her job. She caught the twelve-thirty news.

The carefully coiffed anchorwoman said, "—dential candidate Governor Evan Harkinnon blasted President Roger Kierkstra at a rally in Moline, Illinois, last night, calling Kierkstra a 'do-nothing president and second-rate substitute for deceased President John Miller.'" Helping the viewer who might have spent the last year under a rock, she went on: "President Miller's untimely death from a coronary thrombosis last May propelled then vice president Roger Kierkstra into the presidency."

"Duh," said Brenda to the TV.

The equally well-coiffed anchorman said, "That's right, Sandra. And President Kierkstra, trailing by as much as eight percentage points in major polls conducted over the weekend, is vulnerable to such attacks as a result of the discovery last week that three known terrorists on the prohibited list entered the United States through LaGuardia Airport and vanished into the country."

"The body-recognition system that might have prevented such a lapse has been waiting for the president's signature since July, Bob."

Bob gave a one-second pause to signify a slight alteration in topic. "With only a little over six weeks to go before the ballot, the race is heating up. President Kierkstra met with leaders of industry at a breakfast fund-raiser in Minneapolis this morning."

"Minnesota, Governor Harkinnon's home state, is considered a swing state this year, Bob," Sandra said. "President Kierkstra accuses the Democratic challenger of engaging in negative campaign tactics. Meanwhile, Citizens for Harkinnon have been buying time for television spots claiming the president has funneled contributions from industry in excess of the monies permitted by campaign finance reform."

"As we move into the final weeks of the campaign, many officials are still expressing concern about electronic ballots. Bill Bryant has this report from Cleveland. . . ."

Brenda glanced at the man standing in front of an official-looking building. Courthouse? Image of a courthouse projected in a studio? Nothing was real anymore. "... voter anxiety about the use of computers to vote. We sampled some opinions."

A man appeared on the screen, probably in his sixties, wearing a baseball cap featuring the Cleveland Indians logo. "Don't know how to use a computer. Don't want to know how. A good old paper ballot is plenty good enough for me."

"Right," Brenda murmured. "If the nineteenth century ever comes back." She looked back down at her desk. Lots to do tomorrow. Resumés to look at. An unusually large expense item from the Hong Kong office.

The reporter in Cleveland was back. "... over the 2004 election, in which fraud was widely alleged, though never proved. Officials here have assured us that the new systems have been extensively tested and are guaranteed safe and foolproof. They predict that the election will run smoothly. Back to you, Sandra."

"Well, we'll see, won't we, Bob?"

Bob said, "A recent flurry of polls shows the president's postconvention bounce, which took him to an apparent dead heat with Harkinnon, is fading."

Sandra said, "Kierkstra campaign spokesman Randall Shaw spoke to our Michael Damon earlier today at the White House." The picture changed to the front lawn of the White House and a silver-haired man. Shaw said, "We are pleased with the response to the president. Every venue where the president has appeared shows cheering crowds, and what's more important, Michael, well-informed voters who know what this campaign is all about. They understand what's important here: national security, the economy, and stability—"

Brenda sighed and changed channels. On Channel 5 was Randall Shaw in a studio, saying, "The voters know what's important. Stability, security—"

Brenda muted the TV and switched the channel to CNN so that she could work and watch the streaming news at the same time. It was just more of the same-old, same-old. Posturing politicians in Washington, Boston, and Los Angeles. A threatened strike in the NFL. Hurricane warnings going up along the Texas Gulf Coast. An oil field blown up in Iraq. Brenda shuddered at that one. Then politicians again.

Brenda considered herself politically an independent. She had very much admired President John Morgan Miller, a Republican from Virginia. He had seemed to her an honest man, straightforward and courageous, who had made some hard decisions about national security. But Kierkstra, who was from South Dakota, had been chosen as Miller's vice president to balance the ticket geographically. Kierkstra had a bad reputation in his home state. Rumors of influence-peddling followed him everywhere, and his few months as president had further divided the people of the United States on major issues, even though he had claimed to want to build consensus. By contrast, Governor Harkinnon, the Democratic candidate, looked like a good man to Brenda. He was a little bit scholarly, not given to overstatement or rabble-rousing. His political views were clearly expressed. She might not agree with every single thing he said, but she thought he wasn't just taking positions for political advantage. Nor was he apt to sway with every breeze generated by the spin doctors.

Harkinnon was the "green" candidate, worried about the degradation of the environment. Like the deceased President Miller, Harkinnon pushed in his home state for the development of alternative sources of energy. There were windmill farms all over Minnesota now, and he had urged geothermal, solar, and tidal power to governors whose states had the appropriate resources. Kierkstra was considered a friend of Big Oil.

Brenda hoped Kierkstra might, if elected, be effective in dealing with terrorism. But her hopes were not high. The problem was gargantuan, as she had good reason to know. Just look at that oil-field holocaust. And the other one, the one in New York that no one would ever forget . . .

She put 9/11 firmly out of her mind and picked up a stack of expense vouchers. At random intervals she dipped into the accounting and checked in detail one full day's expenses at one of their twelve offices. She trusted her people. She trusted her accountant. She did it anyway.

In the afternoon, her next task was to read all the resumés, including a couple of late ones Human Resources had just sent up. She settled on one for an interview, a guy named Malcolm Dudley. His name was a little strange—it sounded to Brenda like an English village—but his qualifications were excellent. She told Helen to set up an interview, and then tried to get back to work. But all afternoon, while Brenda should have been working on other things, Sarah's name kept coming into her head. She tried to tell herself that she was simply curious, not exactly suspicious in any well-founded sense. Well, all right, suspicious. But that was because of the work she did. It came with the job to look for hidden causes of apparent coincidences.

And why was it a coincidence anyway? Maybe Sarah had seen Brenda on the street somewhere and decided to renew their friendship. After all, they worked in the same city, less than twenty blocks apart.

Well, why wouldn't she have just called or e-mailed? Making an appointment seemed overly formal.

So maybe Sarah had had a problem at work. Maybe she had wanted to leave AllTech and had wanted to interview at DB Security. That was possible.

And then jumped in front of a bus?

If she had been very unhappy at work, would she have been suicidal?

Brenda tried to remember Sarah from college. She had been what Brenda's mother would have called "a serious little person." But they were all serious little persons, all the girls who were good at math and computers. The boys outnumbered the girls in the field by a lot, and the girls wanted so badly to be taken seriously.

Brenda brought up Helen's data, simply labeled "Sarah Swettenham," in its own file. Yes, Sarah had straight As in college. Better than perfect, in fact—a 4.17 grade-point average, indicating a good many grades of A+.

She'd known Sarah only slightly, but she had never thought her the type to commit suicide. Still, you never knew. Some of the most unlikely people, given sufficient provocation . . . she scrolled further into the info Helen had sniffed out.

The police report on the accident was brief. Brenda had never heard the names of the two reporting officers. With eighteen thousand cops in New York, why would she?

There were four eyewitness statements. The first, a

woman named Anna Hunter, was noted as an FWH (which Brenda translated as female white Hispanic), lived on Ninety-seventh street, and had been on her way to work as a bartender at the Grand Hyatt. Ms. Hunter said that Sarah had "stumbled" into the street. An MW improbably named Arthur Arthur said she had "leaped" into the street. The other two, an FBH and an FW, both said she had tripped. It was a nice cross-section of New York citizens, Brenda thought.

None of the witnesses had noticed anyone with Sarah or anyone running away from the scene. All four had admitted, in various words, that there had been a "big bunch" of people on the corner at the time.

Other than that, there was just the paramedics' statement, which said that Sarah was dead when they arrived. They were required to transport anyway, and apparently started an IV, but they knew she was dead. According to the doctors at St. Francis, she had internal injuries which would have killed her quickly, except that she had died even more quickly of a broken neck.

The drivers of the taxi and the bus were not ticketed. Neither appeared to have been speeding. Brenda assumed that the taxi driver had not been speeding only because there was too much traffic ahead of him. There almost always was.

Brenda chewed on the end of her pen. She would enter her notes in the computer, not on paper with the pen, but you couldn't chew on a keyboard.

After some thought she put in a call to Billie Moldova, one of several detectives she knew. Billie was one of those women with a golden touch for all humanity. Everybody liked her. They even put up with her love of antique slang. Billie had moved through a dozen precincts around Manhattan in the fifteen years she had been a patrol cop, then a detective. She didn't work in the One Eight, where Sarah had been killed, but she would certainly know someone who did.

"Zowie, it's Brenda," Billie said. "When are you gonna teach me to snoop electronically? I'm getting too long in the tooth to run around the streets."

"You love it."

"Oh, well, in another ten years though? Gotta be up to speed."

"Can you find out about an accident for me?"

Billie took the brief facts Brenda gave her. Brenda did not explain that she already had the police reports on the case and the witness statements. Billie probably didn't want to know just how porous the NYPD computer system was. Brenda had done favors for Billie in the past on several cases where Billie needed cybersearches the department couldn't or wouldn't undertake, and Billie was always willing to return the favor.

Brenda said, "All I really want is your take on how it smells."

"You thinking she was pushed?"

"I just plain don't know."

"Will do. Well, twenty-three skiddoo."

"What does *that* mean?"

"I have no idea."

The interoffice line rang. Malcolm Dudley had arrived for his interview.

T wo hours later, Brenda was deep into another project, an analysis of the protection of the medical records of a hospital that was quite sure it had been hacked, when Billie called back.

"I know one of the two guys workin' the case. Bracco," she said.

"Not the other one? I'm disappointed."

"She's new."

"Oh, well, in that case . . ."

"But not so new that she doesn't have opinions."

"Tell me."

"Bracco says it doesn't smell funny to him. His view is you never know what people will do. Cameletti—this is weird because she's the new kid on the block—says it doesn't make sense to her. She says you don't run through a group of people, even if you're in a hurry. Especially if you're in a hurry, you go around. That lets out accident. And you don't go leaping through a crowd to commit suicide either."

"Unfortunately, I agree with both Bracco and Cameletti."

"Me too. Except in a way . . . well, Cameletti is female, like Sarah, and about the same age. So it might be she has a better sense of what Sarah would do."

"True. Anybody see anybody with Sarah?"

"Not that they admit to. In New York it's a miracle that four people stayed long enough to talk to the cops."

CHAPTER 7

Friday, October 17
Eighteen Days before the Presidential Election

"Sarah's parents are not well," Brenda said to the project manager at AllTech. It was just past eight on a Friday morning, and most of the employees were already deep into their work. "Her father just had open-heart surgery. They can't make the trip to New York. So they thought it would save them trouble if I collected her belongings." Brenda had made the call to them when she decided to give in and find out enough about Sarah to put her doubts to rest.

"Well, we were about to pack them up and ship them."

"I can sort out the things they won't want. It'll be less to send. I've known Sarah since we were in school together . . ." She stopped and closed her eyes sadly for a few seconds, a gesture that was not entirely for

effect. She felt a bit guilty that she had let her acquaintance with Sarah lapse. She was beginning to
think that Sarah hadn't had many friends.

"Well, I suppose," the young man said. "Let us pack
and mail them though. We want to pay for the ship-
ping. It's the least we can do. I'm Kevin, by the way."

That and make sure I'm not stealing them for myself, Brenda thought. But that was fair. They didn't
know her, though she'd had Sarah's parents call ahead
and tell AllTech it was okay. They had not wanted to
come to New York. New York frightened them, Brenda
guessed. The note of relief in Sarah's mother's voice
had been unmistakable. The father made growling
noises in the background. What had saddened Brenda
more than anything else was that Sarah's mother recognized Brenda's name. She and Sarah had been only
the most casual of friends, from Brenda's point of view.
But Brenda, to Sarah, had been important enough to
mention to her mother.

Sarah's cubicle—not an office—was larger than the
others on the floor, obviously signaling that she was
more important. But her workstation was plain, a
gray metal desk with a lower, pull-out keyboard, and
a raised shelf over the desk, with reference books and
manuals on it. Other than that, she had the usual
monitor, printer, in-house telephone, swivel chair, and
other office oddments.

Sarah apparently was not the sort of person who
stuck Post-it notes to herself all over her monitor.
Brenda bet that Sarah never forgot her passwords
either.

There were three drawers on the left side of the
desk. Brenda opened the top one, as Kevin watched
from the cubicle's entryway.

An older man appeared behind Kevin. "What's going on?" he said.

Kevin explained. "Mrs. Swettenham called and she said Ms. Grant was okay."

"Well, I see. That's all right, then. You realize, of course, Ms. Grant, that any disks or project notes are proprietary and can't leave the premises."

"Of course. Her family only wants personal things."

"Go right ahead, then." But he didn't leave. With the two of them watching, there was no way Brenda could search Sarah's computer files.

In all three drawers, Brenda found next to nothing that could be called personal. There was a very nice Montblanc pen, probably a graduation gift. There were odds and ends of makeup—two lipsticks, a tube of hair spray, mascara—none of which showed much sign of use.

Sarah's parents could hardly want the makeup. Or the breath mints, lip moisturizer, hand cream, cheap ballpoint pens, paper clips, emery boards, stapler, or half-used packs of gum.

There were six one-dollar bills and a ten. And a dollar and nineteen cents in coins. For a moment Brenda thought of asking Kevin to donate the money to some company charity, but decided against it. She asked him for an envelope, which he fetched, and put the money and the good pen inside. AllTech could send them off to Sarah's parents.

"I guess that's it," she said. "Except . . . I couldn't find her appointment book. Or did she keep everything on a PDA?"

"I have no idea," said Kevin. He sounded bored.

Brenda had wanted to check Sarah's entry for six on the afternoon she died, see if she'd noted anything about the purpose of her appointment with Brenda. Drat! Well, she could ask Billie if a datebook or a PDA had been found among Sarah's belongings at the scene of her death. Meanwhile . . .

"I won't take up any more of your time," she said pleasantly.

"Thank you for helping," the older man said, and as Brenda and Kevin walked toward the elevators, the older man stayed in the cubicle, staring around.

"Tell her parents we'll miss her," Kevin said earnestly. "She was brilliant."

Brenda suspected he would have liked to say something more personal, but just didn't know Sarah well. Maybe nobody did.

Brenda said, "I'll tell them."

"Too bad. It's so ironic. Almost the first time she ever didn't work late and she runs into a bus."

CHAPTER 8

Friday, October 17
Eighteen Days before the Presidential Election

Daniel was on the move in Atlanta. Daniel and Brenda had been approached several weeks ago by the city of Atlanta, which had a problem. The Motor Vehicle Division had decided to leap into the computer age with both feet, allowing people to pay for their traffic tickets online, using their credit or debit card. Presumably this would save thousands of dollars in staffing costs. However, those payments had to go somewhere, and the "somewhere" had to contain the record of the traffic or parking citation, the make and model of the car, and of course the info on the credit card and data about the person who paid the ticket.

Atlanta was worried that it might be possible to hack into the system. Maybe a crook could divert money, or gain credit card numbers, or find out confidential information on citizens. Experienced hackers might get into the system and erase their own traffic citations. Or as one of the police commanders who had done years in fraud said, "A guy could set up a scheme where for twenty percent he erases other people's tickets."

So DB Security had been hired to see if they could break into the Atlanta Motor Vehicle Division's system.

Neither Daniel nor Brenda liked working for a government entity. They both, however, loved being out of the office and in the real world. It was so much less nerve-wracking than cyberchasing terrorists, so much more fun than staring at a computer screen for hours on end. Work in the office took precedence. They could take a break from their routine, though, and work together on the part that could be done from New York.

They tried pretty much every method they could think of to slip through the AMV firewalls. Since they were working on the premise that an unknown hacker with no prior information about the Atlanta system could break into it—the city would not let them posit an insider turning crooked—they started with nothing more than their contract. It provided no background, not even the address of the building that housed the AMV computer.

Atlanta itself would worry about insider break-ins. If someone who had installed the system or someone who used the system turned traitor, that wasn't Brenda and Daniel's problem. And that was fine with them, although both suspected that the city would eventually realize it needed to know more about how an insider could take data and not leave a trail.

So Daniel and Brenda knew nothing about Atlanta's

set-up. They did not know what platform the system was running on. FTP was the old standard.

"I doubt FTP," Brenda had said.

"Telnet?" Daniel said. Telnet preceded Windows, ran on UNIX, and was considered good for remote network operations.

"Maybe. Assume we can't know which." The computer had to have open ports so that it would be open to the Internet. People had to get in to pay their tickets.

Somewhere there was a physical office where the server, whatever it ran on, actually lived. There it would create active server pages, generated from its database.

"When someone logs in with his traffic ticket info," Daniel said, "the SQL has gotta ask them to do specific tasks, like fill in their name, the license plate number, and probably the name of the officer issuing the ticket, and all that."

They needed to get to the server and exploit some security hole. There were always holes. No program was perfect, and people who set up the systems weren't perfect either. Daniel and Brenda even tried inserting a fake patch into the program.

But nothing they tried worked.

Brenda had been burrowing around in the Atlanta city budget and had found the remodeling plans for a building to be used for the AMV computer. Now they had an address.

"You don't suppose it's got a wireless hub and we could pick up signals from it just driving down the street?"

"Simple as that? Worth a try." Wireless systems gave out signals that came "standard" on the equipment.

Like remote garage-door openers, the code could be changed easily, but people often didn't bother to change it. Possibly Brenda or Daniel could get onto the system just by getting near enough to it.

So Daniel flew to Atlanta.

Early Wednesday morning he rented a car and drove past the Motor Vehicles building, but he got no signal. Another good idea that didn't work out. Possibly he should go straight to the source. Get a traffic ticket. He started speeding up and down Simpson and Piedmont Streets. Finally, one of Atlanta's finest spotted him.

"License and registration."

The police officer tore off a ticket.

"Can I pay this online, officer? I've heard you can do that in Atlanta."

The officer gestured with a big beefy thumb. "Yes, indeed, sir. Instructions right there."

"Thank you, officer." The cop left. Daniel proceeded to the laptop in his hotel room, got online and paid using his credit card. Now he had one end of his fishing line, and the other end went into Motor Vehicles.

Daniel had an armamentarium of viruses, one of which he e-mailed to the Motor Vehicles' client server along with his traffic ticket information. The virus should have jammed itself into the system and fired information back to Daniel.

It didn't.

By Friday, if he included the work done at the office and down here, and added in Brenda's hours in New York as well, Daniel thought they had put too much time into futzing around. He drove out to look more closely at the physical building where the data-processing system for Motor Vehicles was housed.

The Atlanta authorities, who wouldn't give them the address, had assured Daniel and Brenda that the building was a fortress, and they were pretty close to correct. "It's a brick shithouse," Daniel said to himself.

Actually, it was cinderblock and reinforced concrete. The large shoebox-shaped structure had a corrugated-roofed lean-to at one end, sheltering a big pile of road salt stockpiled for winter. From municipal records, Daniel knew that half of the building itself warehoused government-agency form sets and city documents, probably even ticket books for the cops. The records also told him it used to house a printing business, which explained its solidity. Old printing presses were extremely heavy.

Daniel walked around the building. There was no entry at all from the salt pile.

There were only two doors, a front door leading into a hall where a guard sat and a back door that had no outside handles. It probably opened from the inside with a panic bar.

Daniel walked in the front door. "Bayside?" he called to the guard. From the entry he could see down the straight central hall to the back door. Yup. Just a panic bar. Very difficult to break into from outside.

"What?" The man had been sleeping and barely opened his eyes.

"Bayside Winery?"

"Are you nuts?" the guard mumbled.

"Ah, southern hospitality," Daniel said, as he left. He had been inside for less than two minutes, but his training in observation served him well. He now knew a lot about the two inner doors, the left one to the paper-and-forms storage side and the right one to the Motor Vehicles side, which were directly across from each other. The paper side had a solid but ordinary brass lockset with a key slot in the faceplate. Apparently the city believed that hardly anybody would want a bunch of government forms. Actually, Daniel could think of a lot of interesting things he could do with those forms, but that wasn't his assignment. And anyhow there was always the guard in the hall. They figured he'd protect the place. Poor fools.

The AMV door was far more complex. There was a card-code slot that Daniel recognized immediately. It would require a secure card, a thing about the same size as a credit card but twice as thick. The cards that worked the lock would encode an entry number that changed at intervals according to an algorithm— possibly as frequently as every fifteen seconds. Only people who were permitted inside would have such cards, of course.

There was no way for Daniel to mock up a card.

He went to a hardware store.

A t eleven Brenda decided to take a break from the office. She could combine lunch with a quick trip to Sarah's apartment.

The apartment was on the West Side, about a fifteen-block walk south and then west. Healthful, Brenda thought, striding along. Sarah's parents had told her it was very nice of her to offer to pack Sarah's possessions and send them. This made Brenda feel a little dishonest, since she was doing it partly out of a sheer suspicious nature. Still, somebody had to. Once she got an idea of how much there was, she could contact a mini-move shipper.

The building manager at Sarah's high rise was a

sharp-edged woman of about forty. She wore a crisply tailored navy suit with a pleated skirt. Her eyebrows were penciled, her platinum hair cut in a diagonal wedge, longer on one side than the other. Unfortunately, the diagonal tended to reinforce the fact that her pointed nose leaned slightly to the left. The woman had a habit of emphasizing her words by thrusting her pen at Brenda.

"Already been done," she said.

"What? The packing? How could that be? I just talked to her parents last night."

"Her office people."

"People from AllTech? How did you know they were legitimate?"

The woman drew herself up to her full majestic height of five feet three inches. "For one thing"—a poke of the pen—"they had identification. For another"—poke—"Ms. Swettenham's employer is listed on her application. For a third"—several pokes—"though why I should need to explain to you, I called her parents, who were listed as next of kin on our forms. We are *very* careful who we rent to."

"Did AllTech ship her computer too? She must have had one." Visions of searching Sarah's files ran through Brenda's mind.

"One? Her living room was all computer gear. Woman must not have had a life."

"But did AllTech take all the computers?"

"Everything except our furniture."

The man in the deli across from Sarah's building was working on his seventh cup of coffee and second sandwich and fingering his earring in boredom. In New York you don't rent a table for several hours unless you keep buying.

He had seen Brenda enter the building and now he watched her leave. He punched a number into his cell.

"She's out now." He listened for a couple of seconds. "No. In there only five minutes tops." He punched off the phone, dropped a few bills onto the table, and left.

CHAPTER 9

Brenda, frustrated, skipped lunch and went back to DB. She dropped in on a few people at the office. Charlie Akira was working on the hospital program, actually writing new code. Maureen Fitzgerald, newly back from a rock-climbing accident, was digging into a buggy firewall program. Brenda gave them a nod of encouragement and appreciation and then went to her office.

She couldn't settle into any work. Puzzled at the speed at which AllTech had cleared Sarah's workspace and apartment, she kept asking herself why. Rubbing the back of her neck, she booted up her computer. Her back had cramped up.

As the computer ran the virus check and she concocted the new password she would enter as soon as the screen was clear again, she reflected on what had, so far, been a frustrating day.

Her virus scan completed its task and reported no problems. She hadn't expected any. DB had created and installed the best firewalls to be had in the industry, but no one knew better than Brenda and Daniel that there were hackers, just as smart as *their* people, hackers whose great delight was destroying other people's systems. So far DB had kept ahead of them.

Daniel, out in the field, was earning his keep at least. What was she doing? Chasing phantoms. Sarah must have been writing code in her head—she'd been prone to that, as Brenda recalled—and had stepped out in front of a cab. That was all there was to it.

But what had Sarah wanted to talk to Brenda about? And why had someone snatched all her personal belongings away before Brenda could look at them?

Did it matter?

She'd never find out, that was for sure. Monday she'd do what she could, go through the motions, call Billie, and find out about Sarah's appointment book, whatever form it was in. Meanwhile there were real baddies out there who needed to be discovered and stopped. It was time to concentrate on them.

She settled down to work, trying to free her mind of everything except what was on the screen in front of her.

Most people would have made little sense of the display. She was looking at chatter, Internet communications that had been selected by a reviewing program because they contained words and phrases that terrorists might use. The selection program was a sophisticated one—she had designed it herself—but it still came up with thousands, sometimes millions, of hits. Daniel and Brenda's most important job these days was to sift through them, taking a closer look at any that seemed truly suspicious and dumping the rest. This, both Brenda and Daniel knew, was the real business of DB, the job that mattered. The security work, the sort of thing Daniel was doing in Atlanta, was simply the moneymaker, the cash cow that kept them alive to do what was really important to them.

The trouble was, you could go crazy looking at this stuff day after day. Everything began to look suspicious. Or else everything became meaningless. That was one reason why both of them took breaks now and then to do fieldwork for the security end of the business.

She was only dimly aware of the growing quiet in the office as other workers left, didn't notice the light outside her windows becoming orange as the sun dropped lower and lower in a lingering October twilight.

As usual, there were many messages too cryptic for interpretation, even for Brenda. Others related to ordinary criminal activity. She ignored those; that area of sleazy human endeavor was somebody else's problem. She had learned, she hoped, to spot the ones that would repay further investigation. Today there were several like that.

One intriguing message referred to a completed job and demanded payment. Probably a drug deal on a large scale, but there were subtle things about the coding that made Brenda wonder. She struggled with it for a little while, then put it aside and went on to the next enigma.

Only when Brenda began to get a headache did she

realize that the office was almost dark and the screen, by contrast, was glaring. She had been sitting staring at it for four hours. She should never sit that long, she knew, stretching her back as she rose.

Brenda was the child of an army colonel and his wife. Her mother, while not exactly cold, should never have had a child. She simply wasn't interested in parenting. As they moved to army bases around the country, and several times abroad, Brenda's mother took language lessons, cooking classes, and opened small businesses—a knitting shop, a French pastry shop, a personal shopper service—and later closed them. She didn't stay with any interest long. Her husband's moves made it difficult to settle to one thing, but Brenda thought her mother's interests didn't go very deep.

Brenda had attended more schools than she could count. When she was eight, routine scoliosis screening in her school near Fort Carson showed she had a severe spinal curvature. She had surgery, then a lot of physical therapy. As for many children recovering from a disability, part of her therapy turned into a way to excel: Brenda became a championship swimmer.

It was after the surgery that her parents decided to let her live with her grandmother, her mother's mother, in New Hampshire. Gram Solto was more motherly than Brenda's mother, but she was elderly and arthritic. Brenda learned to be her own boss.

In New Hampshire, she won increasingly important swimming meets. Her senior year, she qualified for the Olympic swim team. Her event was the two-hundred-meter backstroke. Her time of 2:19.17 didn't win a medal, but it was just under the winning times. She won several national meets after that.

Her father applauded the wins, but never referred to the cause. He was not a man who liked disability.

Now Brenda stretched her torso to the left, to the right, and did two twists, gently but at a good extension. She turned on CNN for a break.

It wasn't much relief. In a tape made earlier in the day, Kierkstra was being charming in the Rose Garden, meeting some little boy who had done something impressive.

"Are you really a president?" the little boy asked. He spoke in a perfectly courteous tone, but his mother cringed and the father said, "James, this is *the* president." Then apologizing to President Kierkstra, the father explained, "He doesn't really understand the full importance of this, sir."

Kierkstra chuckled. "On the contrary, Mr. Fullerton. The importance of this is that a six-year-old boy saved an entire church classroom full of children."

Brenda shook her head and went back to her computer. The moment or two away had cleared her head. She studied what she saw, studied it again, and made a small, satisfied sound. She'd finally caught a shark. The wording of the messages was vague, of course. Terrorists are not stupid, as a rule. They are, however, sometimes a bit unsophisticated in the use of technology.

The first time she noticed the word "Buckingam" in a message, spelled with no "h" and used as a verb, she assumed she was dealing with a translation problem. The message had apparently originated in Brazil. The second time the word popped up, she had been alert, and the third time she was sure it was code. After that it was plain sailing. Brazil, schmazil. There was no doubt in Brenda's mind about where it had really come from.

She was looking at a communication between two cells of a tiny offshoot of Hamas. Although all the references were veiled, it was clear to Brenda that they were planning something new and very dangerous in the way of a terrorist campaign against certain Israeli settlements.

The plans didn't seem to pose any direct threat to the United States, but Brenda despised terrorists—all terrorists. She made some notes, printed them out, and then went to the phone.

It took her a while to reach her friend Sadie in Washington, the one who knew everybody. "Hey, I was in the shower. I've got to leave in twenty minutes. What's up?"

"I have to reach somebody at the Israeli embassy. Somebody influential." Sadie wouldn't ask questions.

Armed with a name and phone number, Brenda disconnected, reconnected, and made the call. Five minutes later she erupted from her office.

A vase full of dried grasses sat on a small table in the reception area. Brenda picked it up and threw it as hard as she could against the wall. It shattered with a satisfying crash. "So take that, Ms. Diplomat!"

"Uh-oh," said Helen. "Trouble with an embassy again?"

"So often! So often, Helen! We come up with something, something important, something that could save lives, for god's sake. And we report it, and what do they do? They patronize us. 'Yes, Ms. Grant. Certainly we'll look into it, Ms. Grant. Thank you for calling it to our attention. Have a nice evening, Ms. Grant.'"

Helen said, "The Scots paid attention, that time with the threat to North Sea oil. And what about the Lugandans? And there've been quite a few others."

"Right. But we could have prevented that suicide bomb attack on the temple in Haifa last summer. We could have kept that ship from being sunk in the Persian Gulf. How many lives were lost in that one? Why is it so difficult?"

"Bureaucracy. Inertia. Stupidity. Are you ready to stop what you're doing, just because progress is slow?" Helen began to pick up the pieces of the vase and collect stray wisps of grass.

"No," said Brenda, stooping to help her. "I guess not. But it gets so damn frustrating."

"You knew that going in. Besides, a lot of your trouble right now is that you're tired and hungry. Let's leave this mess for the cleaning crew and go to Minelli's. Some pasta and Chianti is just what you need."

Brenda allowed herself to be mothered.

The scene Brenda had found on CNN had hit a slow news day. And a day with nice weather. The network replayed it again and again. The White House gleamed in the background. The Rose Garden looked impressive even though it was late fall; Washington had not yet seen a frost. The media videocams were rolling, still photographers snapping the moment, several families in their best clothes on hand, honoring the boy who had saved their children's lives.

Jimmy Fullerton had been in a church classroom when the teacher lost consciousness. The teacher fell against a burning candle, igniting a pile of construction paper. As in many accidents, more than one system failed. The classroom door jammed and the smoke alarm had no battery. The windows were small and near the ceiling. The other children boosted

Jimmy, the smallest and lightest, up to a window, which he broke out with a heavy book. Then he dropped to the ground outside and, with a badly sprained ankle, hobbled around the building to the front office and gave the alarm.

"You were very courageous, Jimmy," President Kierkstra said, shaking the child's hand. "I am honored to meet you."

Kierkstra held the pose for the cameras; he smiled and smiled. Jimmy smiled and then ducked his head.

"You know I need to meet with some people from the national PTA now," Kierkstra said, shaking the hand of the boy's father. "But I thank you for coming." Then he turned to Jimmy's mother and took her hand. "You have a wonderful son there. Raising a child is not easy these days. You can be very, very proud of your accomplishment."

Alexander Cabot, the president's friend and confidant, and Hector Berlesconi, a member of the cabinet, watched from inside the White House.

"He does that very well, doesn't he?" said Berlesconi in a noncommittal tone.

Cabot looked at him but didn't speak.

The president's aides had now escorted the Fullerton family and their entourage off the Rose Garden lawn, and they brought up from behind them a second group, a delegation from the national PTA. Their ostensible purpose was to present the president a plaque for furthering education. Their real purpose was to remind him of his earlier promise to put more funds into programs for special-needs children.

Cabot and Berlesconi watched as the group of parents and teachers lined up for their photo op. The presented award took center stage as the president held one side of it and the PTA president, wearing a pink wool suit, held the other. When the photographers were finished, the PTA head said a few words to the president, which were inaudible to the reporters on the lawn. He smiled broadly and shook her hand. Then he shook the hands of the seven other parents lined up behind him.

Finally, nodding pleasantly to them but ignoring the PTA president's remarks, he strode back into the White House.

As the door closed behind him, Kierkstra turned to Berlesconi and Cabot and said, "Did you see that little monster? That little shit kid had something sticky on his hand."

"We thought the photo session looked good," Cabot said.

"And he got it on the cuff of my shirt! Just look at this!" The president held up his wrist. Neither man saw any discoloration.

"Smarmy little snot! Bet he climbed out of the room to save his own skin and didn't care if all the other kids got burned into little crispy critters."

Berlesconi said, "But he really did take a bad fall and he still ran to get—"

"And that Miss Prissy Prig! Did you see that fuzzy pink suit? Looked like she knitted it outta cat hair. Probably has a dozen cats!" He snorted and whapped his hand against an Abraham Lincoln antique chair. "Plus she was trying to lobby me about special-needs kids. Special-needs kids! Little retards'll outlive us all! Woman needs to get a life! Wish I was out duck hunting."

Neglecting to mention that the woman was one of the strongest, most effective national PTA presidents in years, Berlesconi said, "Nevertheless, now we have to deal with the wetlands issue."

"You deal with it. I'm done with you anyway for today."

Beckoning to Cabot, the president turned on his heel and strode away. Berlesconi cocked his head and watched them go.

In the distance he heard the sneer in the president's tone as he said, "Wetlands! Swamps and mud! God!"

Cabot stretched out his legs. It was very nice that the White House staff, overseen by the Chief Usher, kept the tradition of fires burning in certain fireplaces after Labor Day. Quite civilized. There was nothing as relaxing as tipping the soles of your shoes up to a fire and feeling pleasantly toasted.

Cabot and the president were physically quite a bit alike, tallish, slender, and good-looking. Difficult to elect an ugly president in these days of television. And Kierkstra could pull off an occasion like today's with a certain flair. In private, though, when Kierkstra's attitude became crude and combative, Cabot's morphed from suave deference into subtle arrogance.

Cabot was perfectly comfortable with being arrogant. His family was Old Money. The president, whose money was neither old nor anything like as plentiful as Cabot's, needed Cabot's frequent campaign contributions. But that wasn't the only hold Cabot had over the man.

When Kierkstra was governor of South Dakota, he had accepted payoffs from Cabot's organization, payoffs to water down crossing-safety precautions that would have cost Cabot's railroad a hell of a lot of money. Cabot had all the paperwork on those pay-offs.

They were political dynamite.

"So, Mr. President, with your lawn duties over, how are you feeling?" Cabot always gave the words "Mr. President" a slight ironic twist. Kierkstra had never reacted to this. Cabot wasn't sure the man really got it. He wasn't the sharpest knife in the drawer.

"I'm feeling crappy. I saw the polls. You saw the polls. How do you think I feel?"

"Worried."

Kierkstra got a crafty look on his face, one that his handlers had carefully trained him not to use in public. Cabot always viewed these moments when Kierkstra thought he was going to be smart as the moments he was most vulnerable to manipulation. But right now he didn't want to manipulate. He wanted to make sure Kierkstra understood matters quite clearly.

"So," said the president. "It's a problem, isn't it? We rise or fall together."

"Well, not exactly. I'd still be pretty much the richest man on the planet even if you were voted out of office."

"Suppose I'm retained in office and get rid of you instead?"

"Well, you don't really want to do that."

"I don't?" the president asked, in a voice that missed being presidential.

"No, friend. The Alsatia Petroleum deal has no paper connection to me, not a fingerprint anywhere. But you're all over it like ketchup on fries. And that's not the only case in point either. Remember the railroad crossings."

"You're a bastard."

"Ah, I'm hurt. Cut to the quick." They locked eyes for a few seconds. "We can be bastards together though. Won't that be nice?"

That evening
Atlanta, Georgia

At ten fifteen p.m., just forty-five minutes before he was due to go off duty, the security guard in the hall outside the AMV computer heard a bumping sound. A tubby man wearing overalls that were none too clean slouched into the building. He was carrying a mop and pail and pushing a cart full of cleaning supplies. The guard could hardly be expected to recognize the svelte businessman who had stopped in earlier in the day looking for a winery. Daniel's outer shirt covered a layer of three inner shirts. A tight knit cap, pulled down hard, made his face look slightly puffy.

Daniel set the pail down directly in front of the guard. Fumes of a strongly pine-scented cleaner, almost strong enough to see, rose from the bucket.

Daniel reached into a side pocket, drew his hand back, and, puzzled, reached into a small pocket at the top of the overall bib. "Ah, shit!" he said.

He checked his back pockets. He checked among the bottles in his equipment cart.

"Damn! Hey! Can you watch this stuff? I gotta go back downtown and get my stupid card." He made sure to waft a little more of the fumes toward the guard as he made his gesture of frustration.

"They change the shifts or somethin'?" asked the

guard without much interest. "Never had a cleaning crew come around this late before."

"Just for a couple of days, I guess," said Dan, trying to sound bored and Southern. "Regular man come down sick this mornin'. I'm a sub. But, hey, I need to go get that card, and I don't want to tote all this stuff back with me, so—"

"Forget it," the guard said. "Here."

He ambled over to the door and stuck his own secure card in the slot. The lock clicked open.

"Great. Thanks," Daniel said, moving into the computer room.

"And take this crap with you."

Daniel gazed around with a beatific smile on his face. The Motor Vehicles records center was extremely messy, like many behind-the-scenes offices. A couple of desks were obviously in use, but four more, pinch-hitting as storage units, were piled with papers, folders, stacks of Styrofoam drinking cups in long plastic sleeves, toner, and cartridges. Fluorescent lighting flickered. The air vents hummed, producing nicely cooled air for the health of the equipment.

Well, enough rubbernecking. Daniel was at risk of discovery every moment he spent in this place, and he might have to be there a long time. He was gambling that the guard in the hall would be too sleepy, and too eager to go off duty, to tell his night replacement about the new janitor. He had to get a move on.

He put the bucket of soap and Pine-Sol near an air intake, where the particles it generated would get sucked out of the room. He had too much respect for computers to introduce crud into the air.

He explored a bit.

Aside from the desks, four metal office chairs on wheels, general clutter, and a dead ficus plant, the room held a mainframe, a couple of laptops, some minis that were pushed far enough back on their tables to suggest they weren't used, and two PCs very lightly covered with dust. There were no discarded password notes. The monitors sported no Post-its with passwords written on them. Well, Daniel thought, that would be too easy. No challenge at all.

The mainframe was his patient, of course. He pressed a key and watched the monitor come to life, displaying a logo.

Aha! Windows BackOffice, called BackOrifice by those in the know. They should have used Linux. It was harder to administer but would have been more secure.

But he didn't actually have to monkey around on the computer itself, trying to break passwords. That could take a while, and it was possible somebody in authority might arrive. Who knew when the city techies came to work?

Daniel took from his pocket three small devices, one black, one white, and one cream. They looked like the plugs on the back of the computer. This particular computer had cream-colored plugs and cords, so he selected the cream-colored gadget and put the others away. He pulled the plug from the computer, attached his device, and reset the computer's plug. The original plug plus the gadget looked no different, only a little bit longer.

The little gadget was a keylogger, a keyboard capturing device. It would now record all the keystrokes that went into the Motor Vehicles computer. That would give him the password the operators used to enter the system, as well as a lot of other good stuff, including everything they said to the computer and every keystroke that was entered in this office. But all he really needed was the password.

He started emptying wastebaskets into the bag on his cart, just in case the guard came along.

At 10:50, just before the guard outside would turn over his shift to the next fellow, Daniel quietly moved the cart of cleaning stuff in front of the door, barring the way to anyone entering. He retained a floor-width dust mop and a hand vac with HEPA filters, the type used around computers. He had what he would need when someone came in, and he would have warning if they came when he was asleep. Then he chose the most comfortable chair, put his feet up on a desk, and settled down for a nap.

At 8:30 in the morning, when he'd been awake and ready to look busy for two hours, he heard a sound at the door. He moved the cleaning cart.

"Mornin'," he said to the techie who entered.

"Hey, dude," the young man said.

"Be out of here soon as I get the floor done." The young man nodded, having lost interest in the janitor, just as the guard had done. Then he sat down at the keyboard and brought up the traffic ticket system. The password, of course, didn't echo; it appeared on the screen as a row of asterisks.

Daniel swept diligently back and forth across the floor and under the desk.

"Oh, shit!" the techie blurted, when the power to the computer went out.

"Sorry, sorry," Daniel said. "My fault."

He was already under the desktop, where he'd

been snuffling up dust with the vac. Now he pocketed the keystroke-capturing device and plugged the power cord back into the port on the computer.

"Jeez!" Daniel said, straightening up. "Did I ruin anything?"

"No thanks to you, no. It's backed up."

"I said I'm sorry. Anyway, I'm outta here."

"About time!"

B y this afternoon, he thought, yawning, he would be back in New York, ready to plug in the password and download pretty much everything Atlanta had previously thought was secret. He yawned again. Or maybe he'd wait till tomorrow. Bask a little longer in the world of everyday petty crime before returning to the dark side. Then he could write a report to Atlanta saying that all anyone needed to break into their computer was a little special equipment—plus a bucket and a mop.

CHAPTER 10

Daniel's conscience overrode his personal prefer-
ence. He caught the red-eye. As Atlanta receded
farther behind him, Daniel's sleepy thoughts turned
to New York, and Brenda.

It had been seven years now since the attack on the
towers and the death of Jeremy. In all that time, Brenda
had shown no romantic interest in any man. Daniel
was acutely aware that, while he had Nate, Brenda left
work at night, after dealing with problems that were
often unnerving and sometimes literally earth-shaking,
and went home to an empty apartment.

Not always, though. She had a farm in Connecticut
where she spent as much time as she could, and she
loved her horses and dogs, but that wasn't the same.
Nate's love, Nate's just being there, had got Daniel

through many periods of depression since the towers' collapse. Brenda had no one. He suspected Brenda missed having a man in her life. Someone to talk to, to cuddle with. She hadn't had anyone like that since Jeremy.

Daniel had tried to talk with Brenda about her feelings. She would talk about the collapse of the towers, even about Jeremy, but the words she used were bland. She said she was "devastated" by the deaths. Well, anybody might say that. In fact, it was certainly true. But for a person as intelligent and verbal as Brenda, it was backing away, not meeting Daniel's mind. And that was not like her.

Daniel and Brenda had been friends since they'd started working together back at CGI, but the World Trade Center attacks, and the intense training that had followed them, had made them closer than most brothers and sisters. There was no limit to their trust of one another—with one notable exception. Brenda kept the door to her emotional life firmly shut.

As Daniel's turboprop headed northward over South Carolina, he brooded about Brenda's love life, or lack of it. "Which is not my problem," he mumbled, startling the teenager sitting next to him, an extremely thin girl with nostril studs.

Somewhere over North Carolina, he said, "But what are friends for?"

The teenager had her eyes closed and appeared not to hear. Daniel cast his mind over the good times he and Brenda had had together. Before he had become involved with Nate, Brenda had seen Daniel as lonely and had decided to cheer him up. He had come to New York from Chicago about three years after she had arrived in the city. Brenda had lived within weekending distance of New York all her life, so she considered herself a New York expert. She appointed herself trainer, and took him on explorations of New York, from the famous to the infamous. "We're going to do every naïve, touristy thing you ever heard of. All the stuff New Yorkers never get around to."

They did the 'round-Manhattan boat in July, the Statue of Liberty one August afternoon. She got permission somehow to get the two of them into the New York Stock Exchange. Chinatown was an obvious choice—and a delight. They giggled and ran from place to place and ate at three restaurants in one night, a different course in each. They saw the Rockettes at Radio City. They went to the Rainbow Room and Tavern on the Green and Little Italy. By the time she gave him a tour of New York Mafia hangouts, where they saw John Gotti, the Teflon Don, eating gnocchi and wearing his sharkskin suit, as usual just one size too small, he said, "All right, already. I'm a native."

Then had come 9/11, and their training, and her plaintive "Will we ever be happy again?" Well, he was happy, at least away from work. He had Nate. He had a life. But Brenda . . . she'd been there for him, so he felt uneasy about leaving her in her lonely limbo. He wished he could do something, fix her up with a nice guy. Most of the men he knew were gay, but there was Hal from the gym. And Anthony, who worked with Nate. Both nice, both straight. But she had to have the right guy. She was ready to fall hard for someone.

As the aircraft passed over Chesapeake Bay, Daniel said, "What am I? Her mother?" He had better just stay out of her private life.

As the plane crossed Long Island Sound, descending out of twenty thousand feet, and TRACON, the terminal radar approach control, handed the craft over to ARTS, the local area radar tracking system, he said, "No. I owe her."

When the plane bumped down on the runway, the teenager next to Daniel sat up and yawned, revealing a tongue stud. She said, "Listen up, dude. If it ain't broke, don't fix it."

CHAPTER 11

Sunday, October 19
Brooklyn, New York
Sixteen Days before the Presidential Election

"There is a toxic teenager on the couch downstairs in our living room." Nate's whisper was harsh. The bedroom door was shut. Nate was in jeans and his blue T-shirt with the New York Fire Department logo on the left breast. It was just after noon, and he'd arrived home three minutes before. He was still carrying his jacket. "We talked about him before you left. You said he wouldn't come back."

"He's sixteen. He has no place else to go," Daniel said. His whisper matched Nate's in volume and harshness.

"Nowhere else! There are millions of square miles of land on this planet. He could be on any one of them except the one we're on."

"Look, I got back from Atlanta at two this morning. He got here at three. I haven't been to bed yet. I spent hours trying to talk sense into him, and since he sacked out I've been trying to get hold of his mother, but who knows where she is? My sister is an irresponsible mope. She's addicted to different varieties of painkillers and is the type who throws gasoline on dying embers. And she's a Republican."

Nate knew this last appellation was not a compliment in Daniel's lexicon.

"His father is still in prison for any number of felony drug charges. No matter what I think of the drug laws, he's there and he's not going anywhere."

"The kid is dangerous," Nate said. "His dad is a moronic, homophobic creep. And his mom is worse than both of them. But why does he have to come here?"

"He's my nephew."

"He doesn't have friends or enemies he could torment? You remember what he did last time."

"As clearly as you, especially since you've reminded me of it about six times since."

On his last visit, Drew had stolen Nate's credit cards. It had been the middle of the night. The nephew had gone on a shopping spree on the Internet and maxed out the cards in less than three hours. Drew had returned the cards to Nate's wallet but kept the numbers and the three-digit security codes. Nate wouldn't have known about the theft until his next bill came, except the credit card companies had called. The unusual buying pattern had raised red flags on the companies' computers. Still, it had taken over a week of frustrating phone calls to undo most of Drew's damage, and small problems were still surfacing.

Nate was pacing up and down the floor on the

opposite side of the bed from Daniel. "I'm not trying to take anything away from his tears and tragedy. His parents are as toxic as he is. Fine. That's sad."

"But he's come to us now."

"To his gay uncle. He's a homophobic creep."

"I'm all he has. *We're* all he has. And as crazy as my sister is, I owe her big-time. She wasn't always the way she is now."

"Daniel, we talked about this before you left for Atlanta. Okay, so your sister protected you from your parents. That was then. This is now. We agreed the brat wouldn't be welcome here again."

"I didn't know he'd show up. Was I supposed to slam the door in his face?"

"What did he say when you saw him last time? Just before he stalked out. The last time he was here he slammed the door in your face. Through closed doors, both of us heard the shouted words. And probably the neighbors on both sides."

"Are you going to bring that up every time we discuss him?"

"He said he hated your faggot ass."

"I know what he said."

"And that's okay with you? For someone to say that to you, especially in your own home?"

"No, it's not okay. And you know that." Daniel glanced in the bedroom mirror. He was red in the face. Only Nate could make him this angry. And he was frustrated. He had enough going on in his life without this. And Nate was the one who wanted kids. Why couldn't Nate understand this kid?

"How did he get here?" Nate asked.

"He hitchhiked."

"Why here?"

"He didn't say."

"Did you ask him?"

"Yes, I asked him. He wouldn't say."

They heard footsteps on the stairs and a knock on the bedroom door. Daniel opened it. In his right hand Drew held Nate's helmet, the one he'd worn on 9/11. It had rested on the same shelf in the living room for years. Daniel had seen it the first night he spent with Nate. Nate never touched it. Once when Daniel was reaching for it, Nate had said, "Please don't." Nate had tears in his eyes. Daniel had asked if Nate wanted to talk about the hat or its symbolism. Nate had said no and never said another thing about it. Daniel respected him enough not to ask.

Drew glanced from one to the other. "There's no food." He wore a glittery studded belt that hung low on his butt because it wasn't put through the belt loops. He wore a hooded sweatshirt with the word Element on the front.

Through gritted teeth, Nate said, "There's onions. Potatoes. Five kinds of cheese. Pasta. Tomato paste. Eggs, flour—"

"There's no Cheetos. Or potato chips."

"We'll be calling for takeout soon," Daniel said. He stepped to his nephew and gently took the helmet.

"What is that?" the kid asked.

"We'll talk about it later," Daniel said. "Nate and I still need to talk."

The teenager retreated. Daniel closed the door. He offered the helmet to Nate, who took it and placed it on his side of the bed.

"You've got to listen to me." Nate was hoarse now. "I don't want him here. I'm serious."

"I know you're serious. It's your place."

"It's our place," Nate snapped. "We put both of our names on the mortgage. It has been and will be ours. But I don't want him here."

"For now, it's a package deal. Can't you please understand? I remember helping him with his homework when he was in first grade. He wasn't stupid like everyone tried to prove. He was okay for me. He behaved for me."

"But you weren't enough, and you have no proof that you will be enough for him now."

"I can't chain him to the bed."

Nate said, "If he's here, I can't stay here."

"What are you saying?"

Nate stood, helmet in hand. "I thought it was pretty clear."

"Don't leave, please don't leave," Daniel said. "We can work this out."

"How?"

"I don't know."

"I'll be back when you figure that out." Nate turned and walked out the door and down the stairs.

"*Nate!*" Daniel called after him and took the stairs two at a time. He heard the click of the front door. Drew, who had found a video to watch, lifted his head and looked from Daniel to the closed door. Then the kid asked, "Is he going for food?"

This was the great failing of teenagers. It was their nature to be oblivious to others' feelings and the world around them. If he was fair, Daniel knew he'd been the same way at that age. But he didn't feel fair right now. He was devastated. He'd never thought of a life without Nate. Now Nate was gone. For how long?

Was his nephew worth his life, his relationship? He looked at the scrawny kid sprawled on the couch.

Daniel didn't know what to do. None of his computer classes, none of his antiterrorist training, had prepared him for this. It was tough enough for him to deal with everyday emotions. Now this.

He and Nate had had very few fights. They both worked hard at dangerous jobs. Neither one was a slob. Nate cooked. Daniel cleaned. Like any couple, they had their differences. But this. This was the worst.

Maybe if he waited long enough to get food, his nephew would starve to death. Or maybe Daniel would call Brenda. She liked kids. Maybe she'd have a suggestion. But then he'd have to tell her about Nate.

He remembered he'd been worried about her love life. Oh, god, he couldn't tell her.

Not yet.

CHAPTER 12

Monday, October 20
New York City
Fifteen Days before the Presidential Election

Daniel and Brenda arrived at work at the same moment the next morning and went up in the elevator together. Brenda knew the minute she looked at Daniel that something was badly wrong, but there were other people in the elevator. She waited until they were alone, in the hall outside the office door.

"What?" she said.

"Nothing," said Daniel.

Okay, so Daniel didn't want to talk about whatever it was. He was a grown man. He could make that kind of decision. She'd be ready to listen when he wanted some sympathy.

"Morning, you two," said Helen. "You just missed a phone call."

Brenda held out her hand for a message slip.

"I just hung up the phone. Haven't had time to write down anything but a name and a number. Guy's name is Cooper, Allen Cooper. He's with the NSAA, and he wants to hire DB for some government work. He's in New York, wants to come and see you."

Brenda looked at Daniel. He shrugged. "You know I hate working with the feds," he said, sounding as if he didn't care much. They'd both thought, when they started the business, that they wanted government work. But a few unfortunate experiences had taught them otherwise. Regulations, slow payment, bureaucratic bumbling—it was frustrating business.

"Yeah, me too, but they do pay pretty well—eventually. And we could use a little income," said Brenda. "As I've said before, things are getting kind of tight."

"We're in the black."

"True. Well, I'm not exactly in love with Washington either, but we could at least see him, don't you think?"

"Whatever you want," Daniel said. He went to his office.

Brenda turned to Helen. "Call the guy and tell him he can see us this afternoon about two. And check him out meanwhile."

"Gee, boss, I never would have thought of that."

"Okay, okay. So I don't need to teach my grandmother to suck eggs. Anything else happening?"

"Nothing much." Helen nodded toward the vanished Daniel. "What's eating him?"

"Wish I knew. He's not talking. Trouble with that bratty nephew of his, I'm guessing. He acted the same way last time the kid came to town. He'll tell me when he's ready." She turned to go, saying over her shoulder, "I'm not in this morning to anybody but you and Daniel. Unless the world blows up."

"In that case, you're not in to anybody at all, right?"

"And you can call that applicant back and tell him we'll hire him. Malcolm Dudley."

"Yeah, I was impressed with him too. His background, as far as I've been able to check, is as clean as a whistle."

"Thanks, but keep at it."

Brenda had forgotten all about the afternoon appointment until Helen phoned her on the internal line at five minutes to two. "Mr. Cooper is here to see you."

"Damn! I don't need another bureaucrat right now. I should have had more sense than to let him come." She looked at a screen full of information that needed to be analyzed. "I suppose we'll have to see him, but I'll try to brush him off. Did you run a background on him?"

"Yes, it's fine," said Helen smoothly.

Well, not very informative, but then the guy must be standing right next to Helen's desk. "Right. Did you call Dan?"

"Next on the agenda."

"Okay. Five minutes. The guy's early, anyway."

Brenda had barely turned back to her monitor when the phone rang again. Swearing under her breath, she picked it up.

"Listen," Daniel growled, "I'm in the middle of looking at some decoded stuff from Barcelona, and it's pretty complicated. If I stop now, I'm going to have to start all over again."

"Yeah, well, I'm not exactly idle, you know. It won't take long. We can listen to what he has to say, be polite, tell him no, and get on with work."

"Waste of time." Daniel's growl was even deeper.

"Probably. The sooner you get to the conference room, the sooner we can get it over with."

When Helen ushered Allen Cooper into the room a couple of minutes later, Daniel greeted him with a curt nod. Brenda murmured something and gestured toward a chair.

She watched Cooper as he sat and crossed one elegantly clad knee over the other. He was a startlingly good-looking man of about forty. His nicely tanned face contrasted with hair of a shade somewhere between gold and silver; his eyes were a deep warm brown. His casual black pashmina jacket encased a body without an ounce of extra fat. Brenda was awed in spite of herself. If Gregory Peck's mother met Tom Cruise's father, she thought to herself, under a statue of Adonis . . .

She tried not to let her reaction show in her eyes.

"Ms. Grant, Mr. Henderson." Cooper nodded to both of them. "I know the two of you are busy people. I need your assurance that this conversation will be confidential."

"I would have assumed," said Brenda coolly, "that you would check our reputation before you ever talked to us. But for the record, yes, of course all dealings with our clients are in confidence. And no, before you ask, the room is not bugged."

"Your reputation is impeccable. I hardly needed to check you out. Rapid growth. Very experienced for the few years you've been in business. Everybody knows about you."

"We hope so." Brenda was still stiff.

Cooper inclined his head. "Right. I'm with the National Security Analysis Agency in Washington, D.C. You're familiar with our work?"

Daniel grimaced. "Somewhat," said Brenda, looking at the LeRoy Neiman painting on the wall to avoid staring at Cooper's incredible, almost mesmerizing good looks.

"What we do is analyze data. We don't have the facilities to gather a lot of data. Government agencies do that for us, but we've also begun to employ private firms that do this kind of work."

"Yes," said Brenda. "We know that, Mr. Cooper." Left unspoken, but clearly implied, was the message, *Cut to the chase.*

"Your company has a great reputation in the security field, and we understand that you also collect information about terrorists."

Brenda looked at him. "I see you do have ways of gathering some information," she said.

"Some. The point is, I am authorized to offer your firm a substantial retainer to pass along to NSAA any information you think would be of interest to us."

"What sort of information?" Brenda was wary of this man. She couldn't quite decide why. Maybe it was because he was much too handsome.

He cleared his throat. "We at NSAA are worried about the inability of government agencies to track known terrorists." He spread his hands. "You read the papers. You know the sort of thing I mean. Known Al Qaeda agents get into the United States, take flight training, and wreak havoc. Files are generated on certain people; the files get buried and pretty soon some of those people blow up trains in Madrid and London."

"Yes." Daniel's voice was flat. He wasn't going to give this guy any help.

"DB Security has proven itself to be effective at spotting people no one else seems able to. We'd like to hire you to keep tabs on terrorists around the world, particularly on American soil."

His words hovered in the air. Brenda thought the room seemed somehow darker. Perhaps a cloud had passed over the sun.

Daniel took a deep breath. "That's a tall order."

"Too tall?"

"I didn't say that."

"Mr. Henderson," said Cooper, leaning forward in his chair, "you and your company have reported suspicious activity to various agencies. Every time, these findings have been valuable. In more than one instance, your work prevented a serious international incident. I have confidence in DB's ability to gather information others haven't noticed."

Daniel stood up and began to pace. "Cooper, you made a big deal out of confidentiality just now. We're not real happy that you seem to have information about our private business affairs."

Cooper held out both hands. "Hey, I happen to know a few people in Washington. They know people who know other people. Word gets around. DB is the best in the business, and a few people know the scope of that business."

"Then it's a shame that a few more of those people don't believe it," said Brenda bitterly.

Cooper looked at her. "Meaning?"

She was already sorry she'd spoken. "Nothing much. Forget it."

Cooper nodded. "Meaning, I suppose, that your

information is sometimes ignored. I've heard of a few instances of that too. You have to understand that bureaucracy is a lurching, unwieldy machine, with a strong tendency to keep on doing things the way it has always done them, whether or not that way works. It takes some agencies a long time to acknowledge that the world has changed. I hope, and believe, that the NSAA is not that kind of agency. We could actually help you make a difference."

"All right." Brenda made up her mind abruptly. "Here's a tidbit I picked up a few days ago." She spelled out what details she knew of the Hamas plot. "The Israelis were polite about it, but they brushed me off. I think people are going to die, Mr. Cooper. Can the NSAA do anything about it?"

"No," he said flatly. "It's not our brief. But I personally can do something about it, Ms. Grant. And I will. Will you take on the assignment I have in mind for you?"

"You mentioned a sizable retainer," said Dan, belligerence still in his voice. "Just what did you have in mind?"

"I am authorized to offer you a million dollars a year."

"That's a nice round figure," said Brenda, unable to hide a small smile. "However, we don't usually work with the government."

"I understand that. Of course, we had routine background checks conducted on both of you, and on your principal employees, before making this offer. You are politically independent, slightly left-leaning, and opposed to the present administration. It is natural that you would fight shy of involvement with the government. However, you're also responsible, law-abiding citizens. Aside from several speeding tickets, neither of you has broken any laws that we know of, and you support various good causes. Your politics are your own business, of course. If you agree to work with us, you would be aligning yourself not with the government, but with the safety of this country."

Brenda felt a little as though she was expected to cheer or throw her hat in the air. "I understand what you're saying. Since you seem to know so much about us, you probably also know that we have a demanding business here, and we can't take on much more. I don't know how we'd find time to work with you."

"Remember, we're prepared to pay you well. I imagine an extra million dollars a year would let you hire one or two more employees and take some of the load off yourselves." The man had made his speech. Now he was letting the money talk.

Brenda had to admit that it spoke fluently. She glanced at Daniel. "Of course, Mr. Henderson and I will need to discuss this. How soon do you need an answer?"

"Let's see. This is Monday. Suppose I call you on Wednesday. I'll be out of the office until then—and it'll give me a chance to pass along your information to someone who can act. Watch your newspaper, Ms. Grant."

He stood and shook hands with them both. "I enjoyed meeting you. I hope we can work together."

With that, he left the room, and Daniel growled. "I still don't trust him."

"Yeah, but the first thing is to decide what to do about this offer," Brenda said.

Daniel slumped in his chair. "I don't know. I hate the idea of working with those SOBs in Washington."

"Me, too. But we need the money, Daniel. I hate to admit it, but Cooper's right. Another couple of high-level people could make all the difference. We could assign a lot of the routine security business to them and concentrate on our own thing. And they sure wouldn't cost us a mill. We could pay all our bills, buy that new equipment to make the office more secure—"

"Take a vacation?" said Daniel.

"Well, I don't know that I'd go that far. But it's a thought—someday. What's wrong with supplying information to an agency that will take us seriously? You have to admit we've been pretty frustrated till now. If this guy really does have the ear of people with influence, we'll be a big step ahead. What have we been doing all these years, why have we been knocking ourselves out hunting for terrorists if we aren't going to try to get them?"

Daniel scowled. "What do we know about him? Is he for real?"

Brenda picked up the phone. "Helen, can you come to the conference room for a minute?"

She arrived bringing a small sheaf of printout. "You want to know about Cooper, right?"

"You're prescient."

Helen began reading. By the time she finished, Brenda and Daniel knew Cooper's biography from birth on. Age: thirty-eight. Weight: one-sixty. "Driver's license info," Helen said, with her eyes cast down in pretend modesty. They knew his grades in high school and college, what jobs he had held, and his spending habits. They knew where he had traveled and when, his hobbies (wines and handball), what football and baseball teams he supported, and where he liked to dine. "You want to know what kind of shampoo he likes best?" Helen asked, dumping the file on the conference room table.

"No," said Brenda, "but I suppose it's in there."

"And that may be the most interesting piece of information. Selsun Blue. He apparently has to fight off dandruff. Otherwise, this guy is such a straight arrow, he's about as fascinating as white bread, and I don't mean those lovely white rolls either. Aside, of course, from being the best-looking man on the planet." She winked twice, once at Dan, once at Brenda.

Brenda nodded. "He's so beautiful, it's almost past belief."

Daniel snorted.

Brenda glanced at him sharply, shrugged, and said, "Thanks, Helen. Good job."

When Helen had left, Daniel said, "So what do we know about this outfit, the NSAA?"

"They're supposed to be coordinating all the anti-terrorist efforts."

"I know. But they've only been in business for a couple of years. They don't have much of a reputation for getting things done."

"They're a government agency," said Brenda with a sigh. "What do you expect? At least they don't have a reputation yet for screwing things up. And I haven't heard anything on TV or read anything that suggests they're dishonest. Even the *Times* cuts them some slack, and you know how they love to bash everybody in Washington."

"They're usually right."

CHAPTER 13

Brenda called Sarah's parents. Sarah's mother answered, whispering into the phone, which Brenda took to mean the ill father was sleeping.

"I was just wondering whether the things from her office had arrived," Brenda said.

"Oh, yes." Whispered and brief. Was Sarah's father being as unpleasant as Brenda thought he might? Sick people can be difficult.

"Well, I'm just so sorry," Brenda said. When there was no response, she added, "AllTech sent the things from Sarah's apartment. They should arrive soon, too."

"Oh, they did already. They were so nice to pay extra."

"Well, I guess you have her computers and everything."

"Her clothes. Her kitchen things. The apartment was furnished. But no computers. She must have used the ones at work, don't you think?"

"Um . . . maybe. Well, I wish you well, Mrs. Swettenham. If I can help . . . I don't know exactly how, but you have my phone number."

"Yes, dear. Thank you."

For what? Brenda asked herself as she hung up.

No computers?

On impulse, she composed an e-mail to the dozen branch offices. Anybody out there know anything odd about AllTech or a Sarah Swettenham, now deceased, who used to work there? After a moment's hesitation, she encrypted it before hitting Send. No sense taking any chances. Chances of what? she asked herself. You seeing bogeymen under the bed again?

Anyway, that was done. And probably pointless. But it got it off her mind.

The argument with Daniel continued. But they both knew, really, what the decision would have to be. Even if they hadn't needed the money, they needed, ultimately, cooperation with a reliable authority capable of doing something about any terrorists they might uncover. The government of the United States of America had not, thus far, been spectacularly successful in its efforts, but if the government couldn't do the job, who could? Certainly not DB all alone.

"Okay, guys, let's get started." Brenda looked around the room. Conversation died down.

Meetings at DB were informal but businesslike. Brenda and Dan, who both hated meetings, shared the job of chairing them. Today it was Daniel's turn, but given his state of mind, Brenda had offered to trade. Daniel was closeted in his office doing what he loved best, digging into data to track down terrorists.

Brenda grinned at the man seated on her right. "First of all, I want you all to meet the new kid on the block." New employees were always introduced to the department heads. It was one of the things that made DB different from many growing companies, and Brenda hoped they never got too big to do it this way. "This is Malcolm Dudley, our newest threat analyst. Some of you have seen him around, but he hasn't been formally introduced to all of you."

Malcolm wasn't long out of college, and his curly red-blond hair and gangly body made him look even younger than he was. He half rose, smiled and nodded to the rest of the people in the room, and settled back somewhat awkwardly into his chair.

"Malcolm's working on Bob's team, officially," Brenda went on, "but of course he'll be available to anyone else who needs him. Usual routine. We hang pretty loose around here, Malcolm." She laughed. "I'd love to see somebody try to do an organizational chart of this company. Our motto is—"

"WHATEVER WORKS!" chanted the group.

"So why don't you all tell Malcolm who you are and what you do. Chihiro?"

A small man with unruly dark hair and a round, smiling face nodded to Malcolm. "Chihiro Ogata. I lead the solution architects. I'm also entertainer-in-chief at company parties."

The blond woman sitting next to him said, "He

plays a mean violin. Everything from Beethoven to the Beatles. I'm Sandra Schmidt, and I'm in charge of the maniacs in quality control."

"John Coleman," said the next man. His face was a handsome mahogany, and he was the only one in the room wearing a suit. "Marketing. Don't let the others give you the wrong idea. I may be the only Republican in the company, but I'm also the one who keeps us solvent."

Everyone else groaned at the well-worn line. "Actually," said the man at the foot of the table, "John is about as Republican as Hillary Clinton. He likes to twist our tails. And as for solvency, I can tell you a thing or two about that. Paul Sniegowski, chief financial officer."

"Pilar Estravados," said the woman next to him, who was sitting with her chair pushed well back from the table. She sniffed. "I oversee the technical developers, and I've got a rotten cold, so don't come near me."

"And I told you to go home and get some rest, and stop infecting the rest of us," said Brenda. She was smiling, but she meant it. "Go on. Go write code at home."

Estravados grinned. "Okay, but I've got a code id by doze." She got up and left.

"Workaholics," said Brenda, shaking her head.

"Takes one to know one," murmured Sniegowski.

"Yes . . . Well, that brings us around to Bob Hamilton, and of course you know him, Malcolm—he's your boss. And everybody knows Helen, who is the one indispensable person in this firm. Do you have any questions about anything at this point, Malcolm?"

"Thanks, but I think I've got the basics, and Bob is really helping me a lot. I guess I just want to say . . . I mean, I'm really glad to be here, and I hope I don't screw up."

"I wish I could say none of us ever do that, but I cannot tell a lie. We're glad to have you aboard, and if you have any problems, just come to Bob or Daniel or me . . . or anybody, really. We all help each other. Thank you, Malcolm."

"Now," she said, as the gangly young man left the conference room, "let's keep this as brief as possible. We've all got work to do. Anybody have any problems to bring up?"

"At least he believed us about the Hamas business," said Brenda on Wednesday. They were eating their lunch in a tiny, crowded Thai café. Daniel concentrated on his pad thai, while Brenda held forth, secure in the knowledge that the noise level masked her words. "Did you see today's papers? They're full of the capture of a couple of Hamas types 'rumored to be plotting new attacks that could have shattered the fragile truce between Israel and the Palestinian Authority.' So he kept his word."

"Anything about us in there?" Daniel roused out of a moody silence.

"I suppose we're the 'anonymous sources.' Which is the way we want it."

"Do we have the personnel to take his job on?"

"I hired one guy. With the NSAA money, we can hire more."

"Would that be cost-effective?"

"My look at the figures says yes."

"Okay, you're right. We have to deal with him. Now can we talk about something else?"

Brenda was getting sick of his testiness. She wished he'd talk about whatever was bugging him and get it out of his system, but he remained stubbornly silent. She sighed and began to speculate about the Yankees' chances in the Series this year. Then they walked back to the office.

Allen Cooper was due to call them for a decision this afternoon. They decided that Daniel would take the call. "I think he underestimates you," said Brenda.

"He's due for a little lesson then," said Daniel with a grim smile. "Helen, when the call comes in, send it to me—but let Brenda know. I want her to hear this too."

Brenda checked her interbranch e-mails. Among several dealing with office problems—Hong Kong apparently had a tyrant for an office manager, and two employees were threatening to quit—there was one from the Cairo office.

Yussuf ibn Kareef al Abbas was DB's Middle East expert. Hired partly for his languages, including three Arabian dialects and one Pakistani hill language, he was also a brilliant programmer, and a good enough friend that they were allowed to call him simply Yussuf.

(97) <gs>
S. Swettenham and I both did graduate work at the University of Illinois in Champaign. Kept in touch. She had a recent worry about AllTech. We should speak on secure line.
Yussuf.
(98) <gs>

CHAPTER 14

When Helen called Daniel in midafternoon, it wasn't to transfer a phone call. "Mr. Cooper is here, Mr. Henderson. He wonders if it would be convenient to see you."

"Here! What's he doing here? He was supposed to phone."

"Yes, right here at my desk," said Helen smoothly.

"Meaning you can't talk. Shit! Well, let him stew for a while. He doesn't own this place yet. I'll call you."

There was a connecting door from Daniel's office to Brenda's. He slipped through it. "He came in person, instead of calling."

Brenda was beginning to find Dan's hostility unreasonable. "Where is he?"

"Cooling his heels at the front desk."

"Okay. I'll come in. We'll both deal with him."

When Daniel admitted Allen Cooper to his office, the man was profusely apologetic. "I know this is an intrusion, and I fully appreciate the value of your time, but since other business brought me to New York, I thought I'd call in person. It's good of you to see me, and I'll take only a moment."

Daniel was caught off balance. He grunted something and gestured Cooper to a seat. "Actually, it's just as well you came, I suppose. It's better to say these things in person. Our answer is no, Cooper."

Cooper raised his eyebrows. "You surprise me, Mr. Henderson. This is Ms. Grant's decision as well?" He looked over at Brenda, but Daniel was the one who replied.

"We're agreed. We can't do it for a million."

"Ah. We're haggling over price."

"No haggling. We'll do it for two mill. We need the money to hire more people, get better information. Send us a contract for two and we'll sign. Otherwise forget it."

"You know what you want, Mr. Henderson, and you're not afraid to say so. I like that. I dislike most games." He looked at Brenda for a moment and then turned back to Daniel. "As it happens, I took the liberty of bringing a contract with me, with the dollar figure left blank. We need to move as fast as we can, though I've added somewhat to the parameters of the job. If you will permit me, I will complete the contract and sign it right now."

Brenda drew a deep breath. "You're a fast worker, Mr. Cooper."

"When it is desirable," he said, smiling. "I was certain we could reach an understanding."

Brenda frowned. "You're offering us a lot of money, but you said you've changed the job description. What exactly do you want for your two million?"

"Not your firstborn."

"Don't have one."

"The short answer is independence. Not mine. Yours." He leaned forward. "We know that terrorism can come from within as well as from without. I want you to keep tabs on the worldwide terrorist network, but I also want a second look, from outside governmental agencies, at some of the personnel in some private businesses that do business with the government. I especially want you to vet their new hires."

"Why don't you trust whatever the FBI or the CIA or Homeland Security says about them?"

"I do. I don't distrust them. When I said I want independence, I probably should have said I want a fresh eye. One of the reasons 9/11 happened, in my opinion, is that everybody was looking at everything the same old way. It didn't happen because we had terrorist spies in any of our agencies. And it didn't happen—at least not primarily—because we didn't have enough information on the world of Islamic extremists. We had the information, as I mentioned before."

"Then why *did* it happen?"

"Just what I'm saying. We were looking at things in the same old way. We expected somebody might plant a bomb on a plane, so we were searching luggage for bombs. We expected somebody might hijack a plane, using a gun probably. So we gave pilots instructions on how to go along with hijackers—take them where they wanted to go, so as not to endanger the passengers. Nobody guarded against the human being as the weapon. Nobody thought that people would take over a plane only long enough to fly it into a building and take themselves out with it."

Quite unexpectedly, Brenda felt her eyes fill with tears. She stood up and walked to the window, struggling for composure.

Daniel took over. "Well, we're prepared at least to consider the job."

Cooper took a small sheaf of paper and a pen from his slim attaché case. After making a notation on one sheet, he passed the contract to Dan, who scanned the document quickly.

"This seems straightforward," he said. "We'll need to have our lawyers look it over though."

"Of course," said Cooper. He stood. "I'm confident they will find no flaws. I will have a check for the first half of the retainer sent to you by courier as soon as I have a signed contract. Now, I promised not to take up your time, and I believe in keeping my promises." He looked again at Brenda, who had turned back to face the room. His gaze swept her up and down, lingering a moment. "I'll be in New York for the next couple of days. Perhaps you could call me when you have signed. I'm at the Ritz-Carlton. Could I prevail upon the two of you to be my guests for dinner tonight?"

"I'm sorry, I have other plans," said Brenda. They included a long swim at her health club, followed by *The Philadelphia Story* at an old-movie cinema close to her apartment, but Cooper didn't need to know that.

"What a pity! Cocktails, then? I'd like to drink to a promising new relationship."

"Thanks, but not tonight," she said firmly. Daniel shook his head.

"Well, then, I'll say good-bye and hope to hear from you soon." Cooper shook hands, careful not to crush Brenda's hand in a too-firm grip.

"Well!" said Brenda after he left. "That's going to make life a little busier around here. And a lot more lucrative."

"Yeah," said Dan, sounding morose. "Don't get charmed."

Brenda made a decision. Patience hadn't worked. It was time for shock treatment. "Okay, that's it!" she shouted, smacking the desk. "I've had it with you, buddy boy. Either get it off your chest or snap out of it. We've got work to do, and it drives me crazy seeing you like this. You're acting like you've lost your last friend."

Daniel was quiet for a long moment. Then he said, "Nate's left me." It came out in a monotone.

Brenda was appalled at what she'd said. "Oh god, Dan, I'm sorry! I didn't mean . . . I mean, when? How? Why?"

"I don't know. How do these things happen? I guess it's because of Drew."

The nephew. Nate, Brenda knew, liked kids, but had no time for selfish, devious adolescents who acted like two-year-olds. There'd been trouble before, but she'd had no idea it was this serious. "So when did it happen?"

"Sunday. We had a big fight over Drew, and Nate just stomped off. I thought he'd get over it. Yesterday I kicked Drew out and tried to call Nate at the fire station and tell him. He wasn't there, hadn't been on duty since Sunday, wasn't expected till tonight. I don't know where he is. He hasn't called . . ." Daniel broke off. His voice had become unsteady. "Look, Brenda, I've been a real pain in the ass these past few days. I'm sorry."

"What exactly did he say when he walked out?"

"It's hard for me to remember exact words. It's such a blur."

"Did he say he'd never come back, that your relationship was over, that he didn't love you?"

"None of that."

"So that's good."

"I've never had a fight like this with someone I love," Daniel said. "Sure we fight, but . . . Listen, I know you've been concerned. I appreciate it. Your concern is a comfort. It's hard for me to talk about. I don't know what to do."

"He will call," said Brenda. "Nate loves you. It'll be okay. You know you'll talk eventually. He didn't take all his stuff, did he?"

"No. It was so sudden."

"He'll be back." Brenda saw that his eyes were misty. "You know I'll do anything I can to help. If you need someone to listen, a shoulder to cry on . . ."

"Thanks," Daniel said. "I'll try to be less surly around here."

"Surly to bed, surly to rise. I know it's an old joke. Sorry."

"Every little bit of normal helps, including your feeble puns. I guess right now I'd like to drop it. It hurts too much to talk about it. It'd be easier to throw myself into an encryption that would take a hundred intense hours to figure out."

"Okay, I'll give a shot at a change of subject."

Daniel nodded.

Brenda said, "We may have a problem."

"What?"

"Well, I knew this woman named Sarah Swettenham. Knew her slightly." She told Daniel about Sarah's appointment, her sudden death, the oddity of her apartment being cleaned out, about her computers. "So I kept wondering about it, and just for the hell of it I e-mailed the branch offices to see if they knew anything weird about AllTech or Sarah."

"Not likely."

"Well, see, that's the thing. Yussuf in Cairo did. He e-mailed me back, said Sarah was worried about something, and he told me we should talk on a secure phone."

"Okay." Daniel wasn't much interested.

"I'll call first thing tomorrow. I can't tonight. It's too late there."

B renda, home from her movie, looked around her loft.

It usually pleased her, this quirky living space she'd made entirely her own. It was essentially a single huge room that she'd divided with hangings and plants and bookshelves. Only a little furniture, but supremely comfortable. There was a butter-soft leather couch and chair, with lots of cushions in bright colors. A solid oak table and a couple of dining chairs. A few good paintings and a couple of Edward Weston photographs, original prints that had cost her a bundle. She didn't like imitation anything. Thick rugs on the floor, but no curtains at the windows, because she had no close neighbors and she liked the sun streaming in through windows and skylights every morning.

Tonight the apartment seemed big and shadowy and empty. She shivered. She could light the wood-stove in the middle of the room. Maybe that would make the place feel cozy again, take away the sense of isolation.

Or maybe that would be too much trouble. She should just pick out a book, something she knew and loved, and take it to bed with her. The classic spin-ster's solution: take a good book to bed. She snorted. The next thing, she'd be taking up knitting.

The phone rang.

"Ms. Grant?"

She had never before heard him on the phone, but she recognized the voice instantly. "Yes, Mr. Cooper." What on earth was he calling her for at this time of night?

"I was hoping you'd be home by now, and hoping it wasn't too late to ask again about that drink. For some reason I don't feel able to settle into anything this evening, and I'd love some company."

Brenda was silent. Something peculiar was happen-ing to her insides. She kept seeing those gorgeous eyes, the firm jaw, the strong hands . . .

"Ms. Grant?"

"Oh, sorry. Look, I appreciate the offer, but it's a bit late for me. I'm an early riser."

She half expected him to persist, half expected her-self to give in. Why? She wasn't at all sure she trusted this guy, even if he did things to her hormones that no one had done for a long time.

"Oh, I am sorry. In that case, can I talk you into dinner tomorrow? I'm not in New York for long, and

I do think there are some details we need to discuss about our business, and dinner is far more civilized than a hurried lunch."

Good grief, what was she afraid of? If a handsome guy wanted to treat her to a nice meal, there was no reason at all to think . . . "Thank you. That should work out. Maybe you'd better call the office around noon, just to be sure. Emergencies do come up."

"As they do in my business. But I'm sure it will be a good day. Good-night, Ms. Grant. Sleep well."

She didn't. His voice stayed in her mind far too long and raised far too many ideas.

CHAPTER 15

As soon as Daniel came in Thursday morning, Brenda told him, "Yussuf may be in trouble. I can't get in touch with him."

"Well, maybe he's been busy."

"No, Daniel. I called and I e-mailed. Then I checked the Net news for Cairo, and there was an explosion at the restaurant, the one in our building. The phone lines are out. I hope he'll e-mail."

"Uh-oh."

"The word is that there were deaths at the restaurant, but there's no evidence of anybody else in the building being hurt. But you know how unreliable news is from there. The government always starts out by trying to minimize the problem."

"Yeah, like our government doesn't do that?"

"Whatever."

"I'd better go over there."

"Maybe. Yussuf will probably get in touch three minutes after you leave."

"If so, that's good. I'll call the consulate and check, and if they don't know, I'll pack and get on a red-eye. It's depressing to hang around here."

B renda was cautious. She had agreed to go to dinner with Cooper, but insisted that she would meet him at the restaurant. She had no doubt that he could find out where she lived, probably knew already for that matter, but she wasn't going to help him. Also, she didn't want one of those after-dinner, may-I-come-up? kind of evenings. She would go to dinner and come home alone in a cab.

"How about the Rainbow Room?" he said.

"Well, it's lovely, of course." And touristy. "How about Chanterelle?"

There was a brief pause. Chanterelle was no less pricey, but showed a lot more knowledge of the city. He said, "That would be perfect. I'll make a reservation."

Take that, she thought. She didn't want to be bossy, but she was no pushover either, and he'd better know it up front. In fact, she had thought of inviting him to the EAT-EAT-EAT diner, just around the corner from their office. He would have arrived dressed for an expensive restaurant, and it would have been interesting to watch how he handled the situation. And it probably would have helped her figure him out better. But it would have been just too aggressive, too confrontational.

Brenda owned exactly three good dresses. She was a working woman, not a social butterfly. She decided to wear the jade Jil Sander. Her hair was currently auburn, and so the jade looked good, if she did say so herself.

She was already at a table when he came in, and she could tell by his expression that he liked the way she looked. She had missed that look on a man's face. . . .

Chanterelle was filled with beautiful and powerful people. She fitted in perfectly well, but Cooper shone. Part of Brenda's job was sizing people up by what they were wearing. As Cooper strode to the table, she noted the black pashmina jacket, which she was sure was Dormeuil; Lobb loafers; and the black Prada jeans. Casual chic. Brenda reflected that ordinarily she was put off by men who were dandies, men focused on what they were wearing, but she got a sense that in Cooper's case there was a lot more on his mind than clothing.

He bent over the table, taking her hand, and then sat. He wore a psychedelic shirt with no tie. Inclining her head toward it, she said, "Richard James?"

His eyes widened, but he nodded. "Would you like to order now or chat a while first?"

"I'd like to order." She was pleased that he asked. Sitting in a restaurant waiting and waiting to eat was not her idea of fun. She was much too active a person for that.

So far so good.

There was just one more challenge she ran against him. When he ordered a Château Haut-Brion, she asked, "And you an official of an American federal agency! Salary paid by citizens' taxes?"

"What do you mean?"

"Haven't we been hearing that the American cabernets are the equal of French cabs in blind tastings?"

He laughed. "Yes. But not tonight," he said. "Please?"

While he laughed some more, as if at himself, she decided her initial reaction to this man had been foolish. She liked him. Some men would rather be challenged on their performance in bed than on their wine choices. Cooper said, "You're thinking of the infamous May 24, 1976, debacle in France. The anniversary a few years back was not celebrated over there."

"I imagine not," she said. The 1976 blind tasting of wines in France had left the U.S. wines with the most prizes. The French had agreed to the event in the belief that they would come out on top in virtually all categories. But it was a rout.

Brenda and Cooper studied the menu for a few moments. Brenda had her usual reaction, which was to say yes to everything. But the Moroccan loin of lamb caught her fancy most of all, and Cooper chose the beef filet enveloped in Niman Ranch applewood-smoked bacon.

Chanterelle was all understated elegance: white tablecloths, formal but comfortable chairs. It contained about twenty tables, spaced far enough apart to confer privacy. Its owners, who were also the chef and the hostess, had taken a chance on the Tribeca area thirty years earlier when there was little in the Triangle Below Canal to attract serious diners. Chanterelle continued to flourish, despite being expensive, by the not-simple combination of beautiful food and considerate service. Brenda liked the high tin ceiling and the pale butterscotch color on the walls.

"May I call you Brenda?" he asked. "And could you call me Coop?"

"Coop? Very Gary Cooper."

"One of my favorite actors."

"Okay. Coop it is."

"Mighty grateful, ma'am." He studied her for a few seconds. "Why do you want to be in this business?" he asked.

Brenda watched him as the waiter put a bourbon and water on the table for her and a martini for him. "I notice you ask why I want to, not what it is I do. You've researched everything you can about Daniel and me except what's inside our heads. Is that right?"

"Close to right. We don't get everything. As I told you, your ability to background people is one of the reasons we've hired you."

"Oh, please! With somebody who is really important to you, you can get all the information you need."

"To answer your question, I know about your parents, grade school, high school, college, first employment, and the fact that you were maybe two minutes short of being in the World Trade Center on the morning of 9/11. I know that almost all your friends there died."

Brenda kept silent. If he didn't know about her relationship with Jeremy—and how could he?—so much the better.

"But you see," he said, "that doesn't tell me anything, does it? After 9/11, why didn't you move to Maine and raise apples? A lot of people did things like that. Or take a job in computer development in Seattle? Or move to Florida and go fishing? So many people ran away from terrorism after that. Why did you run toward it?"

"Can you really run away from it?"

"My turn to say, 'Oh, please.' Nirvana, Michigan, is less likely to be attacked than New York City. A dairy farmer is less likely to be attacked than a person who is sticking her nose into every possible hornets' nest."

"You have such a way with words."

He smiled. "But don't you?"

"Poke into hornets' nests? Not intentionally. We keep an ear out for terrorists on the Net. An e-ear, you might say. But we don't go looking for trouble. Most of our company's work is standard anticrime and antiterror advice for corporations and sometimes individuals. And we design systems to protect against intrusion. We even protect against industrial espionage. And we look over and vet programs that companies are using."

"I know all that. In fact, I may have another job for you in that line. But later."

"All right."

"But you're still avoiding answering the question."

"Well, let's say it's also what I'm good at."

He swallowed the last of his martini and looked at her glass, which was still half full. He clearly didn't want to order another drink until she was ready for a refill.

"Go ahead," she said, gesturing at his glass. The waiter saw it and nodded at Cooper without being asked.

"I give up," he said. "You want to be mysterious."

"Not really. I think it's hard to explain your own motives." It was just too early in their relationship for her to explain about Jeremy. For that matter, it was still too painful to talk about. If he wanted to think she was just being coy, so be it. "So, you tell me. Why do you do your job?"

"I'm good at it. Sorry. I will talk about it and shame you for being so reticent."

She grinned back at him.

"There isn't any personal tragedy caused by terrorism in my background. So I can't really . . . well, I can barely guess how you must feel, and I can't claim any emotional reason. Except outrage. Like a lot of people around the world who haven't personally been victims of terrorism, it disgusts me. It's an offense against reason. Maybe deep down there's nothing that scares me more than zealots, people who think they have the only right view of the world, and if you don't share it, you aren't even human. That scares me. You can't reason with them. They don't even hear you."

Brenda liked what he was saying. It agreed with how she felt, or how she had felt until it all got more personal on 9/11. It also seemed honest, so far as she could judge. Cooper seemed to her to be a controlled, logical person. He wore carefully chosen clothing and worked for an agency that might be assumed to want to set things straight. She wondered whether his home was similar, a place for everything and everything in its place. She hesitated to follow that train of thought.

He said, "It outrages my sense of how things ought to be. And frankly, religion seems to bring out the worst of it. Not just Islam. When you read about the Catholics torturing Protestants or the Protestants torturing Catholics, or the Crusaders murdering and pillaging their way across the Holy Land . . ." He stopped. "This isn't a cheery topic for a pleasant dinner."

"Well, I asked."

They changed the subject, chatting through their entrées about the loss of old New York landmarks. "They tore down the Coogan Building," Cooper said.

"I remember the fuss about it. Used to be the old Racquet Club, I think."

"Great brickwork, arched windows, that nineteenth-century gracious look."

"But personally," said Brenda, "I was distressed that the building where Edgar Allan Poe had an apartment was demolished."

"Was it really? What did I hear about that?"

"They saved the façade and pasted it back onto the front of the new building," she said. "Yikes!"

After the main course, which Brenda pronounced wonderful, they both ordered blueberry flan with whipped cream. She sighed with happiness.

Outside the restaurant, on Harrison Street, cabs were passing now and then. But Cooper had a black car waiting. He opened the back door for Brenda. A chauffeur sat waiting in the driver's seat.

"Thank you, Coop, but I'm going to get a cab."

He raised his eyebrows. "You're not afraid to get in a car with me?"

"Of course not. And I'm sure you know where I live. Think of this as maintaining my independence."

"Henry, get a cab," Cooper said.

Brenda said, "Thank you for dinner. I really enjoyed it."

"Tomorrow?"

"I work. I can't take a three-hour dinner every night."

"Monday then? I'm going back to D.C. for the weekend. Or . . . I know. How about meeting me at the office, maybe on Saturday? It's in a beautiful old house. I'd like you to see it. And we never did get around to talking much business tonight. We could go to dinner from there."

A cab pulled up and Henry opened its door.

"Saturday?" Cooper repeated.

"I'm not sure I can get away. I'll call you."

"My cell phone number is here," he said, handing her a card. Then he leaned into the front seat and handed a folded bill to the driver, a twenty-something white guy with dreadlocks and a goatee. "Take the lady wherever she wants to go."

"If I can make it on Saturday, I'll try to have some early results for you by then," Brenda said.

"It's not necessary—dinner is not dependent on business results, Brenda," he said.

"Okay."

"Hey, dude," said the driver. "The lady going any-place or not?"

"Oh, yes. She's going places," Cooper said.

When Daniel called from the air just before mid-night, he asked, "Did you hear from Yussuf?"

"No. I wish."

"Did you go out with that Cooper guy?"

"Yes, Daniel."

"I wish you wouldn't."

"Why?"

"I don't want to be hypercritical, but he rubs me the wrong way."

"I don't see what that has to do with anything.

You're not the one going out with him. What's he gonna do, steal my heart? Besides, it's just a business dinner. And why wouldn't you trust him? We're working for him." Brenda still wasn't sure seeing Cooper was a good idea. She was arguing partly to convince herself.

"He's government. He's going to have interests that are not necessarily ours."

"Like 'I'm from the government and I'm here to help you'? So, he'll murder me between the appetizer course and the entrée?"

"He's slick."

"You talk about slick! I didn't criticize you about that Digby Halliburton creepazoid you were going out with before Nate."

"I didn't date him for long."

"Well, good!"

"And Cooper's not Jeremy."

Brenda drew in a breath, appalled.

Daniel was horrified too. "Oh, god. I shouldn't have said that."

"Nobody else," she said slowly, "is Jeremy. And nobody will ever be Jeremy."

"God, Brenda, I'm just so sorry. I didn't mean that. I don't know why I said that. Jeez! I'm sorry, sorry, sorry, sorry. I'll hit myself if you want."

"Okay, Daniel. Just chill." She thought for a minute, then added, "I mean, it's not your business who I date. If I didn't like Nate, I wouldn't bug you about it, would I?"

"Don't you like Nate?"

"Of course I do. I said *if*!"

"You don't like him."

"I do so! I like him! I like him a lot!"

They both started to laugh then, and Brenda said, "Okay. Okay."

But things weren't quite the same.

CHAPTER 16

The suave Westerner sat in the café on the Seine. He watched the bateaux mouches—the tour boats—float by. His counterpart sat down at the table at precisely ten a.m.

"We agreed not to meet like this," said the Easterner. "You've allowed a breach."

"I know, but I've taken care of it."

"Completely?" the Westerner demanded.

"Yes, yes, it was a one-time thing."

"You are proceeding as planned?" It was almost an accusation from the Westerner.

"Of course. We have played our part well. The payments will continue?"

"If you keep doing your job," the Westerner said. "Daniel Henderson is on the way to Cairo."

"He will be dealt with."

The Westerner left the correct amount of change on the table, got up, and strolled down to the riverbank. The Easterner, looking worried, quickly let himself become part of the anonymous throngs in the street.

D aniel settled in for a long flight from New York. With a stop in Paris, it would take fourteen hours. Cairo was seven hours ahead of Eastern Daylight Time. He had left New York at eight that night and would arrive in Cairo at five the next afternoon, local time. He ate a little, drank bottled water, called Brenda, and then tried to sleep. Instead, he worried and planned. There was more time for the former than he wished and not enough as he suspected he needed for the latter.

No word from the Cairo office. That was bad. He wondered what Yussuf had wanted to tell them. When the company had established its branch offices around the world, it had set them up on two levels. DB Security actually was what it was advertised to be, a security company able to provide services worldwide, and it had made money doing just that. In each office, however, there was also a person assigned to the terrorism watch. Over the years, Daniel's contacts in the antiterrorist world had given him leads on whom to hire. Sometimes these people became the heads of the offices, sometimes not.

Before leaving the United States, Daniel had Googled "Cairo news" but had been rewarded with little more than what he and Brenda already knew. There had been some kind of fire. Definitely an explosion. He would have to examine things up close.

Daniel had been to Egypt before. He'd gone to each country when DB initially set up the offices.

Daniel had seen the pyramids from a distance. He'd traveled down the Nile to Luxor on a felucca. From one of these boats, he'd watched the sunset over the pyramids and the river. He thought someday he'd like to climb the Great Pyramid, though he knew it was forbidden. He wanted a way to connect with a people who had been so dedicated to an essentially pointless task. Why build such great mounds?

Touristy musings couldn't drive away the questions that chased round his head. Had the explosion targeted their Cairo office? If so, what did that mean? He would have to be careful.

The man sitting in the first-class seat never glanced in Daniel's direction. He'd been told to follow him to Cairo. It wasn't as easy as following the ditzy one who changed her hair color every five minutes. He would wait and watch. He was to get information. For now, he was not set to kill.

CHAPTER 17

October 24
Cairo, Egypt
Eleven Days before the Presidential Election

Cairo was warm that afternoon. Daniel knew the cool of the desert would rush in at night. He wore a loose-fitting shirt that covered his arms to below his wrists. His jeans were worn, but not tight. He would fit into the crowds in the city.

He was traveling alone, not with a tour, so he was accosted at the airport by touts for numerous hotels. Almost certainly these hotels were fleabags that charged exorbitant prices to unwary, unaccompanied tourists. Daniel kept his wits and his sense of humor.

Out of the airport in less than twenty minutes, he hailed a cab. Before he got in, he negotiated with the driver for his fare. He knew approximately what it should cost to get him to the center of town, and he had no intention of being ripped off.

Daniel had made his hotel reservations on the Internet. He was staying at the Nile Hilton on Maydan al-Tahrir, the square from which all distances in Egypt are measured. Next door to the hotel was the Egyptian Museum with its renowned collection of antiquities.

The traffic from the airport was nuts. Traffic in Cairo was always a mess. The blat of horns from the seemingly endless supply of Peugeots filled his ears. He caught whiffs of exhaust fumes, incense, and attar of roses.

Daniel hoped to find Yussuf quickly. In the lobby of the hotel he picked up a copy of *Al-Akhbar*, the most popular newspaper in the city, and searched it for a story about the fire. When he found it, details about the incident were minimal, although the story did confirm that it was a bombing and that most of a whole block was gone. What exactly in that block caused it to be a target for bombing was a matter of speculation. The guesses in the paper did not name DB Security.

Daniel took the crowded metro to the Mar Girgis station right outside Coptic Cairo. He walked south, past the Greek Orthodox Cemetery on his left. Just before he got to the Monastery and Church of St. George, he took the footbridge and walked back north to the market. He was in Old Cairo now. Here everyone wore modest clothing, unlike the touristy types at his hotel.

Their office had been on the west side of the market. Now the office and its neighbors were gone. Burnt shells of one- and two-story stone buildings were all that remained. The whole area was cordoned off, and Cairo police still patrolled the square. Daniel saw no one he recognized. He had hoped to find Yussuf here. Now he saw that there was no reason for anyone to be here. Especially, he thought grimly, if Yussuf was dead.

Daniel did not notice a man on the north side of the market who slipped into the ahwa, ordered a chai and a water pipe, and joined in a game of backgammon. The man looked up seldom, just often enough to make sure Daniel was in sight.

After making a tour of the market, Daniel walked up to one of the white-uniformed Cairo policemen and introduced himself as the owner of one of the businesses. Daniel spoke Arabic reasonably well. Arabic is a difficult language, but it had so obviously been needed that during his training he had spent intensive time learning it, and had been taking a once-a-week, two-hour class ever since. He also knew French from school, and enough German to find a men's room and the nearest taxi.

"Was anybody hurt?" he asked the policeman.

The official directed Daniel to Iban Zabul, a plain-clothes Cairo police officer half a block away. Zabul was a heavy man whose white shirt was open at the top and whose dark beige suit coat hung open over matching pants that hung below his protruding belly. Daniel was asked to produce his passport. He showed all his identification. He'd even come prepared with a copy of the rental agreement for the building offices.

Zabul was polite but firm. He took Daniel to a nearby café and questioned him for nearly two hours. Halfway through, they were joined by an officer from the Internal Security Forces. It was he who finally answered Daniel's question. Yes, he said, five bodies had been found in the wreckage.

Daniel gritted his teeth and waited. Nothing, he knew, was ever to be gained by trying to rush an Arab. But he had to be sure ...

The officers told him that the perpetrators had gotten away, but numerous suspects in radical groups had been arrested. Daniel feared this was the classic round-up-the-usual-suspects ploy. No group had yet claimed responsibility for the blast, so no one was sure what the object of the crime had been. It had not originated in DB's offices, but in the little restaurant next door. Which could mean anything, thought Daniel—care and concealment on the part of the attackers, or that it wasn't meant for them, or that the bomb had accidentally gone off too soon. The explosion had taken place during the lunch hour.

Five bodies. Who? *Who?* Daniel knew DB had five full-time staffers, including Yussuf, and several lower-level, part-time computer geeks.

At last the officers got back around to the bodies. They had been identified. One was the owner of the restaurant. Four were DB employees, having their lunch, the officers assumed. No, no trace of Yussuf.

Daniel was stricken. He'd met all of them. They were not close friends, but they'd been part of his life, no matter how peripheral, and part of his business world, and now they were dead. Because of a simple enquiry about Sarah Swettenham? He found that hard to believe. But here were more people he'd lost to terrorism. It wasn't as severe as the shock and horror of 9/11, but the impact of this new loss sank in deep. Daniel left the market, retraced his footsteps.

As he walked, he reflected on the explosion. Was this random Middle East hatred run amok or something more pointed? For his own safety, he needed to assume that they'd been after the DB office. But who were "they"? And why was this happening?

He was as cautious as possible as he walked down the streets, but he knew it would be easy for an enemy to conceal himself among the throngs. Daniel had no weapon.

For a few moments he considered that perhaps he was letting fear overrun his common sense. Bombings occurred in Cairo and other Middle Eastern cities with frightening regularity. Perhaps this one was just a coincidence, but Daniel vowed that no one he knew would die because he incorrectly assumed a "coincidence" had occurred. He walked past the train station and took the bus back to Maydan al-Tahrir.

He went straight up to his room in the Hilton and splashed cold water on his face. He'd had no real sleep for over twenty-four hours, and he needed to be alert. Then he called the homes of company personnel in the Cairo office. People answered who confirmed the deaths. He asked gentle questions, but didn't push them. They showed no indication they knew anything beyond what was in the press. There was no answer at Yussuf's number.

Daniel ordered a meal from room service, scarcely knowing what he ate, and then decided on one last effort. He went downstairs, taking his laptop, and sat on the hotel terrace in the Ibis Café. He examined all the late-evening clientele and staff. He recognized no one. Like good cops everywhere, he was trained to notice people and what they did. It was one of the first rules of terrorist training. He saw nothing suspicious or out of place.

Daniel opened his laptop and scanned the vicinity for any other wireless Internet activity. Detecting none,

Daniel keyed in the codes for the Cairo office. Yussuf could be online somewhere.

No response.

DB had established an emergency contact system long ago. An employee would know to come to a central meeting place, in this case the Ibis, at ten in the morning and ten at night. It was a procedure that guaranteed contact even if all other means of communication had failed. The time ticked to 10:15, then to 10:30, while Daniel searched on his laptop.

At 10:39 he raised his gaze above the keyboard again.

Yussuf stood before him. He was breathing heavily. "I thought I'd never get here," he gasped.

Daniel stood and reached toward him. Yussuf shook his head. "They're after me."

"Who is?" Daniel asked. He heard pops of gunfire. Yussuf's hand clutched his side. He pulled it away. Blood oozed down it, from fingertips to wrist. He shoved a bloody piece of paper into Daniel's hand and then pitched sideways. He crashed into a table with four patrons sitting at it. Daniel heard more gunshots. Patrons, table, and chairs went flying.

Yussuf crumpled to the ground. Daniel dove after him and leaned close, at the same time slipping the bloody paper into his own pants pocket. He saw the hole in the shirt and the welling blood underneath it. Yussuf was silent. His eyes stared, empty. He was dead.

Gunfire shattered the glass on his table, but Daniel was now fifteen feet away. He squeezed past startled patrons. He heard screaming behind him. He slid into a cab on the far side of Maydan al-Tahrir.

He headed north and slightly west for several blocks. At the first red light he threw several Egyptian

pound notes at the driver and shot out the door of
the cab. He ducked into the Ramses Hilton Mall and
walked out a side door, taking the last cab in the line
waiting outside. He ordered it to drive northwest.

Daniel had to get out of Egypt. As the car raced
forward, the driver as usual applying his horn instead
of his brakes, Daniel considered his options. South?
There wasn't an international airport until Luxor. That
was a lot of miles of desert to be trapped in. Same
problem westward without the possibility of an airport. East, the Red Sea and no sure transport, more
desert, and different countries.

He did not take out Yussuf's paper. Patience was
one of the things drummed into you in training. Do
nothing precipitate. Do not give yourself away by the
simplest inadvertent action.

On the northwest outskirts of Cairo, he paid the
cab and got out. He had not seen anyone following
him. He was on the Desert Road from Cairo to Alexandria. He left the road and walked to the riverfront
and then followed the current north and west.

It was the middle of the night when he found the
half-ruined mud-and-brick structure he was looking
for, the safe house. There was at least one in each
country in which they had offices. The houses had
been a drain on DB's finances, but after Daniel's training, he had insisted on them. Brenda was no fool. It
hadn't taken much to convince her. Daniel himself
had set this one up. An old farmer nearby had a few
scrubby, near-famished sheep. A clump of palm trees
clustered around the house. It all looked perfectly ordinary, nothing to attract anyone's attention.

Once inside, screened against any possible observer,
Daniel flicked on a flashlight and examined the note

Yussuf had handed him. Blood obscured some of the words.

> *Went to school with Sarah. Talked sometime . . .*
> *was concerned about vote-tallying program she'd*
> *written. More information is . . .*

Daniel couldn't read the rest. The next words could have been "in Istanbul." They did have an office there. No one from the Istanbul office had contacted Brenda. At least they hadn't before he left. Should he try to stop in Istanbul? Well, first he had to get out of Egypt alive.

Daniel removed bales of hay from around a black Harley motorcycle. He found a change of clothes, several sets of new identity papers, maps, a few simple oddments of disguises, cash in various currencies, weapons, and local guidebooks—the standard stash. He stripped naked, just in case a tracking device had somehow been planted in his clothing, and threw the clothes down the dried-up well next to the rotting farmhouse.

He donned black boxer-briefs, jeans, shirt, socks, boots, leather jacket, and helmet. Of the weapons available, he chose a Glock 19, compact, lightweight, and deadly. After a careful scan of the area to make sure he was unobserved, he climbed on the Harley and started off.

Daniel kept the motor just above an idle, because for now he was not going to take the Desert Road. He was going to try to stick close to the riverbank. He hoped the bluffs and gullies on his left would provide some cover—if he needed cover. If he was being followed. If . . . if . . . if . . .

He kept the headlight off as he motored deeper

into the surrounding night. Eventually he would need to turn west and pick up the Desert Road to Alexandria. For now he wove in and out of the bluffs. He had to have time to think and plan.

Half an hour later he noticed headlights behind him.

An enemy? A late night reveler? A tired parent on an emergency run? He couldn't take a chance. He took the next right, a dirt path that wound down a steep bank to the river. He was forced to slow for hairpin turns. Several times he nearly slid over sandy precipices onto scrub grass hundreds of feet below. He arrived at the base of the hill. The motorcycle slewed left and right as he touched the water's edge.

He let the river cover his tracks. Starlight shone on the eternal Nile and guided him past rocks on the shore. When he looked back, the headlights were behind him on the same narrow strip of land. Daniel sped up. He saw a second set of headlights on the bluff on the left up ahead. They jostled and jumped as they came toward him.

Daniel deduced that the second driver was not following a path down to the riverside but had chosen to career in over the bluffs at speeds Daniel would not have dared. Plainly these people were desperate and deadly. The lights up above seemed to flicker as they appeared and disappeared and reappeared. He'd rather see his enemy. One you can see can be frightening. One you can't see can be terrifying. And who were they? Who, who—and why?

They knew he was there. He could go faster with some light; he switched it on. Revving up the motor, he roared off into the night.

Daniel couldn't hear much over the thrum of his Harley. The lights ahead of him on his left bore relentlessly closer, shining into the night, sometimes jumping out over the gurgling river water, then switching to clumps of bushes, often angling straight down the bluff at dizzyingly steep angles. Must be some kind of all-terrain vehicle.

Now he was nearly abreast of those lights, which at times seemed to be coming down the bluff straight at him. Directly behind Daniel, the lights of the first vehicle he'd seen closed in. Daniel didn't know if he'd get past the vehicle coming at him from above. The lights swung wildly as if someone were riding a giant teeter-totter while trying to focus a laser light. The driver must be passing through the last steep declivities before hitting the shore. Daniel could only hope they would hit it very hard.

He looked back. That car was maybe a hundred yards behind. He looked up and to the left. The lights twirled, pointed straight down, turned back to horizontal, then almost completely vertical, then straightened, roared straight at him for a moment, then dipped and swung again.

Daniel slowed slightly so he could judge better if he had to make a change in direction. He didn't think he'd get far by attempting to charge back up the sandy bluff in the opposite direction from the rapidly closing car. In seconds he would catch up with those lights. Perhaps he would get past them. With any luck the two cars would collide and shoot out spectacular flames.

Then to his left he saw the two menacing beams swing wildly up, then straight down. They held steady for several seconds; then the pursuer's car launched itself into space over the last twenty-foot precipice. It hit, burst into flames, and slid over one last bank of sand. With a shattering crunch, it hit just to his left and then began to tumble. It landed on its hood and began sliding directly toward his path. Daniel gave the cycle as much gas as possible. He roared past the tumbling car with inches to spare.

He didn't have time for a sigh of relief. He turned and saw the lights of the other car behind him swerve, right themselves, sweep around the crumpled wreckage, send up a plume of river water as its right tires caught the Nile, and then head straight for him. Daniel rushed on. The beach was clear. He'd gone at least another two miles when it became evident that the lights behind him were steadily creeping closer. Daniel could now see his shadow ahead of him. They were definitely closing in.

Daniel noted a mass of darkness across his path. He thought it might be a mile ahead. No starlight reflected from it. Was it a headland? A promontory point thrown out by the landward hills? To his left he saw no path. Just brush and sand rising into the night.

Daniel considered his options as he neared the blackness. His headlight was picking up the solid mass. A stop and a sudden turn? Gunfire rang out over the whine of his engines. The erratically fired bullets blew up small clouds of sand. Stop and shoot it out? A shootout in the dark, with how many pursuers? How well-armed? Get off and run into the dark? There could be more of them.

Dirt exploded in a semicircle on his left. The last puff hit less than six inches from his front tire. Any turn and he'd be a better target for the gunfire. Should he head into the river? Take his chances swimming? The river was damn big enough to get lost in. And no doubt filthy, probably deadly. He had seconds to decide. The headland loomed. He let the motorcycle full out. At the last second he saw it. Starlight under the headland.

He caught dim lights on the river. A felucca, one of the boats tourists often used to go up and down the river. He didn't see people on the deck. It was late. Maybe only the owner/boatman would be awake. But the light on the river showed him that the obstruction ahead extended into the river. A pier? On the shore ahead of him he saw a narrow opening in the crumpled remnants of the pier.

Daniel sped straight toward the opening. He leaned as far left as he could. His tires caught the last bits of foam. He tottered, teetered, slid nearly sideways. His laptop slid off into the water, and he kicked and felt around for it, but found only mud. He gave up and aimed his bike under the concrete-and-wood outcropping, an arch dipping into the Nile. He struggled through, dragging the motorcycle. The engine stalled. His head brushed damp wood. The sudden silence of his machine let him hear how close his pursuers were. Then he was through. He righted the motorcycle. He might have spent five seconds under the arch, maybe ten. He tried to start the engine. Nothing.

Tried again. Third time, nope. He switched off the headlight, looked back, and listened. He heard the car that had been behind him crunch into the wall. The opening was far too small for the car.

The sound was not that of a fatal crash, nor was there any sign of fire. The driver must have braked enough to save lives but perhaps not the car. Daniel heard cursing in Arabic and then gunfire, but the shots seemed to be random rather than purposeful. None landed near him. If the car was drivable, his pursuers would have to go inland to get around this obstruction. If it was ruined, they were on foot, and he was in the clear.

Daniel tried the ignition again. This time it caught. Nothing had ever sounded better than the Harley's powerful motor, but he knew they would hear it. He leapt aboard and roared away. Looking back, he didn't see any evidence of car lights attempting to move around the obstruction. Nor were there any lights on the bluffs to his left. He checked frequently. Nothing. He was safe. For now.

The killer listened to the dwindling roar of the motorcycle. The mission had changed to assassination. Missing the kill was bad. But the victim didn't have many options. To get out of Egypt he had to either return through Cairo or go to Alexandria. There would be time.

Helen walked into Brenda's office about 9:30 on Friday morning. Brenda was slouched in her chair, one hand on the mouse, the other groping for something on the desk as she stared at the screen.

"If you're looking for coffee, all the cups are empty," said Helen. "But I brought you some. Here." She held out a tall paper cup with the Brew-Ha-Ha North logo on it.

Brenda pried off the lid, and took a long gulp before she spoke. "Thanks. I appreciate your going to the trouble."

She raised her eyebrows at Brenda's tone. "You pull an all-nighter?"

Brenda swallowed more coffee. "Got home about

ten. Couldn't sleep. Came in about four. Besides, we need to start earning that retainer." DB's lawyer had not only approved the contract in record time, he had slavered over it. Cooper had been as good as his word. With the contract in hand, he'd seen to the immediate issuing of the check. "While you and Chihiro have been working on the backgrounding stuff, I've been working on the terrorist network end. Take a look at what I've found out."

Helen peered over her shoulder. "Doesn't tell me a lot."

"Me, neither, but it's . . . odd. Maybe it's just co-incidence, but I've found similarities in source code in the most unlikely places. Look at this."

Brenda swiveled the monitor so Helen could see more easily. Helen pulled up a chair and peered.

What they were looking at was a screen full of source code, the essence of every computer program. Undecipherable to anyone other than a programmer, it's heavy going even for experts—densely written and full of nonalphabetical symbols. "Right," said Helen. "Pretty klugey code, but I suppose it gets the job done. Where's it from?"

"That little terrorist cell in Uzbekistan."

"Yeah, well, we've known about them for ages. They're small, they're on the fringe, they don't seem to be going anywhere. Okay, they may have links to Al Qaeda, but who doesn't? So what's so scary?"

"See this line?" Brenda pointed the mouse arrow to a long line of code.

"Couldn't get much clunkier than that," said Helen, frowning. "I could figure out a dozen ways to make that more elegant."

"Me too. Now look at this." Brenda clicked on another set of data and arranged the two sets in split screen. She moved the arrow to a line in the new set of code. "Now am I crazy, or are those two identical?"

Helen's interest sharpened. "Sure looks like it. So what?"

"So this one, my dear, is part of a program used by the International Monetary Fund."

"No," said Helen flatly. "It's impossible. No way."

"Yeah, but there it is. Now what are we going to do about it? Report it now, or wait till we find out more? This could be . . . way scary." Her hand shook as she picked up her coffee cup.

"You've had too much coffee, kid. Let's go out for some ice cream. I bet you haven't eaten. Nothing like hot fudge for a midmorning snack And to answer your question: personally, I don't think you report it yet. Not until you're one hundred percent sure. This could blow up in a lot of different directions. You have to be right."

They settled with hot fudge over pistachio ice cream. They both decided Brenda really couldn't have any more coffee for a while. Brenda appeared to relax a little, but she stood up as soon as they'd finished their ice cream. "Gotta get back. Gotta follow this up."

They'd barely stepped inside her office when Helen stopped dead. Brenda bumped into her.

"Sorry! What?"

Helen pulled Brenda inside the door and closed it. "Someone's been at my desk," she whispered.

"How do you know?"

"I line up the mouse on the pad whenever I leave. With the squares." Her mouse pad was printed in a colorful plaid. "It's been moved. Jeez, I wish the camera didn't just focus on the door."

"We can widen it," Brenda said.

"Let's. But it's locking the door after the horse is stolen. Somebody's been rummaging."

"You closed the computer down before you left, right?" Brenda was on a chair, fiddling with the spy camera lens.

"Of course. But look—it shows an attempt to access my files."

"But nobody could have gotten at any data, not without your password."

"No. The point is, somebody tried."

"Next time they try, we'll catch them on camera."

Brenda had about thirty seconds to worry about it before her phone rang.

Helen's voice said, "Line three. It's John Claymore from SafetyBus. He's pretty shook up."

"Ms. Grant? This . . . uh . . . this is John . . . Claymore . . . Safety Bus. I—this is Ms. Grant?"

"Yes, Mr. Claymore. What can I do for you?"

"You've already done it. We had a . . . uh . . . an incident this morning. And if it hadn't been for you . . . well—"

Brenda sucked in her breath. "What happened?"

"See, our people were so impressed with your report that we had some of the work done right away. We couldn't do all the buses, and we couldn't do everything you recommended. Not immediately, I mean. The silent alarm button takes electronics and all, and that takes time. But the door closers and the siren . . . we could do those right away. On some of the buses, not all, of course. And—"

"Mr. Claymore, what happened?"

"Sorry, sorry, I'm sort of upset. One of the buses was attacked."

Brenda's stomach clenched. Those kids! Visions of small faces rose in her mind. Scrubbed little faces, trusting faces, mischievous faces, and none more than five years old. "What about the kids?" she whispered.

"They're okay! That's why I'm calling. I didn't want you to just hear it on the news. They're all okay. See, when the guys tried to storm the bus, the driver hit the siren and locked the door right away. None of the creeps got in. They tried to shoot the bus driver, but those new doors have bulletproof glass, like you said. And the companions are all trained to get the kids into a crouch, down below the windows, if anything happens. So anyway, the driver just took off like a bat out of hell. Well, not really. There's too much traffic in New York for that." He laughed nervously. "But he stepped on the gas to get away from the attackers and went up on the sidewalk. Knocked over a mailbox! And then he went around the corner. By that time the attackers were running in the other direction. The cops someplace nearby heard the siren—it's really loud and scary—and they got there right away. So then . . ."

Claymore went on, excited, upset, needing to tell the whole story. Brenda didn't really listen. The kids were all right. The kids weren't hurt. The details didn't matter.

"Did the police catch the attackers?" she asked, when she could get a word in.

"Well, no. They took off running as soon as the siren went off. We're hoping they can be identified from security tapes. Like I said, the bus had stopped and picked up the little Berlesconi girl at her apartment, and that building has security cameras inside and out. Though I guess the men were masked and dressed all in black, so maybe there won't be much to go on."

"Berlesconi? As in Hector Berlesconi, something-or-other in Washington?"

"His granddaughter. Son's only child. And the grandson of the Senegalese consul, Toussaint Kebede, was on board too, and the grandson of the British ambassador to the UN . . . Oh, your work saved a lot of important children today, Ms. Grant."

All children are important, Brenda thought. "I'm so glad, Mr. Claymore. It's good to know we helped."

When she finally got off the phone, she went out to tell Helen. It made up a little for all the times when DB's information and advice had been ignored. "They'll never catch them though," she added at the end of the story. "They never do, that kind of quick-raid thing. Especially when nobody gets hurt."

Helen nodded her agreement. "But maybe these particular thugs won't try it again with this particular company."

"Maybe. I guess we have to be grateful for that."

Helen gave Brenda a quick hug. "You done good, kid," she said.

Brenda grinned. "Every now and then it's worth it, huh?"

Another call came that afternoon. "Who is it, Helen?" Brenda asked, clicking Save on her keyboard.

"The White House." Helen sounded awed.

"Hot damn! Put them through."

"Ms. Grant?" said a gravelly, unfamiliar voice.

"My name is Hector Berlesconi. I understand my family and I owe you a huge debt of gratitude."

"Not at all, sir. My job—"

"The bus company tells me that if it hadn't been for the precautions you and your company insisted on, all the kids on that bus would have been kidnapped, if not killed."

"Well, sir, we have no way of knowing the intentions of the criminals."

"But we can make a pretty good guess, can't we? Ms. Grant, I have only one grandchild. Little Emily is the light of my life. My son's wife almost died when Emily was born, and they can't have any more children. There's no way I can repay you for what you've done."

"I was just doing a job, sir. But thank you. I love kids, too."

"I thought so. Mr. Claymore told me how you reacted to the news this morning."

"One thing you might do for me. If you ever learn who the attackers were, I'd like to know about it. My firm keeps up on things like that."

"Will do, and with pleasure. Listen, Ms. Grant, my other line has a call for me, but if there's anything more I can ever do for you, please let me know."

The huge bouquet of expensive flowers arrived a few minutes later. The card read simply, *H. B., with gratitude.*

CHAPTER 18

Brenda slipped out of the cab in front of the beautiful old Washington mansion at exactly six-thirty p.m. She had never thought it was cute or fashionable to be late. But then this wasn't a date either.

Wasn't it? Then why was she wearing her best black suit, the Armani she only wore to see major clients in Wall Street offices? Well, this was a major client, in a D.C. office.

Okay, then why wear an indigo raw-silk blouse with it? Oh, stop second-guessing yourself.

Her plane got in early so she spent an hour at the National Portrait Gallery. She loved it, and besides, it seemed so wasteful to fly to D.C. and back for a one-hour meeting with Cooper. That was her conservatism talking. Flying back and forth for two million dollars couldn't really be called foolish.

She strolled up the wide front walk, then climbed the broad steps. They don't make mansions like they used to, she thought. Beautiful Georgian windows, deep, multiple moldings on the door. What this building had seen over the years would make a book. A brass plaque read:

NATIONAL SECURITY ANALYSIS AGENCY

"Identification, please, ma'am," said the guard, bringing her back to the present day.

She showed him her ID.

"Ma'am, your hair is a different color," he said, his thumb pressed firmly on her photo.

"That's right. I thought Wicked Walnut would go nicely with the fall colors. Do you like it?"

"Uh—".

Cooper stepped out of the door. "It's okay, Baker," he said. "The face is the same."

"Yes, sir."

"Sorry about that," Cooper said.

Cooper escorted her across the entry hall. Its two-story ceiling was plastered in deep coves, painted three pale shades of peach to emphasize the design. The walls were linenfold-paneled walnut.

"I could blend in here," she said, placing her head near a wall.

"You'd only make it lovelier."

Compliments? she thought, entering a side room as he swung open the door for her. It was a library as libraries used to be, bookshelves on all sides. However, down the center ran library tables holding monitors and printers, and under the tables were computer towers and other cybergear.

He led her to a pair of wingback chairs near the window.

"I wanted you to see where we work," he said, settling into the chair after she sat down. "And I also want to propose another situation for you to tackle for us."

"Go ahead."

"There is a company that's developed a vote-tallying program. It will be used in polling machines manufactured by 21st Century Polling."

"There are several electronic polling programs."

"True. But this one is going to be used in a whole lot of municipalities in the upcoming election, on voting machines manufactured by 21st Century Polling. The company wants a reliable, independent study of the system to make sure it's kosher."

"Why is it your problem?"

"It isn't exactly, and the NSAA wouldn't be paying you; 21st Century would. I got drawn into it when I heard rumors that the program could be hacked by terrorists. Or if not terrorists, interests outside the United States. Even if that's not true, whoever is president will make a difference in foreign policy."

"Oh."

"But then, with all the media attention to election fraud"—he chuckled without humor—"there has been a push among some people in Congress to double- and triple-vet these things before there's a problem, not after. In any case, DB has a large and growing reputation in precisely this field."

He crossed his legs. "There's only ten days," Brenda said.

"It's just a matter of studying the actual code."

"You have no idea how complicated that can be. The engineers write the program, but then it's compiled and becomes almost unreadable. Plus there are probably thousands and thousands of lines! You can't do it properly in ten days."

"Yes, but ten days is what we have. This is real life, not an academic exercise. Certainly you can study it enough to see whether any problems jump out at you."

"I don't think—"

"Haven't you had time-urgent jobs before?"

"It's true that this is what we do for corporations."

"Then, too, the various municipalities that use the program can point out to the media that it's been vetted." He paused and made a sorry-for-what's-coming face. "Vetted by the very best."

"Silver-tongued devil. You knew I wouldn't buy that."

"You should, though." He clapped his hands. "So may I have 21st Century Polling, the manufacturer, put you on their subscriber list with Internet access?"

"Well, I guess so."

"And of course, you will be able to use the fact that you've been chosen to vet the program as part of DB's advertising."

"Okay, okay. We'll give it a look. No guarantees."

"Excellent!" Cooper stood. "So now let me take you to the best restaurant within a baseball's throw of the Capitol."

"I wish I could." She had decided this was moving

too fast. Better slow it down a little. "But I've got to get back. I've got a full day of work tomorrow."

He raised his eyebrows. "Sunday?"

"No rest for the wicked."

"Well . . . all right, then. Are you on a commercial airline?"

"Yes. Haven't got around to buying the corporate jet yet." She smiled.

"Can you cancel it?"

"Yes—"

"Please do." He picked up his cell and dialed. "Hello, Maurice. Yes, it's me. Can you pack up the dinner and get it to Air Force Seven in thirty minutes? Thanks."

He saw Brenda's face as he ended the call. "Don't worry. It's a small government jet some of us can access. Nothing like Air Force One. You can be as modest as you like."

"Um, fine."

"I wish I could go with you. But I'll see you in New York on Monday. We're still doing dinner, right?"

B renda put her feet up on the footrest that a touch of a button called out from the bottom of the seat ahead. This aircraft should be called *Leg Room One*. What bliss! She could get used to this. It had been a wonderful meal.

A young man in uniform brought her a mochacchino, double the chocolate, topped with whipped cream.

Life would be pretty damn good, if only Daniel would call.

CHAPTER 19

Saturday, October 25
Alexandria
Ten Days before the Presidential Election

Daniel drove the motorcycle into the night. Eventually he slowed down. He felt safer not having to drive full out, but still he kept a careful watch. Next time they might come after him and not put their headlights on. After about five miles he came to a dirt road that led back up over the bluffs and dunes. He followed it. Just before he got to the highway, he turned off the headlight.

When he reached the four-lane Desert Road, stars shone on citrus groves on his right and desert on his left. The full moon rose, starkly huge. No lights appeared on the highway in either direction. Distant lamps showed signs of human habitation in lone farmhouses.

The road climbed into the desert. At times Daniel

thought he could reach out and touch the moon around the next corner. He arrived at a crossroads and thought it had to be Alin of abun-ashair. He cut his engine. He could see the conical roosts where some of the locals raised pigeons for food.

The highway was quiet in either direction. He wanted to take a few minutes to contact Brenda, but he knew it would be impossible. The rule was "silence," and its corollary "never trust anyone." He was not to use technology when there was danger. Any technology could be compromised. He thought of writing a letter, but it would probably get to New York after he did. Also, one problem for the highly trained, lethal fighting machine was that he didn't have a stamp and there was nowhere on this road at this time of night to get one. Daniel kept his lights off as he motored steadily into the heartland of the Nile Delta.

The trip to Alexandria from Cairo normally took two and a half hours along the Cairo-Alexandria Desert Road. The little diversion when he'd nearly been killed had cost him time, but he'd still get to Alexandria by morning. He motored steadily between the fields near the river on his right and the great silent desert on his left. And he thought furiously.

In Cairo there had been a Sarah Swettenham contact. DB's office had been destroyed. Yussuf had been killed at a rendezvous with Daniel. Could all this be connected to Sarah? What was it all about?

He'd been chased north. His pursuers must know he was headed to Alexandria. It would do no good to branch out into the desert.

He let the motorcycle idle at the top of a rise about five miles from the city and gazed down at the lights twinkling off as the sun rose. He looked back. No traffic for the moment. Maybe the bad guys chartered a plane and reached Alexandria ahead of him.

For that matter, the enemy could simply have phoned their minions in Alexandria. Daniel could be cycling into an ambush. He'd need another change of clothes, something to disguise him.

A group that had minions like that—if they did—was one to be reckoned with.

What if they were the government? Spies? CIA? Why would the U.S. government be after him? Why would anybody? Maybe they were the Egyptian police or the Egyptian army or the Egyptian security police? Was he trapped in some kind of sci-fi nightmare, with all of his movements being watched from spy satellites? If so, his position was hopeless.

Daniel wasn't ready to give up yet. His thoughts strayed to Brenda and Nate, the parts of his life he'd rather be dealing with. Daniel's mother, before her death from cancer when he was thirteen, had always said that he was the responsible one in the family—the one they could rely on. Daniel had always been the serious one. Teenage fun had been limited to one or two friends for whom nights of chess and intense discussion on how to fix the world were defined as good times.

Right now he was responsible for getting his ass out of Egypt.

Daniel wanted to be on the first anything out of Alexandria. The motorcycle or a car was hopeless. Westward through Libya was impossible. East through Palestine and Israel would present too many checkpoints, too many problems.

Airports would be watched. Flights would be monitored. Anyone with a little computer expertise could

find out who had purchased tickets and when. He did
have a new identity, but there were only so many entrances to the airport and to the planes. He could be
spotted. He was also tired. He hadn't slept yet. Part
of his training had been endurance. Once a year he
went back for a refresher on basics. Sleep deprivation
had always been toughest on him. It could make him
careless, slow his reactions.

Daniel wished he could talk to Brenda, tell her what
was happening, but he couldn't risk it. A safe haven?
Office and safe house ready for his use? Perhaps, if
they hadn't been compromised.

Daniel decided to take whatever transport was
leaving Alexandria first. A boat would do. Maybe he
could get to Port Said. Port Said to Istanbul? Port Said
to almost anywhere on the planet that wasn't Egypt.

He had his bits of disguise from the Cairo safe
house. He donned the red wig, a pair of clear glasses,
and a burnoose. At a gas station he purchased a water
bottle. In the desert he made mud with the sand and
water and covered any exposed parts of his flesh with
a thin layer. He would look less pink and stand out
less.

The Harley had a GPS. Daniel used it to find less-
traveled roads into the city. He decided to give the
port area a try. Boats could be leaving. Perhaps he
could hire something.

He wanted to do two things first: eat and find a
cybercafé. These days every major tourist city had cy-
bercafés. He motored into the city and was soon surrounded by the daily chaos of traffic. It was, if his
memory hadn't failed him entirely, Sunday, but in an
Islamic city it was just another day. He made his way
to a restaurant on Shakor Pasha, just a short walk

from the Corniche and the harbor, for fuul and ta'amiyya, the popular dishes Egyptians ate for breakfast.

After eating, Daniel left the Harley where it was, hoping it would be there if he needed it again, and then he walked down to the Corniche to survey the possibilities. It was midmorning. He crossed the six lanes of traffic and turned west. He walked the entire length of the Eastern Harbor, all the while being careful to blend in with the hundreds of others enjoying the waterfront. Women wore pantsuits, with scarves around their necks and heads; men casual summer clothes. A few sunbathers were already out. Daniel walked the concrete promenade, then returned along the strip of sand. He dodged tatty plastic chairs, small beach tents, and children playing. He saw nothing suspicious. Nobody pointed to him while wielding a walkie-talkie.

Daniel retreated to the other side of the street, away from the water. He walked past the Cecil Hotel, a famous reminder of Alexandria's glory of the 30s and 40s. Daniel knew there were few reminders of the much earlier and more glorious days of Cleopatra's reign two thousand years ago. He recalled that Michael Palin had said the Corniche was like "Cannes with acne." It was the spots of acne that Daniel was watching.

Daniel found a dingy, art-deco coffee shop with Internet access. He got his coffee, paid for it, and sat down at a computer near the back. From here he could watch both the room and the street. A large clump of people in western dress huddled before a screen, apparently trying to send pictures of somebody's grandkids. They seemed safe enough.

Daniel couldn't send a conventional e-mail. There was too much risk of a wireless intercept. But he had a few tricks in his arsenal. He went to the You Won't Believe This! Penis Enlargement Site and pressed in codes that would allow him to alter the site. He and Brenda had used steganography to conceal data in the .jpg image. Now on the third page of the site, he located the imbedded mark on the breast of the third woman from the left. He altered it. He couldn't leave much of a message in a space of only four pixels, but Brenda would know to check this site, would know where to look and what to look for. He hoped. It would tell her he was alive, at least. A little good news was better than none.

Daniel locked in his changes. Then he searched the Internet for possible options for leaving Alexandria. He was looking for anything likely, but for the moment he concentrated on boats. He found one obscure British tourist agency called Empire and Commonwealth for You, subheaded "Revisit the Days of Empire." It specialized in out-of-the-way tours to former British colonies. It had a ship that would be arriving in Alexandria at about eleven a.m.—in two hours—and it was scheduled to depart again at midnight.

This was at least a chance. But no tickets were available. From the information on the Web site, Daniel couldn't tell whether the tour was sold out or if tickets for just a portion of the tour were simply unavailable. He hunted for another half hour. Nothing. He decided to have a look at the Empire and Commonwealth ship, who got off, see if any possibilities struck him.

He walked back and forth along the Corniche again, checking out the different shops and cafés. Two and a half hours later, the ship had not shown up. He was sure the Web site had said it would arrive at eleven. Another hour passed and finally a largish vessel pulled into the harbor and anchored out at some distance. Was this it?

A good-sized launch made its way out to the ship. Daniel walked to the small dock from which the launch had departed, and loitered. He wasn't a smoker, but now he bummed a cigarette, lit it, and kept it in the corner of his mouth as he leaned casually against a piling and considered his options. How could he get from here to the ship, get on board, and get away without being discovered?

A group of casual but conservatively dressed tourists disembarked. A few had cameras. They chatted amiably in British accents. After them came a group of grubbily dressed men. Both groups turned to the left from the dock and began walking down the Corniche.

The tourists were loud. "I want to try . . ."

"We should see . . ."

"I wonder if Cleopatra walked on this very . . ."

The leader of the group, a darker-skinned man who might have been Egyptian, led them to an ahwa. "You must try the coffee here," he said.

The scruffy men walked mostly in silence. At their rear, a portly older man with a white beard was arguing with a short, slender man. The older man wore a paisley tie and a madras sport coat. Daniel heard him saying, "I don't care . . . I don't care," in a loud voice. They seemed to be arguing in Arabic and English. The group of men walked a block, stopped on a corner, and entered a café.

Daniel waited ten minutes, then followed them

into the café. The place, with whitewashed walls that needed painting, was half full of what he judged to be mostly locals, workingmen who had rough jobs. Ceiling fans weren't moving. He saw that the crowd of men he had followed were ordering food and coffee. A few tourists, made obvious by their cameras and backpacks, were the only loud ones in the room.

Daniel took a trip to the men's room. It might have been cleaned once since the Pyramids were built, he thought. Daniel glanced in the water-and-gunk-spattered mirror. He knew he needed a shave. His wig was matted from the motorcycle helmet. He took off the disguises he'd been wearing and tossed them in the trash. He looked scruffy enough to pass for a vaguely ruffianish person. He didn't wash off the dirt he'd applied. His body movements had rearranged it to a more natural grubbiness.

He returned to the dining room and took a seat between the tourists and the men from the ship. The tourists were gazing at the screen of a laptop computer. A heavyset man who looked to be in his mid-to-late twenties was declaiming, "The man who sold it to me said it was wireless and that it would work anywhere."

"You believed him?" asked another young man. "You always believe what a salesman tells you?"

"It's worked so far," the heavy man said. "It's all so simple. All you have to do is click."

Daniel heard another man in the group say in a stage whisper, "We could shove him out of the plane over the Mediterranean. No one would complain."

"Probably get a medal," came a reply from the other side of the group. The heavy man ignored them and started tapping his fingers on the keyboard.

Daniel hunched over his coffee and concentrated on the men from the ship. At the moment there was a huffy silence among that assemblage as they wolfed down their food.

Suddenly the shortest and thinnest man in the group slammed his fist down on the table. He leaned across the table toward the man in the tie and said in English, "I'm telling you, none of us is going to pick up the slack. You lose somebody in every port. We're not going to do any more work. We're already going twelve hours a day. It's a bloody mess with these hi-falutin nobodies. You got 'em to pay on the cheap, but they're expecting the bloody Ritz. We ain't going to put up with it. You need to find more crewmen or that ship ain't sailing."

The man in the tie said, "This ain't a fucking union."

"We don't need a fucking union," the small man said. "You just fucking need us. We don't care if you don't trust the locals. You need to find somebody and right quick if you want to sail"—he looked at his watch—"in ten hours and fourteen minutes."

Several of the men spoke in Arabic. They echoed the complaints and added their own. The argument continued through the meal. Daniel wasn't hungry, but he ordered a small pastry with his coffee and let himself linger.

Finally the man in the tie said, "I can't hire just anybody. I have to be able to check backgrounds."

"You better pick just anybody or you ain't going and you can give all these royal pretenders their pennies back."

The man glared at each of them in turn. "I'll probably wind up with a terrorist with bombs to explode. My ship will be gone."

Daniel leaned over and said, "May I help?"

The man in the tie gave him a disdainful look. "Who are you?"

Daniel said, "I'm a guy who needs a job. I set out to go round the world. I made it to Port Said when my money ran out. It sounds like you need help. I can provide it."

"It's muck work," said the short man.

"*You're* doing it," Daniel replied. Several of the other men grinned. The short man thought a moment, then smiled. "Hire the bloke, Reginald. He's quick and he's got a sense of humor."

"I don't know this man," Reginald said.

Daniel presented identification papers calling him Jeffrey Garza from Newton, Iowa.

"Garza, huh. Iowa. You ever work on a ship?"

"Crap work is pretty much the same everywhere, isn't it?" Daniel said.

The corners of Reginald's mouth twitched upward. "Well, this isn't properly legal."

"Fuck legal," said the short guy. "Hire the bloke and let's get the fuck out of this dump."

Reginald asked, "Don't you want to know where we're going?"

"Do you pay?" Daniel said.

"I can give you half pay."

"No fucking half pay," the short man said. "He gets starting wages like everyone else."

"Maybe he can replace you, Bruce," Reginald said.

"I go, we all go," Bruce said. Daniel saw the others nod. In union there is strength, at least in a dingy café near the waterfront in Alexandria.

"Fine, we'll do it," Reginald said. "No names, no pack drill."

Daniel hadn't heard the saying. He looked puzzled.

Reginald translated. "We're going to do this se-cretly. We're not going to tell the authorities. Bruce, you're in charge of him."

Abruptly Reginald got to his feet and left.

The others filled Daniel in. Reginald Stanton was the captain and owner of the ship. He had invested in a glorious old yacht, repainted it, and used it to toddle idiot tourists around to former British colonies. He was a man who loved the British Empire and wished it had been preserved.

A slender red-haired man said, "Damn ship was late because Reg can't keep a crew. We spent hours looking for somebody in Mykonos."

"Old Reg was born about a century too late," Bruce said. "Probably wants to marry Queen Victoria and doesn't care that she's dead . . . It's bloody awful work. You're new. You'll get the worst end of it. You look like you can deal with it. Have to."

Quoting Annie Proulx, Daniel said, "If you can't fix it, you have to stand it."

Two hours later he was on board. The ship looked like the next gale might sink her. In her day she might have been something. The six men who had been in the café made up over half the crew. On board Daniel met a cook and a steward. He was then put to work cleaning the latrines, washing and waxing the interior floors, and swabbing the deck. Daniel found it a little hard to believe that he was actually swab-bing a deck. It was all to be done before the tourists returned near midnight.

Daniel took some comfort in thinking that one of

the last places he would be looked for was as a crew-man on a ship. No one would talk about him being there since the captain/owner was doing something illegal.

Daniel asked a couple of questions. He learned their destination was Cyprus. Good enough. He could jump ship there and get a flight to Istanbul.

Mostly he kept his mouth shut and worked hard. When the tourists filed back on about ten that night, he was assigned the duty of seeing to the comforts of those in cabins one and two. Cabin one bedded down easily. Cabin two wanted late-night drinks and a dip in the Jacuzzi.

Daniel had to turn on the Jacuzzi, make sure it was the right temperature, and find the towels. When the two men from cabin two got to the Jacuzzi, they decided it was too cool out, and they would have their drinks in their cabin. Daniel swallowed his annoyance. The rudeness of the tourists didn't matter. He was leaving Egypt without a trace.

He'd gotten the order. Find him. Use all available personnel in the area. Find him. Kill him. And don't fail. The man began to sweat. The price of failure was high.

CHAPTER 20

"I'm the fucking president of the fucking United States. I can have a fucking press conference if I want to have a fucking press conference." President Kierkstra was in a full-blown, angry-bull, maddened rage. The press secretary, Bret Culligan, didn't know what to do. The president had stormed in, brandishing newspapers and demanding to see the latest polls.

Culligan had been with the president ever since they cheated and lied their way to a win in their first race in South Dakota years before. Now Culligan had just about reached his limit. He had never seen Kierkstra so out of control. Their internal tracking showed them rapidly losing ground in some of the key states.

The only one who seemed able to control the president these days was Alexander Cabot, and he wasn't around. The arrogant, aloof, austere gazillionaire flitted in and out of their lives like a demented fairy godfather. Culligan hoped the son of a bitch had a miracle up his sleeve because right now the Kierkstra presidential express was up to its axles in shit.

Culligan had urged the president to dump all press conferences for the duration of the campaign. They were disasters waiting to happen. It was a miracle the man hadn't already blundered into on-air stupidity. Culligan wondered, not for the first time, how he'd gotten himself into this job. How had he gone from an idealistic journalism student at Northwestern University to a flack for probably the stupidest man ever to be president of the United States?

It was eight days before the election and the president was in Columbus, Ohio. On a Monday evening the president should be getting ready to ease back and watch football. That's what he did on Monday nights. He watched football. That's what he did all day on Saturdays and all day on Sundays. He liked advisors around him, male advisors who could talk about football and the players. He liked calling coaches and feeling part of victories. But Kierkstra wasn't thinking about football right now. He was insisting on a press conference.

The president swept all the food, plates, and papers off the table in the suite's living room. In both hands he flourished the stacks of newspapers he'd stomped in with. "Look at these!" He was nearly shrieking. If Culligan had more nerve, he'd cover his ears.

"Look at these! It says I'm a crook! I am not a crook." The press secretary wondered if the man knew who had made that simple phrase into a joke. He doubted it. The president seldom showed the slightest interest in history or reading. The press secretary needed to fire whoever had left those papers around where the headlines had caught the president's eye. Probably some idiot holdover from the Miller administration who knew they would upset this less-than-bright man.

"I am not going to lose. I'm going to talk to these people. I'm going to set these people straight. I'm going to show them I'm the one they have to deal with. I'm the one they have to fear. I'm going to win this election." The press secretary had no idea how the president could be so confident. Culligan couldn't tell whether this was the delusion of all politicians just before an election or the usual pointless rhetoric given to the press before the polls opened. Culligan was on double-strength pills for his high blood pressure, drank antacids by the gallon, hadn't eaten real food in a month, and hadn't seen his family since he wasn't sure when. He hoped they still lived in the same house. Alexander Cabot wasn't around to calm the man down. Where the hell was he?

Kierkstra rounded on Culligan. "You're a hack. Why did I ever hire you?"

Usually Culligan brushed off these in-his-face attacks. He'd endured them through every campaign so far. Tonight, however, Culligan thought, screw it. Let the asshole fuck it up. He said, "You're right, Mr. President. You're the one to get out there and tell them." A last shred of conscience forced him to add, in an attempt to forestall a disaster, "But, Mr. President, are you sure you want to do it this late on a Monday?"

"Yes, now. I've got to get this out. I'll be done before the kickoff."

"We might not get full press coverage."

"You arrange it! Goddamn it! They owe me. Get those fuckers from the networks to move their asses."

As they always did, the networks preempted regular programming for the president. Hell, they'd even interrupted Oprah once. All the cable news channels toadied along. And so that night, many Americans sat down to dinner accompanied by the face of the president.

Kierkstra's opening remarks were full of confidence about his agenda for the country and his certainty of winning the coming election. Culligan watched and groaned quietly so the mikes wouldn't pick it up. The president had that crafty look again. How many times had they told him never, never, never to get that look on his face? They'd trained him and trained him, even had him practice in front of mirrors. Culligan wondered if either he or the president would get back to private life without being indicted. He surreptitiously guzzled from his bottle of strawberry-flavored antacid.

The president opened the floor for questions.

"Mr. President, Sumner Welsh, AP." This president always made the reporters identify themselves. "You're behind in the polls."

"Election day is the only poll that counts."

"Mr. President, Joseph Townsend, UPI. A poll out yesterday says Governor Harkinnon's lead here in Ohio is insurmountable."

"I find you lead by being out in front. The people are behind me."

What? A number of reporters shook their heads in puzzlement.

"Mr. President, Nancy Sorenson, *New York Times*.

There are reports in the Sioux Falls *Argus Leader* that while you were governor there your administration was rife with corruption."

"That's a smear from the Democrats near the election with old charges that have long ago been proven false. That shows how desperate they are. They'll rake up any old muck. Don't you people know how to be fair and balanced?"

"Mr. President, Kathleen Norward, *Chicago Tribune*. Aren't we talking about facts?"

"Facts made up by who?"

"Mr. President, Dorothy Kmetz, *Los Angeles Times*. Isn't that what your campaign has been doing against Mr. Harkinnon, bringing up old charges that have long ago been proven false?"

Culligan knew the questioners were getting bolder. The press sensed a loser.

Kierkstra said, "I've had nothing to do with that. If Concerned Citizens for America has found some mistruths in my opponent's life, they are free to exercise their constitutional right to speak about it."

"Mr. President, Roger Kruse, *Time* magazine. All those who head Concerned Citizens for America are, or were, members of your staff back in Dakota or now in Washington."

"I'm lucky to have loyal people working for me."

"Mr. President, Shawn Lubell, the *Wall Street Journal*. How are you going to prevent vote fraud?"

"We've worked on it for years. Everything has been taken care of."

"Mr. President, Guy Glick, *USA Today*. Our correspondent here in Ohio says there are chances for major fraud at the polls on Election Day."

"Nonsense. It's been taken care of. How many times do I have to answer the same question? Don't you people have better things to ask about?"

"Mr. President, Evaline Gleason, *Sacramento Bee.* What is more important than ensuring that every person's vote is counted accurately? In Canada they use paper ballots to make sure there is a paper trail."

"Canada? Who cares about Canada?"

"The Canadians," a voice called from the rear. The room erupted in laughter.

Culligan tried to see who it was. They'd never attend another press conference. He sighed. Or maybe he'd put them up front if Kierkstra was ever stupid enough to have one of these again. Or if he was able to have one as a sitting president after January. Culligan could see that the laughter had done its damage. The president considered himself a wit. He didn't like it when he was the butt of laughter. The crafty look was gone, replaced now with a goggle-eyed stubbornness.

"Listen to me," Kierkstra said. "We've had people on this. We have people on this."

"Mr. President, Rose Lin, CBS. Who is 'we'? Aren't local people in charge of what programs and machines they use?"

"Of course. Everyone knows that. I mean the FEC. They've been monitoring everything. All those computer programs have been examined. Your government has made sure this election is going to be honest. Every single nanobit is going to be checked and double-checked. The federal government is working closely with all the state and local governments. We know what we're doing. I have faith in the American people. The American people know we've rested assured that we can find any perpetrator in a computer and program beyond change and ferret out the Internet and clean a firewall . . ."

Culligan wished he had a hook. The president was lost in his syntax. That didn't matter so much really. Most of the idiots who supported Kierkstra had the same problem when they tried to speak publicly. They liked it when he misspoke. Made him seem more like them. And they didn't listen most of the time anyway. They knew he was one of them. They knew he watched football. In a burst of anger, Culligan wished he could take those people and shake them and say to them, "The man could destroy life as we know it with a snap of his fingers, but your judgment is based on who you want to have a beer with. Don't you get it?" It never seemed to sink into their heads that it would take several million dollars plus the beer to ever get them within a pop-top opener of the president. What mattered to them was that they knew he was a good guy who shared their peeves, prejudices, and stupidity.

The digital readout on the lectern, which could be seen only by those behind it, was moving toward nine o'clock. Culligan knew the press conference would end soon. The president liked to have his feet up well before kickoff.

CHAPTER 21

Monday, October 27
New York City
Eight Days before the Presidential Election

Having stood up to Allen Cooper's food-wine-and-restaurant one-upmanship, Brenda had a new idea for their second dinner date.

She wasn't entirely certain why she was being so contrary and so careful. After all, as she had said to Dan, what was the worst that could go wrong?

Well, one obvious thing was that she could be too eager. She didn't feel desperate for a man, but you never could be quite sure what your reptile brain was working on while your rational brain thought it was in full control. But even if she were more eager for male company than she thought, how bad could that be? It was many years since Jeremy had died, and in all that time she had not dated anyone.

Since Coop lived in Washington, the fact that he was coming to New York for a second time made it pretty clear that he was courting her. Wow, a courting couple, she thought. I should feel like a teenager again. She had decided on black spiked hair tonight, and a black sweater and black skirt that any Goth would be proud of. Way spiky heels on calf-high boots.

Brenda again suggested the place to meet for dinner, giving him just the street address, a place she often lunched at since it was near work. He'd find out soon enough it was the EAT-EAT-EAT diner.

She arrived at the EAT-EAT-EAT early and sat at a table in the window, just in case when he drove up he thought the address was a horrible mistake. Her table was one of five along the window wall. It was topped with light turquoise Formica, flecked with gold bits. The counter ran along the other wall and had ten round stools upholstered in lime green bellying up to it. The grill was behind the counter, in full view. Lenny, who owned the EAT-EAT-EAT and also did most of the cooking, was standing at her table as a limo drew to the curb. The driver ran around to the rear passenger door, getting there just as Cooper opened the door for himself. Hands on hips, he looked at the diner, saw Brenda in the window, recognized her despite the change in hair color and the spiking—he's unusually observant, she thought—cocked his finger, and pointed. In a few seconds, he was at her table.

He gave her a lopsided grin, which she felt was fair, given the circumstances. Lenny stood waiting as Cooper sat down.

"Welcome to the EAT-EAT-EAT," Brenda said.

Lenny said, "We were going to call it the EAT!

EAT! EAT!"—he made the exclamation points with his index finger—"but that would have been inexcusably arrogant."

"Oh, surely not," Cooper said.

"And also we felt that raising expectations that high was just asking for trouble."

"I'm sure the expectations would have been amply justified," Cooper said.

"I like this guy, Bren," Lenny said.

She thought, I guess I like him too.

Brenda ordered a potato pancake and applesauce, with a Sprite. Cooper, after quickly studying the menu, ordered pastrami on rye with a Coke.

"That's the way to go," Brenda said. "Dark-colored soda with red meat, and I'm having a light-colored soda with my veggie selection."

"Well, Coke is full-bodied and stands up well to pastrami."

She nodded, pleased. "My Sprite is a modest little vintage with a subtle aftertaste."

"Brenda, this is dinner we're having. Is a potato pancake enough for you?"

"Wait."

They chatted briefly, and then Cooper said, "How is the investigation coming along?"

"I have a list of people at several of the companies who fudged their resumés. Mostly it's just puffery. They claim better schools than they really went to. More experience. Or they happened to leave out minor youthful arrests. It's a long list. Do you want me to e-mail or snail-mail or fax it?"

"I'll send a courier to pick it up."

"There are a few who had arrests for felonies. Don't employers check anymore?"

"Most do."

"And I have a much shorter list of people who just might have terrorist connections. Or terrorist sympathies. You realize, of course, that a lot of truly dangerous people don't have connections in any real sense."

"The bombings in London proved that. Some of what we used to call cells don't have any connection to anybody. They're just a bunch of like-minded people with murder on their minds."

"Haters. Which is why I've flagged some whose histories make me suspicious. Do you want us to actually investigate them or just point them out to you?"

"Let me have the list first, and I'll see whether we already have them under surveillance. No sense duplicating effort."

"If you decide you want us to look into them, I have a couple of very subtle investigators." She was silent for a moment, then said, "There's something else. Or there may be. I found it a few days ago, and I haven't nailed it down for sure, but . . . well, maybe you'd better know about it."

Coop raised an eyebrow and glanced around the room.

Brenda lowered her voice to barely audible. "I was trolling possible trouble sites and looking at source code, if you know what that is."

He shook his head.

"Okay, you don't need to, really. To put it in simple terms, it's the basis of all computer programs, the language in which they're written. And it's almost as individual as handwriting. I mean, there are usually a lot of different ways to achieve the same end. Some programmers do it one way, some another. Once you know that, you can usually tell who wrote what, or at least if the same person wrote two different programs." She took a deep breath. "I've found a possible connection between two pieces of source code—you may not believe this."

"Try me."

"One is from a program the IMF uses for routine money transfers."

"You can access that? How?"

"Don't ask, but yes, we can. And the other—this is the part you're not going to believe. I'm not even sure I believe it, and that's why I haven't said anything before. The other is from some chatter sent out by a small cell of Al Qaeda."

Coop sat very still. Brenda wondered if he had heard her. Finally he let out his breath in a small soundless whistle. "That's . . . very important, potentially. What have you done about it?"

"Nothing, really. Things have been moving pretty fast at DB. There hasn't been time to check it out thoroughly. And it's the kind of thing I'd have to do myself—or Dan, of course. It's too sensitive to let out of our hands."

"Yes. Well, I can have some checking done from my end. Not the computer stuff. The Washington bureaucracy would take much too long. But a connection between the IMF and Al Qaeda . . . whew! That's explosive and will take some very, very careful handling." He shook his head. "Brenda, you were right to let me know. Now stop worrying about it. I'll take it from here." He looked her in the eye, his face set. "It could be very dangerous for you, you know. Seriously, I want you to leave it alone."

"That's a bit of a relief, actually. Not because I'm worried about us—we have the best firewalls in the business. Nobody can trace the query back to us. But we have enough to do as it is without chasing that down."

"Good. Do you have enough staff with the extra work I've handed you? There are a couple of people I could recommend."

Brenda thought, but did not say, that she wanted to keep her staff totally separate from Cooper. She was willing to trust him, maybe quite a bit more than she had at first, but she wasn't going to take any chances. She was aware that she was attracted to him, and that made it even more important to be cautious. It could distort her judgment.

Suddenly, she remembered that old dumb joke: How do porcupines mate? Very carefully.

She laughed until her eyes watered.

"Did I say something funny?" Cooper asked.

"No. No." She laughed some more and then got control of herself. "I'm sorry. I thought of something unrelated. Sorry."

Lenny's waitress, Sonia, appeared with Cooper's seven-inch-high pastrami sandwich, and Brenda's potato pancake. The pancake was the size of a fourteen-inch pizza. The applesauce came in a huge soup bowl.

"I see what you meant," Cooper said.

As she cut into her potato pancake, Brenda studied Cooper in a way that she hoped was not rudely obvious. She was surprised to see that his hands appealed to her. She hadn't noticed before, because she had been so focused on his facial expressions. They were solid, square hands, with an almost invisible sprinkling of hair on the backs of the fingers. She'd never been especially attracted to long, thin fingers on a man—"pianist's hands" were not her thing.

Why do people have these unreasoning preferences? And why do I care? I like what I like.

She liked hands with muscles and bones in them. It wasn't that she wanted a man with Neanderthal hands. Big hairy-creature hands, no.

She noticed with satisfaction that he didn't show signs of an expensive manicure—no varnish, which some men used, but she thought wasn't sexy. For a man who dressed well, his hands were very natural. In fact, he had very, very sexy hands. For a few seconds she thought about being caressed with those hands.

"How is the election program looking?" he said.

"So far I don't see anything wrong with it."

"That's good."

"So far. But I have a lot more work to do on it. I assumed you didn't want any of it farmed out to any of my assistants."

"Well, unidentifiable chunks, I suppose, couldn't hurt."

"Okay. That'll make it go faster."

After they ate, they walked part way into Central Park and watched the horse-drawn carriages pass by. Coop bought two Sno-cones from a street vendor along the path. It was a warm fall evening, and the carriages looked particularly old-fashioned under the lights. Neither of them suggested taking a ride. It would have been too romantic. Brenda didn't know whether their caution was a good thing or a bad thing.

"Did you notice," she said, "that all the carriage drivers are men?"

"I've seen women drivers too."

"In the daytime. I wonder if they only hire men for after dark."

They walked to where they could look down at the

Central Park Pond, a sunken comma-shaped pool below street level. In the darkness, it was a black hole in the earth.

They hailed a cab in front of the newish Ritz-Carlton.

"You want me to take a separate cab and let you go home alone, don't you?" Cooper asked.

"I'm afraid so."

"I'm a grown-up. I can stand it. But let's have dinner when I'm back here on Wednesday."

"All right. I'm not playing hard to get, really. I'm just . . . there are some things—"

"Don't explain." He put his hand behind her head, drawing her to him. He kissed her forehead, then her lips.

Brenda kissed him back. It felt good after all this time. Cooper broke the kiss and let her go. "Wednesday," he said.

"Wednesday," Brenda said.

"Yeah, definitely Wednesday," said the cabbie. "Which this is Monday. We all clear on that now? I'm starting my meter."

CHAPTER 22

Tuesday, October 28
New York City
Seven Days before the Presidential Election

Before Brenda started working that day, she checked the penis-enlargement site and found Daniel's message. She was more frustrated than pleased because it contained no information other than that he was alive. It made her wish even more that she could talk to him. Where was he? What was he doing? Was he okay?

Next, Brenda returned to the vote-tallying program. She had been back and forth through the code. She could find nothing that would tell the machines to give extra votes to any person or, in fact, to alter votes at all. Nor were there any obvious bugs that might cause a crash. In fact, the program was beautifully written.

She reflected on the fact that computers "know" the

date. In protecting her client companies against viruses that could disrupt or destroy their records, she frequently used a technique called the "canary in the coal mine." It traded on the fact that a lot of viruses used a "time-bomb" effect, setting the virus to break out at a certain preprogrammed date in the future. So she would set one of their hard drives to a date a week ahead. If it was attacked, the client would know in time to save the real data on the other drives.

The vote-tallying program might have a "virus" set to go into effect on the date of the election or the day before. Of course, it wouldn't be a real virus, in the sense that it was an invader, but it should look like one.

But she couldn't find any such thing.

It was time to give parts of the program to someone else to look over. She'd try the new guy, Malcolm Dudley. He was a sharp cookie, and he needed something more to do.

Istanbul

The trip to Cyprus took twenty hours. He'd finally been able to get a night's sleep, with his gun under his pillow. On Cyprus he'd gotten off with the other crew members. At an opportune moment, but not without a shudder, he'd dumped his gun over the side of the ship. No point in even trying to get a weapon onto a plane. He'd picked up a disguise in a used-clothing shop in Famagusta near the harbor, taken a cab to the airport, and using the identity papers from the safe house, boarded a flight to Istanbul.

Now Daniel stood in the aisle of the plane waiting for the passengers ahead of him to disembark. It was very early evening. He was back on high alert. The enemy must know DB had offices in Istanbul. It was a logical place for Daniel to go. If *he* were the bad guys, he would station someone here.

Right now he looked like a thin old man with straggly gray hair, his face hidden behind dirty glasses. On the plane he'd sat and knitted and shuffled his beads.

Daniel saw two men at the international terminal exit. They set off his alarm instincts. As the passengers disembarked, these men examined each tourist too carefully. Of course, they might not have been looking for him. They could have been police officers from Istanbul looking for a criminal or taking ordinary antiterrorist precautions. But if these two were connected to the group that had killed Yussuf and had tried to kill him, he needed urgently to find out who they were and why they were dealing out death.

As Daniel unobtrusively kept them under surveillance, he also watched the local television monitors. The channel was turned to CNN. It had a voice-over in Turkish, which Daniel did not speak, but the crawl was in English. The fifth item was about a bombing in Istanbul.

Daniel became even more uneasy. But bombings happened all the time, right? His line moved slowly to the checkpoint. At his turn the security guard inspected his tattered shopping bag and wished him a good day.

The many other monitors in the terminal were set to a local station. This time he understood neither the words nor the crawl, but the picture was clear. It showed the street and building where their Istanbul offices were. Daniel swore. Not more dead bodies. Not another haven destroyed.

He could try to get to the safe house and then simply flee Istanbul and fly west, but the note from Yussuf had said Istanbul. He needed to follow that lead. Now his people in Istanbul were in danger. Daniel wasn't the kind to run from danger. If there was something he could do to help or save his employees—his friends—he would do it. He was not about to abandon them. Until he knew what was happening to them, he would stay in Turkey.

Meanwhile he'd tail these men. Maybe he would learn something valuable. If he lost them, then he'd see if it was possible to check on DB's offices.

Hours passed in the airport lounge. Daniel didn't sit there idle all evening. He went to the washroom, hoping the two men wouldn't leave while he was in there, and returned as a swaggering teenager with a tuft of goatee at his chin, aviator sunglasses, and a T-shirt a size too tight. His pants were slung down almost to indecency level; his butt, encased in red boxer shorts, hung out the back. The men were still there.

He decided to take another chance and left the building to go rent a car. It wasn't easy, looking the way he did, but a healthy cash supplement settled the deal. When he pulled it around to the front, the men were still inside. He waited until a security guard asked him to leave, slipped the security guard money, and waited some more. Wonderful what bribery would do.

Finally the men left. They'd examined each set of arriving passengers. Daniel figured they were staying until the last international flight, and he'd been right.

Now he followed them as they drove through the Istanbul night.

As he drove, he divested himself of most of the teen trappings, although he was stuck with the jeans. He could feel the red boxers hanging out the back. Nothing for it.

It was clammy and dank, early autumn on the Bosporus. Daniel enjoyed the change of being the one following those who were out to kill him—if these were the right guys. He'd had enough training to do a reasonable job of tailing them.

Daniel wondered how these people managed to have so many agents in so many places. There was a limited number of spots to catch trains and planes, but it would still be difficult to watch all of them adequately. At least here, for now, they hadn't glommed onto him yet.

Eventually the two men followed the E5 highway west out of Istanbul. It was just after eleven and traffic was light. Daniel fell quite far back. No need to arouse the slightest suspicion. The moon was clear in the night sky and might reflect off his windshield. About thirty miles past the last suburban lights of Istanbul, they came to the town of Olukai. The car ahead took a left turn south. Daniel was forced to close in, but within two miles of taking this new road, the car made a right turn and headed west again. Daniel switched off his lights and continued following them. As soon as his tires hit this new road, Daniel realized it wasn't paved. He heard bits of stones and scatterings of dirt rattle against the car's undercarriage.

Daniel slowed considerably. He could see the tail-lights bobbing ahead of him. The men headed deeper into the Turkish countryside, and the rough surface forced Daniel to grip the steering wheel tightly. More than once the bottom of the car scraped against some obstruction.

As Daniel kept his eyes on these strangers, he thought about home. Did these guys really have anything to do with him? What was Brenda doing? Where was Nate? Did Nate think of him as often as he thought of Nate? Even in the midst of this chaos, he missed him.

Five miles on, he saw the lights turn. He slowed, stopped, and turned off his engine. The lights seemed to be going up a slight rise. Then they halted.

Daniel got out of his car. He could see lights coming on in a small house, but he saw no other lights and no other dwellings. His guerrilla training allowed him to make an easy trek of the half mile over the uneven ground.

From his hiding place behind a low stone wall, Daniel could see that the men were grilling some sort of bread dough. It looked as though they lived here. This might be the break he needed to find out who they were and who they worked for.

They had switched on one electric light in the kitchen. He noted the windows swung outward. One was open a crack. The feeble kitchen light spilled into an adjoining room. In there Daniel saw what looked like surprisingly up-to-date computer equipment. He could use the equipment to get in touch with Brenda using the enemies' own computer and codes. He'd also hack into their system and get some valuable information.

Daniel crept nearer. No dogs barked. A bird rustled. Insects whirred. From twenty feet away he was able to hear the men. They both spoke French, one with a strong New York accent. Daniel thought, are they stationed here or did someone fly a New York City denizen around the world just to look for him? Very possible. Something that he and Brenda had—or knew—must be a threat to someone. A huge threat. You don't send people halfway round the world to assassinate someone because you don't like his ties.

The one with the New York accent, taller than the other by at least a foot, spoke. "If he comes through here, we've got to kill the fucker. Instantly. Our highest priority. He's got to be dead." His voice was high-pitched and squeaky.

The second one spoke in French. "Why do I have to stay on watch?"

"Somebody's got to challenge him."

"I can't do it. I don't speak English."

Confirmed then. They were after him. Daniel noticed how cold the night had become.

"*Bien sûr,*" said the tall one, biting into a piece of bread. "You're here to help me. Then tomorrow . . ." Daniel listened to them cheerfully plan their schedule for the next day, which consisted of being at the airport to track him down and kill him.

They finished eating. Daniel heard the sound of a flushing toilet and then saw lights go on in two small rooms. He noted their placement. Within five minutes all lights were extinguished. He guessed they weren't into reading in bed before dropping off to sleep. Daniel waited for an hour. Then he crept to the tall one's window.

He listened to the quiet inside and out. He circled

the house on hands and knees. Working in the dim moonlight, he checked for electrical connections and alarms. He paid attention to every nuance of the night: a gentle breeze, a few birds and animals calling, insects in their nighttime symphony. No human sounds. He listened and waited. One hour. Two. He wanted to talk to these men if he could.

And he wanted to keep them here. He opened the hood of their car with exquisite care, pulled off the distributor cap, and threw it deep into the bushes. Then he crept back and made another careful circuit of the house. Moving noiselessly across the porch to the front door, he put his hand on the knob.

Just out of the corner of his eye, Daniel caught a tiny flicker of red light to his left. He held his breath. He heard a soft noise. They had an alarm system. He heard steps coming around either side of the house.

The tall one came first. Daniel felled him with a titanic blow to the nose. He heard crunching. Felt a warm stickiness spatter on his hands. Blood.

The smaller one used this distraction to attempt to get away. Daniel tackled him, landing on the short guy's gut. He heard a whoosh. Then he put a foot on the man's neck and said, "Who is trying to kill me?"

The short guy said, "*Va te faire foutre,*" and spat at Daniel. Since Daniel's face was nearly six feet away and the guy was supine, the spittle didn't reach.

Daniel applied more pressure to the neck and spoke in French. "Who, motherfucker? You tell me, and I let you live."

"No matter what I tell you, you die."

Daniel kept the pressure on his neck while he turned to the taller one. He was still unconscious. The small man squirmed under Daniel's foot. Daniel took the man's belt, secured his hands, then shoved him into the house, sat him on a kitchen chair, and tied him to it.

Returning to the taller one, Daniel dragged him to the room with the computer and tied his hands to either side of a cold radiator. He secured the feet to separate ends of a weight-lifting bar and added as many weights to the end as he could find. Then he picked up the shorter man, chair and all, and brought him into the room. He turned the short guy on his side, then secured the chair and both wrists and both ankles to the same workout equipment.

Daniel turned on the light next to the computer. He got some water and splashed it on the tall guy's face. He came to groggily. He glared at Daniel. "You hit me, you fucker."

"You're trying to kill me."

"Fuck you," he said.

"This is stupid," Daniel said. He moved to the short guy and asked, "Who wants to kill me?"

"Fuck you and your faggot boyfriend," was the reply.

The mention of a boyfriend disturbed Daniel. They knew a great deal about him, and Nate could be in real danger.

Daniel said, "You really need better training in the you're-the-one-tied-up etiquette of the killing profession."

"You are going to be dead."

Daniel made sure both men were tied tightly, then searched the house for weapons. He found a machine gun, several AK-47s, a couple of shotguns, a few assorted handguns, and an arsenal's worth of ammunition. He placed the trove on the table the computer sat on, far out of reach of the prisoners, and checked to see if the guns were loaded and ready for use.

For now he'd try to get information from the computer. He was good. He knew he might be able to hack in.

No Post-it notes full of passwords stuck around the monitor frame. Of course it wouldn't be that easy.

They didn't use Windows either. He could almost hear his teacher saying, in a voice slightly tinged with an English accent, "Windows is insecure and insecurable. Bad guys will use a BSD variant or Linux."

There was no wireless gear here either. Too easy to spy on.

So these were sophisticated bad guys. That was not a surprise. If so, they'd have long passwords that mixed upper- and lower-case letters and numbers. He didn't have any password-cracking programs with him, and in any case it would take ages to decrypt, if it was even possible. The feds might be able to, but it would take them a while.

Frustrated and furious, Daniel strode over to the man with the mashed nose.

"I want your password. Now!"

The man tried to kick him.

Daniel placed one hand over the man's mouth and the other over his flattened nose. He pressed on both so that not only was the nose painful but the man would also start to smother. He waited while the thrashing got more violent, then stopped. He took his hands away. The man gasped and came to. Daniel did this four more times. After the last try, the man croaked out, "A . . . 72 . . . brd . . . 41 . . . Xmn . . . 80, uppercase A and X."

"It better be," Daniel said.

As soon as he was sure the password was correct, he found some duct tape and gagged both men. Might as well shut 'em up.

Daniel called up several files. He discovered the path through the Internet to the home port—or one of the home ports—for the network the computer was using. He discovered plans of DB's satellite offices and some of its safe houses. Daniel and Brenda had never put all of these in one file or even in one computer. The sickening thought hit Daniel. There was a traitor somewhere up in their organization. A traitor. Devastating. Who? He had no idea. Another top-level, A-one priority that would have to get in line with all the others.

He found the orders for killing him and plans for covering all the airports he could have gotten to, all the trains he might have had access to, with entry and exit points and orders for a variety of people to be on duty. The network he was uncovering was vast, with enough personnel to indicate he was dealing with a huge organization. One lone terrorist with a couple of demented friends couldn't operate on this scale. This was big. This was sophisticated. Very, very sophisticated.

Finally, he tried e-mailing his finds back to DB. He was afraid there would be strong encryption on a VPN to protect the data as it crossed the public Internet, but if so, they'd have to worry about decrypting it later.

He found a jump drive and saved each file he managed to open. Daniel knew he had to tell someone about all this. If governments didn't know about a network this big, they were criminally negligent. Then again he and Brenda were unaware of it, and they specialized in uncovering just this kind of plan and organization. Maybe some government was supporting these people or helping to cover it up? Or maybe some branch of a government was hip deep in lethal conspiracies. Daniel recalled all the boneheaded CIA schemes to depose dictators. A lot of people got dead for no good reason in many of those cockamamie clandestine disasters.

Who in any government would be on which side? He hated to imagine any of the western democracies doing something on this scale. He realized he wanted to blame a Middle Eastern country. But he had no proof. He had to keep an open mind no matter how odious the answer. Whatever it was, it could hardly be worse than the deaths of thousands of innocents in the streets of Manhattan.

Daniel knew DB's network wasn't nearly big enough to combat this kind of operation. He wondered why an obscure port outside of Istanbul would have this sort of information available. Of course, it was connected to a network that might be headquartered ten miles away or ten thousand miles away. But in this day and age, you couldn't take a chance on plots uncovered being anything but real. If he believed in the nonsensical color coding of terrorist alerts, he'd have long since passed despair, but this sure seemed real.

Daniel looked out the window. No strange sounds. No lights. Good so far.

He looked at his captives, who both glared at him. The tall guy flipped his middle finger at Daniel. Daniel gave him a bright smile and returned to work. He hunted for references to Sarah Swettenham. Plans were fine, but someone was willing to kill, and the only connection was Sarah.

Daniel broke though some of the encoded areas quickly. Others he might be able to get through if he had the time and equipment like that in his office in New York. But he didn't have either here. And these men certainly weren't working alone. The signal he tripped when he first entered the house might have alerted others who were already on their way.

CHAPTER 23

Monday, October 27
Near Istanbul
Eight Days before the Presidential Election

Daniel changed into a black T-shirt and black jeans and black running shoes. He carefully peeked out the window. Moonlight covered the countryside. He returned to the computer, rubbed his eyes with his knuckles, rotated his shoulders, cracked his knuckles. Then he hunched over the screen. The hours of the night crept past as he tried to make the computer reveal what it knew.

The clock on the computer read 2:17 when Daniel decided to try interrogation again. He'd saved everything he could to his jump drive. He'd try to decipher the rest in New York.

He looked at his prisoners. The short guy glared at his captor. Daniel asked, in French, "Who sent you?"

His captive shook violently. If his enemy hadn't been gagged, Daniel guessed he would have been spit on.

He tried the tall guy, who, once his gag was removed, said, "We will kill your faggot friend first. We'll cut off his balls and make you eat them as he bleeds to death."

Daniel reached down and tweaked the bloody mass that used to be the guy's nose. He screamed in agony. Daniel said, "It's time for you to stop making threats. I'm not going to kill you, but I will get answers."

"Geneva Convention!" the man wailed.

Daniel's fury erupted at what had happened to the people in the twin towers and his fear for Nate. He needed to make believable threats.

"I'm not an army," Daniel said, "or an official government representative. Like you, I'm freelance. I'm just a guy who is tired of people trying to kill him. So here's what I'm going to do. I'm going to work on your nose for a while. That will be kind of fun. Frankly, it shouldn't take much pressure for that to kill you in and of itself. Some bone fragments might do some real damage in your brain. I'll break both your kneecaps, shatter your ankles, then cut off your fingers one at a time. If you're lucky, I might leave the thumbs."

Suddenly the tall guy's head jerked. Blood blossomed out of his right ear. Daniel flattened himself on the floor. Half his captive's face disappeared. Daniel heard a series of distant rifle shots. The computer monitor ten feet from him burst into shards. The computer continued humming.

Crouching behind an old dresser for protection, Daniel shoved it across the room to the desk. He grabbed weapons and ammunition from it, flicked off the light, and dove for a newly made hole in the wall that looked out on the front of the house. Poking the machine gun's muzzle out the hole, he emptied a clip in the direction from which the firing had come. Before the sound of the last shot had faded, he dove, dropped, and rolled. Gunfire roared.

Crawling along the floor, Daniel checked the short guy. He was squirming madly. With the butt of the machine gun, Daniel knocked him unconscious. Then he reloaded.

Daniel stopped behind the old dresser. The hail of bullets resumed from the front of the house. A direct frontal attack? He scrabbled down the short hall to a window in the second bedroom that faced the backyard. Amid the din of gunfire, he glanced out. Two shadows were running full tilt toward the house. They were not firing. Daniel let fly a spray of bullets from the machine gun in his right hand.

Screams of agony mixed with the sounds of gunfire. When Daniel let up for a moment, there was silence and the smell of cordite. Both attackers were lumps on the ground ten feet from the house.

Daniel dashed toward the front of the house. Too late. Enemies were inside.

Daniel changed tactics. He reloaded, stood up, strode forward, and just kept firing. His mind was on autopilot, focused on survival, on being the last man standing.

He caught them by surprise. The sound of gunfire stopped. Daniel eased slowly into each room. One body near the front door had eyes staring, a bullet hole in its cheek half an inch below its left eye. Blood stained the wall behind it. Daniel heard a sigh, caught a subtle movement. The second man, flat on the floor, was raising a weapon to fire. Daniel emptied his gun at him. Seconds later he was standing over a body riddled with holes and covered in blood.

Five dead. Two in the back, two here, one in the computer room. Daniel checked the short guy. Breathing and still secured. Six. That was a lot of minions. They must be hiring locals.

As his pulse slowed, he crept cautiously from room to room. Then he checked the yard. He needed to be positive no enemies were left. All was silent inside and out.

If there were neighbors, they showed no sign of their presence. He eased back to the computer room. As he passed his victims, his elbow scraped through undried blood on one wall. He flinched. A shower would take care of the blood. But he'd need more than a shower to remove the stain of this night's battle from his mind.

As a little kid, he'd wanted to be a superhero, vaguely invincible and always doing in the bad guy, but he'd never pictured actual death. In high school and college Daniel had never dreamed of himself as a killer.

He'd killed people tonight. He wasn't proud of it. It was what he'd been trained for. He didn't stop to think before he had to pull a trigger. He'd been forced into the same type of situation before. He had the nerve to get through it. But he wasn't sure he had the nerve to survive the memories. He had vowed never to let his commitment to his liberal ideals overwhelm his determination to protect himself or those he loved. Now, if that encompassed ball-busting training and death, he was ready. Maybe not reconciled, but ready.

Daniel sat on the floor and took stock. He was a little bruised, but had no serious wounds. More important, the computer tower remained intact. He pulled in another monitor from the front room and put all the computer equipment on the floor. Using chairs, two desks, a blanket, and several paperweights, he created a blackout space under which he could work. He made sure he had an opening to observe the short guy.

Daniel crossed his legs in a lotus position, leaned over, and pulled the keyboard close. The monitor came to life.

He examined more files. Among the last, he found his and Brenda's names and a list of their employees. He found additional references to their offices. Finally, he found notes about Sarah, but no hard data that told him what the hell was going on.

Daniel crept out of his hiding place. Flies were buzzing around the corpses. As the insects neared his face, Daniel gently swatted them away. He approached his only undead captive, the short guy. He unbound him from the chair and flipped him on his back. Then Daniel knelt astride the tied-up terrorist and ripped the duct tape off the man's mouth. Hunks of beard came with it. The man's eyes followed Daniel's every movement. The man looked more angry than scared, ready to attack whatever part of Daniel he could reach.

"Give me your secret code and password," Daniel said.

"Fuck you," his captive said. Daniel, ready for the spit that followed, dodged. Daniel resisted backhanding him. It wasn't efficient, and it wouldn't help him get his answer.

Daniel replaced the duct tape. He hunted around the house for several minutes and found a toolkit in a storage closet. He took out a pair of pliers and returned to the computer room. Squatting next to his captive, Daniel showed him the pliers. The man's eyes followed the rust-encrusted metal object.

Daniel said, "I could yank on several significant parts of your anatomy. And while there are probably a few places in this world where that kind of thing is a big turn-on, I'm guessing this isn't one of them." Daniel wasn't into needless cruelty. He was doing this to get information out of a son of a bitch who wanted to kill him. "I think we'll make this simple." He yanked off the tape with his left hand. Then he grabbed the captive's left ear with the pliers and twisted slightly. He got a yowl and a short string of obscenities.

When the man stopped to draw a breath, Daniel said, "We can make this easy or hard." He slowly swung the pliers in front of the man's eyes, like a metronome on its slowest speed. The man's eyes followed the pliers as far as they could. When they were out of sight, his eyes sought Daniel's. The metal came in contact with the ear. The man began to bellow even before Daniel applied the slightest force. Daniel held his captive's head and clamped the pliers to the ear. The man tried to shake his head, which caused the pain to intensify. Then Daniel twisted the ear slightly. The man closed his mouth and held his head very still.

"Like I said, I need information," Daniel said.

The man began to bellow.

Daniel twisted. Hard.

Silence. Gasping for breath.

Daniel assumed the bellowing was an attempt to

warn or communicate with someone. "I don't know if they were your friends or just fellow killers, but they're all dead. Nobody is going to hear you. The louder you scream, the harder I twist."

The man drew a deep breath. Daniel twisted. Bits of blood appeared around the tips of the pliers. For a few seconds Daniel felt guilt about the cruelty. Then he thought of the World Trade Center. He thought of a bombed building in Cairo. He clamped down tighter and twisted again. The man began to cry. Daniel smelled the acrid odor before he looked back and saw the stain spreading on the front of the man's pants. Daniel increased the pressure.

"Okay." The man gasped. "Okay."

Daniel let go. The man blabbed.

Daniel reapplied the tape, made sure his captive's other bonds were secure, and returned to the computer. For several moments he wondered if the man might have been lying to him or given him a code that would betray an interloper's presence. But it didn't matter. He had to try something. He wasn't planning to live out his existence in a bullet-pocked hovel in Turkey.

Daniel typed in the code. The screen went blank for a second and then filled with data he hadn't seen before.

He shut the door between himself and the corpses. The flies were atrocious. No matter how single-mindedly he applied himself to the work, he stayed intensely aware of his surroundings. Even with the mind-absorbing work and preparedness for an attack, at times motes of fear for his friends and loved ones seeped into the unengaged neurons in his brain.

He found a mass of encrypted data that he had to

assume was important. He wished he had the software to decrypt it, but that was back at his office. He downloaded everything.

He worked until full light. It was time to get out of there. Daniel took the wallets from all the men, returned to the computer, and began reserving seats on every mode of transportation out of the city in each of their names as well as his own. He worked one credit card until it would no longer give him access and then switched to another.

The organization trailing him knew he was here. Since they did, there was no reason not to send an e-mail to Brenda. He didn't say what he'd done or where he was. He wrote simply, "Having a great time. Wish you were here." She would know he wasn't dead and that he would be home as soon as he could.

He examined the view out each window: broken rocks and barren ground. As the morning shadows receded, they revealed golden, brown, and gray boulders, stunted trees, and sparse vegetation. Crumbled stone walls made a poor delineation between fields and yards. He saw no nearby dwellings.

Before he left the house, he solved the problem of the short guy bound in duct tape by calling the police and giving them the location. Let the short guy try to explain the mayhem. Then Daniel took one of the shotguns and blasted the hell out of all the computer equipment. No one would be able to discover if he'd found anything or not.

As he walked out of the house, he sniffed his left armpit. He had flecks of blood on his shirt and pants. He needed a shower and a shave and another change of clothes.

Daniel also needed to check DB's local secret rendezvous. He'd have to be circumspect. He wanted no more of their own to die. Daniel made sure his prisoner was completely secure. He found a blue Ford, which the other attackers must have arrived in. The hood was cool but the keys were in the ignition. He drove to the safe house. It was ten miles back toward Istanbul and fifteen miles to the south of the E5 highway.

Daniel was tired. He found himself humming tunes to himself as he drove. At least they weren't Broadway show tunes. Those drove Nate nuts. He'd give a great deal to be fast asleep in bed next to Nate.

This safe house had once been a monastery. It had lost most of its roof, and the walls were crumbling. In a small, still-intact shed, Daniel found another pair of jeans, another Glock 19, a clean black T-shirt, a black leather jacket, and another disguise. He took the gun. He wasn't planning to fly out of Istanbul. He might have killed every agent the enemy had in Turkey. Or not. Travel by plane still seemed too great a risk.

It was midmorning when he stood among the dead at Lone Pine, one of the most moving of all the Anzac cemeteries of Gallipoli. He was to be here by ten at night or ten in the morning. It was after ten, and he was late. He watched the few other people from a clutch of pine trees that hadn't been destroyed in the catastrophic 1994 fire. He saw Gezasa Escabra, his contact, at some distance. He circled him from afar, watching all the people in the cemetery. At ten-thirty, Escabra began walking back to his car. He was giving up. Daniel got to the parking lot far ahead of him. Once again he checked out every person within sight. Nothing raised a red flag. Was the organization against them rushing in reinforcements? Maybe they weren't all-powerful. Had Daniel, for the moment, crippled them in Istanbul? He hoped so.

Daniel followed Escabra, who took the route back toward the city. Daniel checked over and over again. They were not being followed. At a quiet spot in the road, he sped up and came up behind Escabra and passed. He didn't want to scare the hell out of him, so Daniel waved as he passed. Escabra looked alarmed, then pleased. They turned off at the next cross highway. When they were hidden from the road, they stopped.

Escabra said, "Are you okay? We received frantic e-mails from New York. We have been expecting you."

"What happened to the Istanbul office?"

"No one was hurt. I saw a man across the street who looked suspicious. I got everyone out of the office by a back way and called the police. We were gone when the bomb went off. We've been in hiding. You could not have found us."

"At least you're all safe. Stay hidden. We'll let you know when it is safe. That will most likely be when I am out of Istanbul. I've got a way out this afternoon."

"Who are these people?" Escabra asked.

"I don't know. Obviously they mean business. Get back to our people. Wait for word."

Escabra nodded.

They got in their cars. Daniel drove off first and he sped away. He'd lied about leaving that afternoon. He trusted no one now, did not even trust Escabra enough to ask about Yussuf's note. He had to be at the Sirkeci Railway Station in Istanbul to catch the express train to Budapest at ten p.m. If a lie gave him a little bit of an edge, he would use it.

CHAPTER 24

Wednesday, October 29
New York City
Six Days before the Presidential Election

On her third date with Coop, Brenda relaxed her vigilance. Not so far as to let him pick her up at home, but she agreed that he could meet her at work. She had warned Helen he would be arriving, and when he did, Helen sent Brenda's office the "Look at your e-mail" message light instead of an intercom message, which would have been overheard by the visitor.

The e-mail from Helen said, "Wow!"

And he did look great.

Again he was casually dressed. Brenda had gone to pale, fluffy blond hair, which Helen this morning had said was "very Marilyn Monroe."

When Coop spread his hands as if amazed, she sang a breathy "Happy birthday, Mr. President." Coop laughed and Helen applauded. Helen looked absolutely delighted, Brenda thought. Of course, Helen had been worried for a long time about Brenda's all-work-no-play life. Helen had discarded her old boyfriend and taken up with two new ones in the time Brenda had gone on two dinner dates with Coop.

Brenda and Coop stood on the sidewalk, looking up and down Madison Avenue. New York had been in one of its nicest moods all day, crisp air and crystalline blue skies, and even though it was dark now, the crisp clean smell remained. There were even stars visible, a rarity in Manhattan. Brenda had a sense of unlimited potential. Maybe Coop was good for her.

He said, "Let's walk."

"Sure. At least we won't offend a cabbie this time."

They passed a drugstore, a gallery of Central American art with Moche pots in the window, a cut-rate scissors-and-knives store, and a Thai restaurant, all cheek by jowl.

There was a discreet brass sign, lighted with a single small spotlight, advertising an antique store upstairs from the restaurant, and two blazing fluorescent red arrows in a hardware-store window, pointing up to a second floor where one could get "Expert Massage—No Appointment Necessary."

"We're approving the polling program, but for ethical reasons we're going to have to include a caveat that we haven't had time to study it thoroughly," Brenda said.

Cooper smiled. "I admire your principles. Thank you for doing a good job in such a short time."

A ground-floor store near an alley, called Vintage Neon, displayed dozens of neon signs. Most were turned off, as the store was closed for the night. But there were three in the front left on for advertising: a six-foot martini glass, all bright amber except for an intensely green olive; an eight-foot-wide hamburger with red ketchup and yellow mustard; and a thing of concentric blue circles around the red words "TIRES CHANGED WHILE YOU WAIT."

"Bought from stores that closed, I guess," Brenda said.

"Or just picked up when buildings are demolished. Neon isn't popular anymore."

"It's popular in interior decoration. People buy these things to put in their living rooms."

"But it's not used for outdoor advertising."

"No, everything's digital now. And neon doesn't blink fast enough."

Looking around, Coop said, "Remember when there used to be phone booths? I haven't seen one in ages."

"You're right. They were removed because people could leave bombs in them."

"No lockers at train or bus stations anymore either."

"The legacy of terrorists," Brenda said. "I think about an attack every time I go in the subway. Or a high-rise. God, I love New York! And sometimes now I hate it! This makes me so damn furious!"

Coop reached out and put his arm around her shoulders. Then he drew her to him and kissed her. Brenda tensed for a second, and then she kissed him back.

She saw motion over his shoulder as a man lunged out of the alley. Coop must have noticed the reaction in her eyes, because he whirled around, keeping himself between her and the threat.

The man said, "Give me your wallets!"

In a wild moment of disbelief, Brenda thought the man's head looked like a tomato. Round cheeks, a small rounded chin, and a smooth round brow. He was bald or had shaved his head, which was now lit by red neon, making the tomato illusion complete.

This thought took less than a second. Tomato head or no, he was not an amusing sight. Muscles bulged under a black shirt, and his torso tapered to a slender waist. He looked like a very hard, strong man. In his right hand was a knife. Coop was a fairly tall man, but this guy was taller.

Coop yelled, "Get away!" and charged the attacker. Brenda saw Coop reaching for the wrist that held the knife, but the man outweighed Coop and was grabbing for Coop's shirt with his left hand. She leaped forward and seized the left hand in a double-handed grip, twisting it over and backward as if she wanted to wring it from his arm.

Mr. Tomato Head shrieked. He dropped the knife and ran down the alley. Coop chased him ten yards or so but gave up. The man was lost to sight behind Dumpsters and trash bags. "Shit!" Coop barked.

"Don't chase him," Brenda called. "It isn't worth getting killed for."

Coop came back limping. "Did he cut your leg?" she asked.

"No, no. Thank god. These just aren't running shoes." He was wearing tasseled loafers, clearly the last choice anyone would make to sprint in.

"Jeez!" he said, frowning. "I think you broke his wrist!"

"I hope so."

"I didn't know you could do that."

"Scare you?"

The frown faded, and Coop smiled. "Actually, I kinda like it."

"Dan and I both did a lot of defense training. Well . . . we'd better find a cop."

"You want to take the time?"

"No. But it's the proper civic thing."

"You're right. For whatever good it'll do."

A patrol cop took the information, and then they met with a detective, who took the same information all over again. Neither one gave them much hope that Mr. Tomato Head would be found, not even with Brenda's description of his unusually round head.

"You saw him in bad light though?" the detective asked twice.

"Pretty bad."

"Well, then."

An hour later, Coop and Brenda, having done their civic duty, walked back along Madison Avenue.

Brenda said, "You want to know what I was thinking? I was thinking I was glad he wasn't a terrorist. He was just an ordinary mugger."

"I was thinking the same thing."

"It's like—with a so-to-speak normal mugger, you know where they're coming from. They just want money."

Coop laughed. "An honest type of dishonesty?"

"Yup."

There was a lull in the conversation. Brenda hesitated before breaking the silence. She and Coop had gone to restaurants she had never been to with Jeremy. After the catastrophe on 9/11, she had lived almost entirely in central and north-central Manhattan, avoiding the area around the World Trade Center's ghost.

But Jeremy had come to her apartment. Her apartment, which was just three blocks away.

She drew a slow breath. Decision time.

"Would you like to come up to my place for . . . and send out for dinner?"

CHAPTER 25

Thursday, October 30
Istanbul
Five Days before the Presidential Election

Daniel knew his enemies might figure out where he was going, just by process of elimination. There were only so many trains and planes from points near where he'd last been seen. He had to assume other thugs had been contacted before the recent battle had even begun. Someone would be trying to pick up the trail. The problem for the bad guys was they had to have enough personnel to check out every train and bus station, boat dock, rent-a-car agency, and airport. Daniel, operating on the assumption that they could do it, donned the nun's disguise from the safe house in the Turkish countryside.

Daniel waited at the Sirkeci train station. The combined Byzantine, Seljuk, and Muslim architecture intrigued him. This was where Agatha Christie had boarded the famed Orient Express, but it hadn't run from this terminal since the seventies. He would be taking the Bosfor Ekspresi through Sofia and Bucharest, with a change in Budapest for Venice. He was headed for the safe house outside Rome.

He watched his fellow passengers carefully. Nothing struck him as odd. On the train he shut his eyes and listened. Tried to sense any unusual movement. The train rolled quietly out of Istanbul, was soon through the Turkish countryside and into Bulgaria. Daniel bought snacks and bottled water from machines. He overheard conversations in six languages. At the few station stops, he did his best to observe carefully everyone who came on board.

The lights in the train were dim as it rolled through the night. Only one person had on a reading light. All was quiet, and Daniel was fighting sleep, until they arrived at a tiny station, barely a blip in the road, in Bulgaria. It was just after two, and Daniel was dozing. As the train slowed, he wakened. He saw two men on a platform. The station was little more than a hut, certainly not a place an express train should stop. The men stood in the shadows, but as they moved toward the train, they were forced to traverse the only lighted portion of the platform. Both seemed to be in their late twenties. One was thin and had short brown hair cut evenly all the way around his head. He might have been five foot nine and weighed perhaps one thirty-five. The other was shorter, with dark wavy hair slicked back. Daniel saw that they didn't look sleepy or tired. Instead they looked alert and grim. They spoke with the conductor for an unusually long time. Inquisitive tourists? Or danger? The delay wasn't much—maybe three, four minutes—but those three or four minutes weren't in the timetable.

The two men boarded the train.

Daniel guessed they would inspect the train. He trusted to his disguise and the weapons under his habit. The two men began at the front of the train. Finally Daniel saw them making their way through the car in front of his.

He felt a tug on his rosary. His heart slammed against his chest. He took his eyes off the men. A four-year-old girl with two pink bows in her hair gravely gazed up at him. She said something to Daniel in a language that was unfamiliar to him. Then she tugged again. Daniel whispered, "Can I help you?" in every language he knew. Instead of trying to disguise his voice, he'd decided that when he was in the nun getup, he would always whisper. Let the listeners come to whatever conclusions they would.

The little girl pointed up ahead. Daniel saw a woman in her mid-twenties with children clustered around her. They were in the front seat nearest the door between the two train cars. The oldest, a girl, was asleep in a seat. The youngest whimpered almost continuously. A boy of about three seemed to be in continuous motion, as he tried to climb the armrest and the backrest, and squirm down onto the floor all at the same time. The fourth child was in the aisle. He was smiling happily as he waved to his sister. The little girl tugged on Daniel's rosary again. Daniel marveled at the surprise she'd caused him. He'd been trained to be alert to everything around him, but he'd dismissed the little girl as she'd made her way toward him. She tugged more insistently and pointed ahead.

Daniel wasn't great with kids. He often didn't have the patience, but these five looked ragged and forlorn. Daniel rose and moved forward. It would be in character for a nun to assist a family in distress. He walked up to the woman. They managed to communicate in French. The six of them, mother and five kids, were on their way to visit the father. But now two of them were sick, and she didn't know what to do. Could the nun help her? Could the good sister watch them for her while she took the littlest one to the lavatory?

Daniel's primer on how to travel had included practical and specific courses on how not to be taken in by scam artists and bunkum peddlers in foreign countries. He saw none of the signs here. He wondered briefly if his enemies had the cleverness to disguise a female agent as a traveler with five children. He had serious doubts about this, but he didn't relax his vigilance.

He took a seat. Clutching a bag of diapers, the woman took the child to the lavatory at the rear of the car. The little girl who had approached him sat on Daniel's right. The boy from the aisle sat in his lap. The one who had been squirming was crammed between Daniel and the train window. When Daniel smiled down at him, the boy began to scrunch up his face to cry. Daniel began to hum softly and then to sing in a low voice an old Scottish ballad about children gone amissing. The child might not understand the words, but he stopped scrunching. The boy in his arms stirred and settled, and the little girl nodded off.

Daniel sensed a presence in front of him. He didn't look up. The woman had gone toward the rear of the car, not forward. He rocked the little boy and sang softly. The two men barely noticed him. He did not meet their eyes, but instead concentrated on the children in his charge. He observed as much as he could. The men were unshaven. He saw bulges under their jackets that suggested they were armed. Neither one spoke. They made three trips past him.

As the men passed Daniel a third time, the mother returned, thanking him profusely. She offered him tiny cakes and cookies. Daniel used the tips of his fingers to delicately enfold small bits. He saw the men take up positions at the exit doors at the far end of the car ahead of him, one facing toward him and one facing the car behind. They would be able to see everyone from there.

Daniel now undertook the most difficult part of an antiterrorist's job. He waited. He had no choice. He could not betray nervousness or give in to a twitch, yet he couldn't hold himself rigidly silent. He swayed with the train, closed his eyes as if to nap, but through slitted eyes he watched every passenger and the two men guarding the exit doors.

In Bucharest early the next morning, two older teenagers in leather bikers' jackets rushed to board at the last second. Their heads were shaved, their eyebrows plucked, and their faces pierced and punctured with studs and earrings. Your clever terrorist tries to blend in. Your average thug anywhere on the globe doesn't much care who notices him. "Clumsy" was the word that came to Daniel's mind. They looked too carefully over the passengers they passed. Then they spoke to one of the men Daniel had identified earlier in the car ahead of him. That man now made his way farther forward. Nearly every car on the train would now have an enemy posted in it.

Daniel saw the two new arrivals in the car ahead

of him, lurching from seat to seat, swaggering, leering, and jostling passengers. Either they were inept or they saw no need to conceal their behavior.

So they weren't perfect. That was reassuring. Their organization might be large, but it wasn't omnipotent.

He glanced around. The man who had been in the car behind him was moving farther back on the train. When the two new ones reached his compartment, Daniel realized they were loud as well as rude. They swore at each other and at anyone who glared or even dared to glance at them. They were speaking German. One was taller and uglier, with a thick ring clamped through the connecting point between his two nostrils. The shorter one had two ugly scars running from the top of his shaven head to just above his right eyebrow. Multicolored rings were scattered along these two trails of dark purple.

When the two thugs got near their seats, the young mother Daniel had been helping leaned into the aisle to retrieve a small truck which the two-year-old had just dropped. The taller of the two thugs, the one with the nose ring, lurched into her. The train swayed at that moment and Nose Ring almost fell into her lap. His crotch banged against her oversized diaper bag. The large, ugly brute let out a yowl, then backhanded the woman. The child teetered in her arms as she frantically clutched at him and tried to right herself. Daniel caught the child, but the motion exposed his wrist, and Nose Ring saw it. He might not have been too smart, but he knew that a nun with a hairy hand was suspicious.

Daniel didn't hesitate. He righted the woman, and with his free hand he grabbed the guy's crotch. He didn't want to use a gun. If there was any way to avoid drawing attention to himself, he certainly wanted to play it that way. It took him only seconds to hustle Nose Ring out the door and into the space between the train cars.

Daniel didn't let go his firm hold. His captive began to bellow. Daniel moved him out of the line of sight of the passengers, one or two of whom looked up. But they couldn't see around the nun's habit to observe Daniel's very non-nunlike grip on Nose Ring's family jewels. Scarred Guy, who hadn't seen the telltale wrist, had stumbled after them.

Daniel heard the click of the train wheels and the rush of the wind. Scarred Guy grabbed Daniel around the waist. He managed to knock Daniel's wimple askew. Nose Ring gasped and swore in guttural German and added, "It's him."

Scarred Guy said, "Kill him."

Daniel fought grimly. He kept a firm grip on Nose Ring and tried to swing him around into Scarred Guy.

The train swayed. Together the three men tottered back and forth in the small passageway. Scarred Guy pulled a twelve-inch, serrated-bladed knife from his boot. He tore a gash in Daniel's habit from shoulder to knee. The fabric caught the knife long enough for Daniel to counter the measure. He grabbed Scarred Guy's hand and bent it back toward the accordion-folded canvas wall connecting the cars. The knife gashed the plasticized fabric, and now Daniel could feel the wind rushing past. He twisted and yanked. The train lurched. The knife went into Nose Ring's left thigh.

Daniel stepped near the door. His attackers were entangled for an instant in blood and anger and screams. Daniel unlatched the window, pulled it down, reached outside, and threw open the door. Scarred Guy, unwounded, rushed toward him. Daniel sidestepped, grabbed him by his coat, and heaved. At the last moment he loosened his grip, and the man's arms flailed like pinwheels as he flew into the foliage on the side of the rails. Nose Ring swayed on one foot, but instead of grabbing a purchase to steady himself, he tried to shove Daniel, a mistake for which he paid when Daniel assisted him in joining his partner.

Daniel stood between the cars and breathed deeply. He looked through the windows into the cars before and behind him. No conductor. No one seeming to take notice. Most of the passengers had been asleep, nestled into their uncomfortable pillows. Had he killed the two men? Very likely. He didn't know them nor they him, but the whims of the world had brought them together. And now those two were likely dead instead of him. He straightened his wimple and refastened his rope belt to hold the damaged robe around him.

Daniel returned to the car. The woman with the five children gave him a strange look. Of course, she was in a position to have seen some of what had happened. Daniel said to her in French, "Are you okay?"

"Yes. You have helped. Who were those men?"

Daniel shrugged. "I think they may have been on the wrong train. I gave them some advice."

An hour or so later the two other men met in the car in front of Daniel's. They engaged in dialogue Daniel could not hear. Certainly the consternation on their faces was real. They began examining each of the passengers closely. Squabbles broke out, and the conductor and several other railway employees were summoned. Even though Daniel suspected the two searchers were well armed, their orders did not seem to include creating an international incident. They walked back through Daniel's car. He did his best to look saintly.

In Budapest, still in his nun's habit, he changed trains for Rome. What more logical place for a nun to be going than Rome?

CHAPTER 26

Hector Berlesconi was extremely uncomfortable.
He was physically uncomfortable. His blocky
figure didn't fit easily into the storage closet. Although
it was roomy as closets go and although he had removed the shelves, put them on the floor, and stacked
the boxes of paper and other supplies, he was still
jammed in. The air wasn't too good either.

Worse than the physical discomfort though was his
acute distaste for what he was about to do. The idea
of spying on the president of the United States of-
fended his every notion of propriety, not to mention
the probable illegality of the action. And he could
imagine several disastrous things that might happen
if he were to be caught.

Nevertheless, he intended to know more about what

was going on, and if this was the only way to do it, then this was what he had to do.

He'd been vaguely uneasy for a while now about the president's attitude, but the early-morning campaign-strategy meeting had focused his anxieties. Oddly enough, it was the president's civility that had disturbed him. The latest polls had been presented, and they weren't looking good. Governor Harkinnon appeared to be gaining on all fronts.

President Kierkstra had simply sat at his desk and nodded, not even appearing to pay attention. No temper tantrums, no screamed obscenities, no threats. "Yes, well," he'd finally said, "we all know the polls can be wrong. Even exit polls."

There was a small nervous titter. Everyone in the room knew that elections had been manipulated before this, by means as simple as making sure there weren't enough voting machines in key precincts, or as complicated as going to the Supreme Court.

It was the exchange of glances between the president and his crony Alexander Cabot that had set Berlesconi's systems to high alert.

Hector stood in his closet and sweated. The meeting had been over for about half an hour, just about long enough to fix up the closet and get himself hidden. He knew Cabot and Kierkstra often repaired to this small office for private conversations after the glad-handing that always followed formal meetings. He hoped he wouldn't have long to wait.

In fact it wasn't more than a minute or two later that footsteps sounded on polished wood, then were muffled as the person reached the thickly woven rug.

Person—or persons?

Persons. President Kierkstra and someone else. Unless the president had taken to talking to himself. Which, thought Hector almost despairingly, might be the next step.

But it wasn't happening this time. To the president's "Hurry up," a voice replied, "I'm right behind you. And are you carrying a gun again?"

"None of your damn business!"

"It might be as well to keep your voice down, Mr. President. The walls have ears, you know. Especially White House walls." It was Alexander Cabot's voice.

Hector wished he could wipe his brow. Sweat was dripping into his eyes, making them sting.

"Oh, siddown, for god's sake. And stop nagging me about ears. The staff knows enough to stay away from this office when I'm using it. They know it's private." The president was back to his usual petulant self.

Cabot sighed, loudly enough that Hector could hear him through the thick oak of the closet door. "You should know by now that nothing a president says or does is guaranteed to be private, not for long."

"Well, this damn well better be private. You promised me!"

"And I keep my promises. You know that. I am merely advising you to use some elementary caution. I am your friend and advisor. I keep you informed about the world of big business and high finance. It would be most unfortunate if there were any hint of any other sort of relationship."

"Whaddya mean, relationship? You make me sound like some goddamn pervert!"

"Oh, but ours is a beautiful friendship, isn't it? Based on complete mutual mistrust."

The president muttered something Hector couldn't catch.

"Indeed. But we didn't come here to exchange insults, and it would be unwise to prolong this meeting. I wanted simply to let you know that the system is in place. It's being checked out by the best security firm in this country, DB Security, and so far they've found nothing suspicious. As soon as the press release goes out—and it's in the works now—the public can be assured that computerized voting across the country is simple and utterly foolproof."

There was no sound for a moment, and then the president began to chuckle. Cabot joined him. The laughter turned to guffaws.

The sweat dripped down Hector's face. He hoped they would leave soon.

He also hoped he was wrong about what he had heard. But he knew he wasn't. His suspicions of Alexander Cabot were confirmed.

Hector's first actions after he left the cupboard were to go to his small White House office to take a quick shower and change into the spare clothes he always kept there. The ones he had put on that morning were soaked through, and he didn't need anyone wondering why he had sweated so much on a cool day.

His next task required finesse. He wanted a photograph of Cabot, the man famous for his avoidance of cameras.

Cabot had always claimed that a man of great wealth was also at great risk. Any number of people might want to harm him, for any number of reasons. He wanted to be anonymous, invisible. He never consented to be interviewed, never allowed cameras anywhere near his presence. So far as Berlesconi knew, Cabot had somehow managed to evade the paparazzi all his life. So where was a picture to be found?

The press office was out. Berlesconi didn't want anyone to know what he was looking for.

Suddenly he snapped his fingers. Surveillance cameras! The White House bristled with them at all entrances. Taking care to move at a casual saunter and making up a story as he went along, he made his way to the well-hidden security office, the nerve center of all the precautionary measures meant to protect the president and the executive branch. Very few people knew where the security office was. Fewer still were allowed into the area, but back when Berlesconi had been one of President Miller's closest advisors, he had often dropped in. His philosophy was that you might as well make friends with everybody possible. You never knew when it might come in handy.

"Hi, guys," he said to the guards. "Doing a great job down here, as usual. Making good use of all the money we spend on this operation, I hope?"

"Doing our best," said the oldest man, who had been on the job forever. "Gets harder every year, with all the crazies around. We could use more staff, more cameras—more of everything." The man was aware of Berlesconi's role in budget decisions.

"Aw, c'mon, you've got the best equipment there is, and you know it." Berlesconi moved closer to one of the monitors. "I've never seen myself on one of these things. Bet I look like Public Enemy Number One, with my build. I'd like to check myself out. How long do you keep the tapes?"

"Years, but you wouldn't see a lot. See, that's what I mean about needing better equipment. The resolution isn't good."

Berlesconi looked skeptical. "Show me. If you've got time to run a tape, I mean."

"Don't have to look at a tape," said the guard. "Just take a look at the monitor here." He pointed. "That's one of the doors from the Rose Garden, see? And there's the president just going out. You can tell from the way he walks, but even if I zoom in"—he magnified the picture—"it's still a little fuzzy. You can see who it is, but not clearly. Same with the guy with him." The guard chuckled. "Good thing, too, with that man. He's not wild about being photographed."

Berlesconi swore under his breath. The man with the president was undoubtedly Cabot—also recognizable from his walk—but even if he had been facing the camera, the resolution was only so-so.

"You have to be able to identify people," Berlesconi said. "It's vital to security."

"They've got a new IFRSUUTI out too, and we could sure use it," continued the guard, determined to make his point.

"What's IFRSUUTI?"

The guard explained, then went on with his complaint. "We got one when it first came out, but the resolution . . . well, here, I can show you." He turned to a different monitor. "Now, look. This one's in the anteroom to the Oval Office. Anybody comes in, their face shows up on this thing. The president's secretary can see it, and we see it down here too. It has to match up with the image we have on file or . . . well, let's just say a lot of questions get asked."

"Hey, you mean you have an infrared image of anybody who's ever gone into the Oval Office? Lemme see mine," demanded Berlesconi.

The guard punched a few keys and a pattern of colors, vaguely resembling a human face, came up on the screen.

"That's me, huh?" said Berlesconi with a grin. "My own Italian mama wouldn't know me. Hey, you got one of Cabot?" He chuckled.

The guard laughed too. "Yeah, we do. Bet he wouldn't like that, would he? Not that it looks much like him. Here." More keys. Another peculiar face-like image appeared.

Berlesconi broke into a belly laugh. "Man, that's amazing," he said, when he had recovered. "Tell you what. Can you give me a printout of that? And the other Cabot pictures? I wanna make a bet with Cabot. I want to tell him I can produce a picture of him."

"You won't tell him where it came from, will you?" said the guard with sudden caution. "On account of nobody's supposed to know about this system. I'm not sure Kierkstra knows, even."

"Cross my heart," said Berlesconi, making the gesture.

"You'll see what I mean . . . even better in the printout," persisted the guard. "We really need the update. The company that makes 'em says it's a lot better, and harder to fool."

Berlesconi promised to take the matter up with someone in authority. In fact, Berlesconi had nothing whatever to say about White House expenses, but people sometimes assumed that the guy who ran the Budget Office could perform miracles. At that point Berlesconi would have promised anything in order to walk off with the printout.

It wasn't much, he thought, studying it later, but in a weird way the printout sort of looked like Cabot. Somebody who knew the man just might be able to recognize it, might be able to tell Berlesconi more about Cabot and just exactly what he was up to.

Daniel arrived in Venice and, still dressed as a nun, took the four-and-a-half-hour express train to Rome. The news monitors in the station showed war deaths, the U.S. president making a statement, and local news. The announcers spoke in Italian. None of the pictures showed bombings or fires in business establishments.

Once in Rome, Daniel purchased a bus ticket for Avezzano, east of Rome, where he finally divested himself of his habit and walked five miles into the hills. In the moonlight he passed Alba Fucens, the ruins of an ancient city. What had happened to it? he wondered. What did happen when the system breaks down?

Daniel stopped on a bluff overlooking an unsown field with an isolated farmhouse in the middle. He waited for any sign of movement, any whiff of suspicious activity.

It was what he didn't see that gave him pause. Every safe house in the organization had a visible signal that all was well. So every safe place was visited once a day. It wasn't a perfect system, but it was the best they could do. Not only would an enemy have to know that there was such a signal, they would have to know the code.

Daniel scanned every square foot of the moonlit pastoral scene below him. Time ticked slowly by. He was sweating despite the chill. He took enough time to make a thorough examination. Halfway up the hill behind the farmhouse, he saw the marker: a tumbledown well had a pinprick of laser light that did not blink. The lack of a random blink warned him of the danger.

Daniel heard a bird chirp in the forest behind him. A bird? In the middle of the night? He didn't hesitate. He dashed in a zigzag pattern down the bluff in front of him. Trees and bushes offered less and less cover as he neared the bottom of the hill. He planned to skirt the farmhouse in a broad arc, using the stand of trees at the bottom of the slope for a shield. Halfway down, he saw a glint of moonlight in the middle of the trees. Moonlight, hell. The moon was behind him. The red flash moments later proved him right. Something hostile was down there.

Daniel ran toward a low cement wall. Not much cover, but it was all he could find. They must have nightscopes, and how many of them were there? Any number of enemies could be hiding at windows and doorways, or on the roof or around a corner. He ducked his head, hunched his shoulders, and headed for the hill behind the house and the trees that began fifty feet beyond it. He zigzagged wildly in his desperate dash to safety. The moon—the real moon—shone brightly enough for him to see puffs of dirt as shots spread around him. Moments later he was in the woods again.

Daniel stopped fifteen feet inside the trees. He inched his way up the slope, leaped across a small path, miscalculated, and landed in a ditch.

It was an expensive mistake. He had landed awkwardly and twisted his ankle. It hurt like hell. He bit back a cry and touched the spot on his ankle. He wiggled his foot. Nothing seemed broken. He tried putting weight on it and got a sharp flash of agony.

Daniel had been taught how to deal with pain. He blanked his mind to everything except the pain. He concentrated on each bone, on each moment of agony. He compartmentalized it. Focused on the fact that if he did not overcome it, he would be dead. It helped. It would, he thought bitterly, help more if he could turn himself into a robot. Robots don't feel pain. Humans do.

He knew he needed to move and keep on moving. He wrenched his concentration from the pain to the world around him. He could smell the sweat of a man moving on the far side of the path about twenty feet below him. One antagonist had shot from behind him. At least one other had fired from the farmhouse. Daniel had at least two enemies, three if the man on the far side of the path was not the man who shot from behind or from the house.

As quietly as he could, he pulled off his undershirt and wrapped it around his ankle in a makeshift bandage. Then he waited for the man ascending the slope to come opposite him. Neither his five senses nor his intuition gave any indication of another human's presence. He threw a stone fifteen feet in front of the man and another the same distance behind him. He saw a flash of red and noted the shooter's turn toward the back. Daniel hustled twenty feet ahead in the woods then hurled himself across the path, taking pains not to put excess pressure on his injured ankle. He kept going into the woods on the far side. After fifty feet he stopped; then he slowly circled back.

The glint of moonlight on the gun gave away the

location of the enemy. Daniel crept closer. The face opposite him was covered with a black ski mask. Daniel inched nearer. He saw the man's chest rising and falling.

Daniel leaped. The fight was brief. In moments Daniel's knees were crammed into the armpits of the recumbent figure; he had his enemy pinned to the ground. He hadn't expended much energy. The man was nearly unconscious.

Daniel yanked off the man's ski mask. Other than reinforcing that he was in control, the gesture was futile. The moonlight wasn't bright enough for Daniel to see the face clearly, and anyway, out of the billions of people on the planet, why should he recognize this one? He didn't really expect to know his assailants.

"Who are you?" Daniel asked.

"I'll be dead soon and so will you."

"Who sent you?" Daniel asked.

No answer. Daniel smelled coffee and cigarettes. He grabbed a hank of the man's long greasy hair and with the other hand grabbed at the man's crotch. With both hands he pulled and twisted. The man gasped. "Who sent you?" Daniel whispered again as he inflicted pain. But there was no reply.

Daniel had to act quickly. The noises the wounded man was making would give him away, and Daniel was going to draw any other enemies to his position if he stayed there much longer. Daniel reached for the man's right leg. He placed his fingers in three strategic locations on the man's kneecap, pressed, and dislocated it. The man screamed. He wouldn't be chasing Daniel around the mountains any time soon.

Daniel felt the man's weight shift. A knife appeared in the man's left hand. Daniel easily grabbed the wrist.

There was a soft thud. The assassin's hand splintered into a bloody mass, and the man fell unconscious. Was someone firing at Daniel? Or at the injured man?

Daniel grabbed the man's gun and crawled away.

Behind the first large tree, Daniel hesitated. He didn't know if further movement would put him in the lap of an enemy or take him farther away from them. He heard shots thudding into a tree above his head. So far, not so good. But he could see flashes of red from the gun. He fired to the left and right of what he'd seen. He moved up the slope of the hill. His ankle ached. He had to ignore it, but it hobbled him and made his usual fluid movements less than what he wished.

Again he circled.

And listened.

And breathed.

And felt the agony in his ankle.

Daniel had nearly reached the top of the slope. He came to a derelict shed. He crouched on the ground in the deepest shadows, on the farthest side, and took time to think.

They'd been here waiting for him. He had hoped that not all of his and Brenda's codes had been compromised. Okay, so how did these guys get here? Daniel circled again, then began making his way down to the farmhouse, figuring it was the place they'd least expect him to go.

Daniel examined the farmhouse. He found the computers smashed, the monitors crushed, and trip wires attached to bombs. Someone hadn't finished rigging them. Apparently he'd interrupted them. In the garage he found a van. The driver stared straight ahead. Daniel recognized Antonio Manzoni, the safe-house custodian, whom he'd hired a few months ago. His body had been duct-taped to the seat, and he had a bullet hole in the head. Blood, everywhere blood. He'd been shot here.

There was a broken section of wooden fence in the garage, and a piece of it was usable as a crutch. Daniel seized it gratefully.

Dawn was still hours away. Daniel didn't know if sunlight would be his friend or enemy. He waited for the men to return to finish rigging the bombs. But minutes passed, then an hour. No sign of them. Had he killed the explosives guy? He dug in the corner of the garage for his stash of supplies. He grabbed more cash, new credit cards, new identity papers, and a few more elements of disguise. He hobbled to the exit.

His ankle was swelling badly and beginning to throb. He knew he couldn't walk five miles. He'd have to risk the van. After careful observation, he went back to the garage, pulled Antonio's body out of the driver's seat, and laid him gently on the floor.

"Sorry, friend. I wish I had time to bury you." He saluted, then climbed into the van and drove with great caution to Avezzano. From there he took the bus to Rome's Leonardo da Vinci airport, where he showered, changed once again, and napped until the first flight out.

Daniel's clothing now consisted of a garish flower-patterned shirt, pink-shaded sunglasses, and yellow pants. It took every ounce of his energy to smile and be loud and boisterous while ignoring his ankle. The first flight available going in the right direction was to Buenos Aires. He would have to change there for Miami, then take another flight to New York.

He boarded the plane and found the seat next to

him was empty. The attendant was willing to give him a plastic bag with ice cubes. He eased his ankle onto the seat, placed the ice over it, and went to sleep. As Daniel dozed off, he couldn't resist a smile of satisfaction. He hoped he had a piece of the puzzle. He was alive. For now.

The next day the skyscrapers of Manhattan never looked better.

CHAPTER 27

Friday, October 31
New York City
Four Days before the Presidential Election

He got a taxi at LaGuardia and directed the driver
to take him to a Syrian restaurant in Queens.
More than anything, he would have liked to go right
home, but he had to know whether he was being followed. Certainly if the enemy knew all about DB's
offices abroad, they knew where he lived. But he
wanted to be forewarned.

The restaurant was near Park Forest Hills Hospital, where he knew you could get a taxi anytime. He
walked through the restaurant and out the back door,
saying, "Excuse me, excuse me," then down an alley,
all the while toting the small carry-on he had bought
back in the Rome airport.

Nobody seemed to be following. The taxi he picked
up at the hospital deposited him in Brooklyn at noon.

Daniel hoped he would find Nate there, but the house was silent, and there was no sign that Nate had been in while Daniel was gone. He pushed his sadness into the back of his mind as he dropped his bag, grabbed his spare cell phone, transferred the note from Yussuf and his jump drive to his shirt pocket, went back outside, and hailed a taxi.

The ride to the DB offices took half an hour. God, Manhattan looked good.

CHAPTER 28

Same Day
New York City

Hector Berlesconi made a couple of phone calls to cancel appointments and then got himself to Reagan National Airport, where he boarded the first plane for New York.

He arrived a little before noon and went straight to the offices of DB Security.

Helen was about to go to lunch when Berlesconi walked in the door. Her "May I help you?" carried the clear implication that she very much doubted it. People didn't just walk in off the street.

Berlesconi dredged up all his charm. "Gosh, I'm sorry I dropped in without an appointment, but I just flew in from Washington and I hoped that maybe Ms. Grant would be free for lunch. I owe her a lot and I'd like to make a tiny repayment. My name is Hector Berlesconi."

Aha! That's why he looks familiar. "Oh . . . well, of course, Mr. Berlesconi. I know about you and your grandson."

"Granddaughter," he corrected gently.

Helen, who had made the mistake deliberately, smiled and shook her head. "Darn. I'm so forgetful. Elsie, isn't it?"

"Emily." Berlesconi was smiling broadly now. "And now that we've pretty well established that I am who I say I am, am I going to get lucky and find Ms. Grant in?"

"I'll check." She picked up the phone.

Brenda had just decided to take a break and order in a sandwich. "Mmm?" she said into the phone.

"You have a visitor. Mr. Hector Berlesconi. He wants to know if you're free for lunch."

"The guy from the White House? What does he look like?"

"Yes, he surely looks like himself." On her end, Helen grinned at Berlesconi, who sighed melodramatically.

There was a limit to how much information Helen could give her with the man standing right there. "I'll be right out."

Brenda, who had learned over the years to set aside her first impression of people and wait to see what experience taught her, wasn't sure why she warmed to Berlesconi at once. Maybe it was because he was so much older. Maybe it was his jowly face or his crumpled clothes. He carried a thin briefcase, but while it may have been fine leather, it was scuffed and supple from years of use. He looked like a grandfather. She walked up to him and held out her hand. "It's an honor, Mr. Berlesconi."

He grasped it firmly. "The honor is mine, Ms. Grant. As I was in New York, I took the liberty of hoping you'd be available for lunch. I know how busy you are, but—"

"It's true, unfortunately. I'm up to my ears today, and I'm not dressed for a fancy lunch." With no appointments today, she'd dressed for comfort in slacks and a loose purple shirt. "I'd actually planned to eat at my desk."

"I know a great little Italian place near here," said Berlesconi coaxingly. "Couple blocks away. Owned by a cousin of mine, third or fourth or somewhere down the line. Good food, very casual. Would that suit you?"

"Not Minelli's!"

"That's the one. You know it?"

"One of my favorites. Okay, you've got a deal. I really do have to get back here pronto though."

She collected her purse and they breezed out. Brenda had a hard time reminding herself that this friendly, laid-back guy was a member of the cabinet.

Berlesconi confined his comments to the weather, which was overcast, until they were greeted at Minelli's with Italian exuberance and ensconced in the best booth, the big, quiet one in the corner. "Glass of wine?" he suggested when they were settled. Giorgio Minelli hovered solicitously.

"I don't usually drink in the middle of the day. Makes me sleepy all afternoon. Water will be fine."

"Right. Make that two Pellegrinos, Giorgio. And have Marco bring us some antipasto quick, while we decide what else we want."

"I know already," said Brenda. "Minestrone. It's wonderful here."

Berlesconi beamed. "Good girl! You know good Italian peasant food."

Their meal arrived, a huge platter of meats and cheeses and olives and peppers borne proudly by Giorgio himself, along with a basket of crusty bread and two steaming bowls of soup.

"Ah, Giorgio, that's what I call service. Now leave us alone so I can enjoy my lunch with this lovely lady." Berlesconi and the proprietor exchanged some rapid Italian and a couple of broad winks.

Berlesconi waited until they had nearly finished eating; then he sat back. His face lost its jovial expression and became sober, even formal. He dropped the informality of his speech as well. "Ms. Grant, I hate to introduce an unpleasant topic, but I had a reason for coming to see you today." His voice was quiet, easily covered by the boisterous conversations around them.

Brenda put down her soupspoon. "You came especially to see me? I thought you were just in New York and happened in."

"I'm glad I was able to give that impression, but the fact is, I had a definite mission. I would like you to undertake a short investigation for me. Your company's advice has been very solid."

"Thank you."

"This is extremely confidential. The person involved is very highly placed."

"We are very discreet."

"I know that. Your reputation is sterling. I've learned something I think you and Mr. Henderson should know, and I'm afraid it's pretty serious."

Brenda could not imagine what was coming. "Have we done something wrong?" She tried, and failed, to think what it might be.

"It's possible. I don't know how, but I think— there's no easy way to say this—I think you may have put your okay on election software that has been deliberately sabotaged."

Brenda sat in silence for a long few seconds. Then she said, "I think I'll have that glass of wine after all."

She drank it slowly. Berlesconi let her brood. Once or twice Giorgio glanced their way, frowning. He looked unhappy about the turn his cousin's pleasant lunch was taking, but he knew better than to interrupt.

Finally Brenda said, "I want to know as much as you can tell me."

"I know nothing for certain. All I can say is, when you've spent as much time in Washington as I have, you develop a keen sense of smell, and this whole election thing has a powerful stink of trouble. There's something else. I would like you to research a man for me. His name is Alexander Cabot."

"Cabot!"

"You know who he is, of course."

Brenda shrugged. "I've heard of him certainly. President's confidant, richest guy on the planet, finger in all sorts of pies. Bebe Rebozo squared."

Berlesconi's eyebrows rose. "And what does a kid like you know about Bebe Rebozo?"

"I've always been fascinated with the Nixon era. Used to read a lot of history back when I had time. I always thought Nixon's pal Rebozo was sleaze—and probably mafia." She looked again at Berlesconi and his very Italian features. "Sorry. Stupid remark."

"He was Cuban, you remember, not Italian. But

hey." He spread his hands and shrugged. "So you think Cabot's another Rebozo? That's interesting."

"I don't really know anything about him at all."

"Very reclusive. He's enormously rich, of course, amazingly rich for a guy who's not that old. Forty-five. He inherited a gigantic fortune from his parents, but he's at least quadrupled it."

"Oil, right?"

"Now, yes. His grandfather was a lumber baron, as they were called in those days. His father was in both coal and oil, and Cabot was in railroads for a while. I think now he's mostly divested himself of everything except oil."

"He's global. I mean, he's not just into U.S. oil."

"Right. But if you're thinking terrorist connections, global isn't unusual these days. Most oil companies are global." Berlesconi pointed to his briefcase. "I have a couple of rare photos of him in here. And I mean rare."

"Mr. Berlesconi." Brenda rolled the stem of her wineglass between her fingers. "Why are you telling me all this? If you think there's something wrong with the vote tabulation program, I can tell you that there isn't any that I can see. I've been all over it. I've had staff studying isolated chunks of it too. And Daniel Henderson is on his way back from abroad and will be going over the whole thing afresh today. But it looks like clean code. And beautiful, incidentally. Whoever wrote it wasn't just a genius, but an artist as well. I'd like to shake his hand. Or hers," she added, thinking of poor Sarah.

"Shall we go for a walk?" he asked.

Outside, the weather was raw, threatening rain. Brenda wrapped her coat around herself. After a block or so, she stopped. "Let's sit," she said. "Mr. Berle-sconi . . ."

"I think we're past that stage, don't you?" said the man. "Hector's a lot easier to pronounce."

"If you're Hector, I'm Brenda." Or the White Queen, she thought with a touch of hysteria. Is it possible that I'm sitting here freezing and having a first-name-basis conversation with a cabinet secretary? Somehow I've stepped through the looking glass.

"You saved Emily's life, Brenda, and I owe you. The future of your company and the company that designed the software depends on the quality of that vote-tallying software. The election may be rigged. The future of the country depends on the honesty of our elections."

"But what has Cabot got to do with it?"

"Let me tell you what I happened to overhear this morning."

She listened. When he had finished, she shivered.

"You're cold. I shouldn't keep you out here," said Berlesconi.

"Doesn't matter. I'll be just as cold inside. What you're saying is that you think Alexander Cabot, maybe the wealthiest man in the world, and Roger Kierkstra, president of the United States, are conspiring to steal the next presidential election?"

Berlesconi nodded wordlessly. They both stood up.

"Brenda, don't just recheck the program. I want you to do a complete background on Cabot. Find out what he wants and why he wants it. Find out whether he's linked to a foreign power or to terrorists. Go over him as he's never been gone over before. And now, I've got to get back to D.C."

He pulled a manila envelope out of his briefcase.

"Here's everything I have on him, which, unfortunately, isn't very much."

"Dan! Oh, Dan! I am just so glad to see you!" Daniel lifted Brenda up and swung her around. "It's good to be back." He picked Helen up and swung her around too. Then he staggered slightly and hobbled to Helen's chair and sat.

Helen and Brenda stared at his drawn face. "You're hurt," they said, almost in unison.

"Ah, it's a sprained ankle. Not a bullet in the brain."

"Sometimes I think it would only improve you—" Brenda said, mock severely. "Let me look at it."

"I kept ice on it during the flights home."

She touched the swelling. "You can step on it? Obviously. Move your foot." It moved. "I don't suppose you'll go to a doctor?"

"Nope."

"Didn't think so. Okay, be a hero." She trekked down the hall to the ice machine and came back with ice wrapped in a towel.

Then she said, "Bring me up to date. Come into my office. There's a reclining chair."

He sat down wearily in the recliner that faced Brenda's desk and applied the ice to his ankle. She turned down the sound on her always-running television. "I have some things to tell you too, but you go first," she said. "Come on, narrate."

He did. Helen brought in doughnuts and coffee. Daniel ate doughnuts ravenously. Brenda could hardly swallow her coffee when she realized what danger he had been in.

It took Daniel more than an hour to describe what had happened to him.

"Oh, my god," she said. "It just gets worse and worse. Poor Yussuf. I think he was only twenty-eight. How horrible."

"And here's Yussuf's note."

"'Went to school with Sarah.' Well, we knew that. 'Talked sometime'—probably sometimes—'was concerned about vote-tallying program she'd written. More information is . . .' I can't make out any more of it. Can you?"

"I think that says, 'in Istanbul,' which is why I went there. Only I didn't end up learning much—not yet, anyway. Now it's your turn."

CHAPTER 29

Same day
New York City

It took another hour for Brenda to describe to
Daniel her meeting with Berlesconi.

"I think Cooper must have reservations about the
program too, since he asked us to vet it. If it's the one
Sarah worked on—"

Daniel interrupted. "And if somebody was willing
to kill me to keep me from finding out that she was
worried about it, plus kill our people in Cairo, there
probably is something wrong."

"Well, I haven't been able to find it. Malcolm didn't
find anything either."

"Could they give you a 'good' program and then
just send out an altered program to the voting districts?"

"I don't see how," Brenda replied. "It would go out

over the Internet to subscribers' LANs. We can access what's going out at any time. I suppose they could send a patch if a bug turned up. Everybody does that. But we'd see that too."

"Then there must be something in the program itself. If there's anything at all."

"Take a fresh look at it, Daniel. Starting right now."

A lone in her office, Brenda glanced at the television, but CNN was showing a special on prisons, and the streaming news didn't seem to suggest any more catastrophes than usual.

She might as well get to Hector Berlesconi's assignment. Helen could do all the backgrounding on Cabot. Nobody knew much about him, but as far as Brenda could remember, the man was just reclusive, not some kind of deeply hidden spy with false credentials. He was young for his wealth. His father had left him an immense fortune, which he had rapidly multiplied.

She opened the clasp on the manila envelope and slid out the contents. Some xeroxed news clippings. Some actual documents, including a report card from Choate, of all things. Some fuzzy printouts of surveillance-camera tapes.

The man was tallish, slender. Damn the resolution on these things. He resembled somebody she knew, but she couldn't put her finger on the memory. Somebody she knew, but this man had darker hair, dressed extremely conservatively—

There was an infrared printout too. Berlesconi had certainly done his homework.

That, too, kicked off a little buzz of memory.

Not . . . certainly not—

No. What a silly idea!

But once you thought of something, it wouldn't go away unless you disproved it.

Resolutely, she typed in the access code for their IFRSUUTI program and its stored images.

"Coop! Oh, god! Not Coop!"

W hen they heard Brenda's angry shout, Helen was in the hall, handing a cup of coffee to Daniel. She managed to set it down and not spill it before they both bolted for Brenda's office. They found her, her arms hugged around herself, staring at the screen.

Daniel looked at the screen while Helen put her hand on Brenda's shoulder.

"Oh, my god," Daniel said.

Helen took a look.

"Holy shit!"

"I 'm all right! I'm all right! Don't fuss over me."

Daniel was holding a glass of water for Brenda. It seemed stupid, but what else was there to do?

Brenda said, "Dan, I know you mean well, but I'm not fainting."

"You can if you want to."

She almost smiled. "Just let me breathe here a minute, will you?"

Helen and Daniel stood next to Brenda, all three of them stunned. Helen glanced at the television. "There's—"

Then she froze. The next picture was of smoking wreckage in a field. Brenda lurched up and turned up the sound.

". . . was on board when the plane crashed near Glen Rock, New Jersey. The Boeing was en route to Reagan National Airport and is said to have been carrying a hundred and eighty passengers and crew. Hector Berlesconi, a longtime cabinet member, was director of the Office of Management and Budget under President Miller and now President Kierkstra. Terrorist activity is a possibility in the crash. More details as we get them in. Once again, early this afternoon, American Airlines flight 1947 from Kennedy International Airport to Reagan National Airport crashed shortly after takeoff . . ."

Brenda slumped over her desk, tears trickling through the hands she pressed to her eyes.

Daniel's cell phone rang.

"A fine time for a phone call. But—"

He pulled his phone out of his pocket and flipped it open. His face changed. "It's Nate."

He hit Answer, listened for a moment, and clicked off. His hands were shaking. "That was Nate. At our house. He's hysterical and he faded out on me at the end. Let's go!"

CHAPTER 30

Same day
Brooklyn

They found a cab right away, but traffic was as bad as usual, and the Brooklyn Bridge was nearly at a standstill. Brenda sat tight-lipped, her fists clenched, willing the cab to move faster. She didn't want to talk when the cabdriver could overhear. Maybe she was paranoid, but she was beginning not to trust anyone. And she welcomed the chance to digest the idea that Coop was Cabot.

Daniel swore at every red light, every double-parked car, every jaywalker. Two blocks from his house, halted once more by a lane closure and a delivery truck, Daniel wrenched open the door and flung some money at the driver. "Come on! It's quicker to walk!"

"Look, man, it's not my fault—" began the driver,

in a thick accent, but Daniel and Brenda were halfway down the block. Daniel had given the cabbie directions to the street behind his. Maybe he was paranoid too.

They ran down the alley, Daniel limping badly, Brenda's heels clicking like castanets.

A group of workingmen were chopping up the street in front of Daniel's brownstone. Brenda felt as if the jackhammers were drilling a hole through her skull. At the door of his house, Daniel fumbled for his keys. Brenda rang the doorbell. "Quicker this way," she mouthed, though she couldn't be heard over the din.

There was no answer.

Daniel found his key at last and opened the outer door. He didn't need his key for the inner one. It stood open. Daniel banged it back so hard it bounced off the wall. They rushed in.

"Bloody hell," Brenda whispered.

The place was a shambles. There wasn't a piece of furniture left whole in the living room. Hunks of stuffing lay like snow over the slashed Persian rugs. Paintings hung in shreds from their frames. Tiny shards of glass from broken light bulbs sparkled all over the floor. Nate's helmet lay forlorn in a corner.

The louvered closet doors in the front hall stood open, one wrenched off its hinges. Coats and jackets were tossed in piles all over the hall, and on top of one lay a white Stetson, a jagged hole through its crown.

"Nate! Nate?" Daniel charged up the stairs. "Hey, where are you?" He headed for the master bedroom. Brenda, trying to avoid broken glass, strode through the dining room to the kitchen at the back of the house. Same scene, different details. Broken china and glass everywhere, food and wine and beer and liquor mashed together in pools. No Nate.

Back to the hallway. The only window was a small one. She turned on a light and put a hand to her mouth.

"Dan, he's here," she called up the stairs. "Bring towels. Hurry."

Nate lay in the back hall on the floor near their office. His head was up against a small table. A cell phone had fallen from his hand. Blood ran in rivulets down his face. Even with the light on, the area was dim, but Brenda could see a stain spreading on Nate's shirt.

"Oh, god!" Daniel knelt near him.

"If he's bleeding, he's alive." Brenda wadded the towel against Nate's chest and held it there, pressing hard. "Wipe off his face so we can see how badly his head is hurt."

"He's unconscious," Daniel said. "We've got to call an ambulance." He picked up the cell phone.

"No!" said Brenda. "Dan, we can't!"

"But he needs help fast!"

"I know." Brenda tried to keep her voice steady and calm. "But we both know this was no simple burglary. Somebody came here, probably looking for you and/or our data, and I don't think they intended to leave anybody alive. It's a miracle Nate made it. Maybe they think he's dead. Anyway, I think it's one whole hell of a lot safer to deal with this ourselves."

"Oh, right. And just how are we supposed to do that?"

"Chill, Dan. We do have training in this sort of thing, and you don't really want to take a chance of letting the thugs who did this know he's alive. First we have to stop the bleeding—" She stopped as Daniel made a sudden noise. "What? What?"

"His eyelid moved. Good sign. I'll get some water."

"You stay with him and keep the pressure on his wound. I'll get the water."

She returned with a pitcher of water and another towel.

"Okay, wet it," said Daniel. "I want to wash his face."

With infinite care, Daniel wiped away the blood from Nate's cheeks and from his forehead. New blood appeared from a network of small cuts.

"That's what I thought," said Dan, sounding a little less strained. "He must have fallen into some broken glass. Those cuts aren't serious. I'll wrap a towel around his head, and then you can help me get this shirt off."

A pair of scissors lay open on the floor next to a ravaged computer keyboard. Daniel cut away the Ralph Lauren shirt, and he and Brenda removed it.

Brenda laid a clean towel against the left side of Nate's chest, pulled it away after a moment, and then sat back on her heels, her relief so great she thought she might faint. "Look," she said, pointing.

Before the blood welled up again, Daniel saw two holes, a small one just below and to the left of Nate's left nipple, and a larger one below his left arm.

"It just missed anything vital," she said. "In and out. And see—no bubbles. They didn't even nick a lung. Two inches nearer his heart, and . . ." She swallowed and applied the towel to the wounds again, meanwhile gently lifting one of Nate's eyelids. "His pupils are reactive. His color's okay. We need some bandages. You got any gauze?"

Daniel took a deep breath. "I think so. Somewhere." Daniel found some supplies, and between the two of them, they managed to get Nate's wounds more or less clean and bandaged.

"Now what?" asked Daniel. He had decided to let Brenda take over. She was calm and well-organized. He felt as though he had just stepped from a roller coaster into a wringer.

"I've been thinking," she responded. "He needs skilled attention. He's probably got a broken rib or two, and he'll for sure get an infection if he doesn't get a ton of antibiotics into him."

"But . . . doctors have to report gunshot wounds."

"I know. What we're going to have to do is take him to my place in the country. We'll have to take a chance that they—whoever *they* are—don't know about that little hideaway."

"They seem to know about everything else," he said bitterly.

"We can't think that way. If we do, we're defeated from the start. Whoever's running this may be brilliant, but he isn't omniscient. What choice have we got?"

"Yeah. Okay. I guess But even out there, a doctor—"

"No doctors. My caretaker looks after the horses. He's in tight with the vet in town, so we've got a supply of drugs and stuff. A wound is a wound, and penicillin is penicillin, whether you're dealing with a horse or a man. And Jasper'll keep his mouth shut."

"You trust him?"

"Absolutely. We go way back. He and his family would do anything for me. And the other way around."

Daniel accepted that. "How are we going to get Nate into a car? It's pretty conspicuous, carrying a guy."

"I know. It would be a lot easier if he'd wake up. Try sponging his face again."

Daniel brought fresh cold water and gently applied it to Nate's cheeks, his neck, his wrists. His eyelids fluttered once, twice. His breathing changed. His eyes opened. He looked up at Daniel.

"Hi, guy," said Daniel thickly.

"God, I hurt," said Nate.

Brenda stood. She looked at Nate lying on the floor. She looked at the ruin of the office. "Bastards," she said softly, and then louder and louder, building to a scream. "Bastards. Bastards. GOD DAMNED FUCKING BASTARDS!" She picked up a chunk of chair and threw it with vicious accuracy through the hall window.

"I hope nobody was out there," said Dan, after a shocked moment.

"I hope so too," said Brenda. "Sorry." She was back in control of herself, but she was shaking. "I also hope the neighbors didn't hear."

"Nobody much is home in the afternoon. Anyway, the jackhammers cover up everything. That's why they didn't hear . . ." His gesture took in the scene of disaster.

"I walked in while they were . . . couldn't stop them, they . . ." Nate's weak voice trailed off.

"Hey, guy, don't try to talk. We're getting you out of here as soon as we can." Daniel looked around helplessly. "I'd love to make him more comfortable. Can we give him a pillow or something?"

"There's one in the living room. Better put it under his knees. We don't want to move his head just yet." This accomplished, Brenda said, "Look, Dan, your garage isn't far from here. Give me your keys. I'll go get the car and park as close as I can."

She turned to go and then turned back and looked at them both. "I love you guys," she said, and left.

Getting Nate to the car was bad. Daniel had put more bandages on Nate, taping them down tightly to apply pressure to the wounds and support the ribs. He had managed to button him into a large, loose wool cardigan, and then half carried him to the front door. The effort had almost exhausted both men.

"Okay, bud," said Brenda, "you're gonna have to walk from here. We can't carry you down the front steps."

"Nothing . . . wrong . . . with my . . . legs," Nate gasped out.

"Oh, god," said Daniel.

"I don't suppose anybody could manage a bleary chorus of 'When Irish Eyes Are Smiling'?" Brenda said.

"I like . . . 'Melancholy Baby' . . . better," said Nate. Brenda couldn't figure out whether to laugh or cry.

The drive to Connecticut was no picnic. The distance was only about seventy miles, but traffic, as usual, was horrendous. They crawled to the Brooklyn Bridge and across, then crawled across Lower Manhattan to the Henry Hudson Parkway, where the cars stood bumper to bumper. Horns blared. Drivers yelled.

They had come to a complete stop. Five lanes of cars and vans and cabs and semis sat belching noxious fumes and road rage. "I've never hated New York traffic so much," said Daniel.

The traffic didn't open up until they got into Connecticut, and even then Brenda held the car to a mile or two below the speed limit.

"Okay, I can feel what you're not saying," she said to the backseat. "And no, I'm not going to pick up speed. We can't risk a ticket."

"Like you usually do," said Daniel.

"Like I usually do," she agreed. "But not this time. A speeding car with a bleeding man in the backseat? I don't think so. We'd either get a police escort to the nearest hospital or get arrested for an unreported gunshot wound. Probably both."

When they finally reached Brenda's farm, after what seemed like years, Nate was in a lot of pain.

"I'm sorry," said the man with the earrings. "We missed him."

"Sorry doesn't work."

"I know that. If you don't mind the attention we'd get, we could bomb DB's office."

"I do mind the attention we'd get. Plus god only knows how many people know now."

"But what can they know? Our mole doesn't believe Henderson found anything in Istanbul."

"Yes. They can't have more than a quarter of the story. Our best bet right now is to let those pitiful people think they're doing their thing."

There was no need to worry about secrecy here in the middle of Brenda's thirty acres of farm and woodland. Except for the caretaker's family, the nearest neighbors were three miles away, the nearest town fifteen.

She raced up the drive blasting her horn. Before they got to the house, a lanky gray-haired man in overalls had come out to meet them. Daniel could see, in the swath of the headlights, a somewhat younger carbon copy of the man running toward the car. Two golden retrievers cavorted around the doors, barking a glad welcome.

"Jasper, we've got trouble," said Brenda, jumping out of the car. "Down, kids, and shut up!" The dogs' barks changed to whines at her tone of voice. Their tails dropped down and hung between their legs. "My friend here has been shot and needs attention right away. I think he's in shock. He's lost some blood."

The caretaker was a man of few words. He turned to his son. "Blankets and a couple of clothes poles," he said. "And my old slicker."

On the improvised stretcher they got Nate into the house and put him into bed. "Use mine," said Jasper. "First floor." Then he shooed away everyone except his son, Zeke. "I'll see to him."

Brenda could have kissed him. No questions, no fuss. It was a blessed relief to hand Nate over to someone competent, to rid herself of part of the problem for a little while.

She and Daniel collapsed onto chairs in the kitchen, too tired and spent even to speak for a few minutes. The dogs settled at Brenda's feet, whining now and then. A fat orange tabby surveyed them coolly from the top of the refrigerator.

"Do you think he's going to be all right?" asked Daniel eventually.

"I don't know." She didn't have to be strong anymore. "Jasper's pretty good, but if it looks really serious, he'll let us know."

"We're the same blood type!" said Daniel eagerly. "We found out when we both got tested for HIV, ages ago. I could donate."

"It's a possibility, I guess. Jasper has the equipment. We can tell him you're available."

Then Dan said, "Do we have the energy to talk about this mess?"

Brenda shook her head. "Later." They lapsed into a weary silence until Jasper came into the kitchen and pulled up a chair.

"Got him warm and stable, gave him a shot of penicillin and a little morphine. His legs are propped up—that's on account of the shock—and I'm pumping some glucose and saline into him. He's got two broken ribs, but there's nothing much to do about those except keep him quiet. Wounds are clean. Doesn't seem to have any lung damage. Could have been a lot worse."

Daniel looked at him in wonder. "Thank god. And thank you, Jasper. You knew how to do all that? Just from working with horses?"

"Humans aren't all that different. Just easier to deal with. They'll mostly do what you tell 'em, and they're smaller."

"I told you he could handle it," Brenda said to Daniel. "I've never seen anything Jasper couldn't deal with, from delivering puppies to fixing old tractors to chasing hunters off the place. Jasper, is Nate going to need blood? Dan's just told me he's a match."

"Don't think so. Looks like he's doing okay, but have to wait and see." He looked at Brenda hard, his blue eyes meeting her green ones. "Can't tell nobody about this, right?"

"Right. I'm sorry to dump this on you, Jasper, but it's a big mess and we can't get the authorities involved.

We didn't do anything illegal, except for not reporting it. And there's a lot of bad stuff going on, but I don't think there's any danger for you or the boys."

"Don't need to tell me that," said Jasper gruffly. "Don't need to tell me nothin'. You wouldn't do nothin' to hurt us or anybody else. What'll we say to the grans, though?"

"Jasper's grandkids . . . Zeke's boys," Brenda explained to Daniel. "Tom's ten and Rick's twelve. They live up the road, but they play over here a lot. I think we'll just tell them part of the truth, that a friend of mine is sick and I brought him here to get well. And that it's a secret. Boys that age aren't much interested in sick people. I don't think they'll ask questions."

"I'll handle 'em." Jasper gave her an appraising look. "Any reason you can't get some sleep? You look done in."

"No reason at all, come to think of it. Come on, Daniel. We'll think better after we've had some rest. I'll make up a bed for you."

"Zeke's done it," said Jasper.

Brenda laid a hand on his shoulder, tears in her eyes. "I owe you, Jasper."

The caretaker ducked his head. "Nope. T'other way 'round."

CHAPTER 31

B renda had planned to sleep for an hour or two and then get up to check on Nate and make plans. When she stirred restlessly, she opened her eyes to find it still dark. She struggled out of a dream. She couldn't remember its details, but the panic she'd felt was still with her. Awareness of the situation rushed back. Nate shot. Their security, both personal and corporate, compromised. And Cooper! What about Cooper? She was far too fidgety to sleep, so she got up.

Somebody knew way too much about the activities of DB Security. Somebody from inside. There was no other explanation. She groaned. The dogs, which had been sleeping on the floor, rose and put their chins in her hands, whining softly.

"Thanks, kids," she said, fondling both heads. "It's

nothing to do with you, and I can't explain, but I appreciate the sympathy. C'mon, I need some exercise."

She peeked in on Nate, who was breathing easily. Dan, his bad ankle propped up on a footstool, was asleep in the chair next to the bed.

Still too tense to do anything productive, Brenda called to the dogs and went out into the cool misty air to run. Familiar with the path around the orchard, she ran without worrying about tripping in the dark. The dogs, thrilled to be out, kept just ahead of her, making her even more sure of her footing.

Five laps around was about two miles, not as much as she could have run, but enough to burn off some of her anxiety.

She found Daniel in the kitchen, a cup of coffee steaming in front of him.

"Have some," he said. "I made it. It's good."

"How's Nate?"

"A lot better. He's still out for the count—Jasper gave him some more morphine—but his pulse is back to almost normal and he's pink again. For a while there I really thought . . ." His voice shook. He took another sip from his mug. "He woke up for a few minutes, and I told him I loved him."

She poured herself a cup of the strong coffee, added brown sugar in lieu of the caramel she loved, and sat down at the table. It wasn't Brew-Ha-Ha quality, but it did the job.

"So," she said, "I assume they were trying to get Yussuf's note."

"Well, or get me before I told anybody about the note or what I downloaded in Istanbul."

"They wanted to kill you, but not Nate?"

"Alive, he's a bargaining chip."

"Maybe. If they can find him. They won't find him out here. I tell you, nobody knows about this place. It's officially in Jasper's name. He pays the taxes and the bills. I pay him in cash. He does the shopping, he picks up the mail. There is nothing to connect me with this piece of the planet."

"What about those kids? The grandchildren. And their mother. Don't they ever say anything about the rich lady who owns this place?"

"They don't have a mother. She died giving birth to Tom. Jasper's wife is dead too, so there aren't any women involved in the family. That's one reason they spend so much time here. And they've been told not to talk about me. I told you before; I trust them, all of them."

Daniel couldn't leave it alone. "What about somebody following us out here, all the way from New York? Or a homing device on my car?"

Brenda tried to be patient. They were reasonable questions. "Nobody followed us. I watched. As for electronic surveillance, it wouldn't matter even if somebody did plant a bug. When we first got into this antiterrorism stuff, I got paranoid and put a sensor at the end of the driveway. In any case, the bad guys have to know now that you've told me about the note, and we could have duplicated the data from Istanbul. So it's too late to stop the flow of information."

"That doesn't mean we're safe," Daniel said.

"No. But we're safer. I can't imagine any reason why they'd be in a huge rush to kill us now. More likely they'd find a way to use us."

Through the open windows came the sounds of laughter. Daniel started.

"Relax. It's just the kids. They like to climb around in the apple trees, especially at this time of year. They can have all the apples they want for the asking, but it's more fun if they pretend they're stealing them." Brenda rose from the table and went to the back window. "Hey, robbers!"

"Yikes, they're after us," one of the boys yelled. She watched as they began to scramble down from the tree. Apples fell like hail as the tree rocked.

"Bring me three or four pounds and I'll bake you a pie," Brenda shouted.

"Hey! Deal!" The older boy started inspecting the fallen apples for wormholes. "Tom, you go and get a basket from the barn."

"Is it a good idea to have them come in here?" said Daniel.

"It's what they usually do. Better to keep to routine."

Daniel looked around the room. "You know, I'm seeing you in a new light. This just doesn't seem to be your setting. Rag rugs, checked curtains, plants on the windowsill, a cat. And baking pies? Playing mommy with a couple of kids?"

She made a face. "You think you know me. You only know one side. Yeah, I'm good with computers. Yeah, I'm ambitious. The big-deal corporate exec in the fast lane, that's me. But out here I can drop the briefcase and the persona and just be a woman. The kids aren't mine, but they'll do until . . ." She swallowed and looked away.

"You want kids?"

"Why does that surprise you so much?" Brenda

bristled a bit as she measured flour into a bowl and found the lard in the refrigerator. "Just because you don't?"

"Yeah, but Nate sort of does. He wants to adopt. I just can't see it. Aside from the fact that anyone under twenty-one gives me hives, what kind of parents would we make, with our jobs? We're both gone all the time, and either of us could be dead tomorrow."

There was no answer to the last remark. "So that's why you don't want kids," said Brenda, sprinkling a little salt into the bowl and beginning to wield a pastry blender. "But how about me? I've got enough money to retire tomorrow. I could move out here for good, play with my dogs, ride my horses, farm my land. Marry, have kids. Why not?"

Daniel didn't speak. How serious had she been about Cooper?

Brenda worked her dough in silence, adding water a drop at a time. When the dough's consistency suited her, she said, "Trouble is, the only men in my life are you and Nate."

"But you're gorgeous! And kind, generous, brilliant, competent—"

"Trustworthy, loyal, and obedient," she finished, dumping the dough onto a floured board.

The two boys burst into the kitchen, carrying a peck basket between them. "Is this enough?" asked Tom.

"Lots more than enough," said Rick, with the superiority of being two years older. "But some of them have a few worms, so I thought we'd better get extra."

"Right. Now you have to wash them and start peeling."

They groaned in unison.

"Hey, I'm no Little Red Hen. You want to eat my

pie, you help make it. Kids, this is my friend Daniel, and he's going to help too. Dan, Tom's the runt and Rick's the long drink of water. Knives are in that drawer. Go to it."

When the pie was in the oven and the kids had gone back out to play, she scrambled eggs, fried bacon, made toast.

"I'm not very hungry," said Dan, looking doubtfully at her preparations.

"Neither am I, but we should eat. Heaven only knows when we'll get another chance for a real meal."

Daniel toyed with his food. Brenda knew what he was thinking. Here he was with a savory home-cooked meal in front of him, while Nate lay in a morphine-induced sleep, getting his nourishment through a vein in his arm.

"We need to talk, make plans," said Brenda when she'd finished her breakfast.

"We need to reach the office," Daniel said urgently. "I keep forgetting. I've been worrying about Nate, and then last night I slept like the dead. We need to warn everybody there that there could be an attack."

"I warned them already. Told them to get out of there and watch their backs. I've got a secure phone here."

"All right. So now what?"

"Well, I went out for a run while you were still asleep, and I did some thinking."

"And?"

"Cooper doesn't know that I know who he really is, right?"

CHAPTER 32

Same day
On the highway

"Don't do it!" Daniel said.

"Dan, we've been over this and over it. I think I have to do it." Brenda moved into the left lane and sped up. They were getting back to the New York office as fast as they could. Daniel let Brenda drive his car because she was the more aggressive driver, but he was beginning to doubt the decision.

He curled his toes and tried to concentrate on the conversation. "He's a creep and a crook and a killer."

"I know that. That's why we have to stop him."

"But Brenda, to think of going out with—"

"It's my decision." She zipped around the car in front of her, muttering something uncomplimentary as horns blared in her wake.

"Hey, watch it!" Daniel's voice went up another

notch or two. "You almost hit that guy coming up in the next lane. And we need to keep a low profile, remember? Even if we don't have a bleeding person in the car anymore, I still don't think getting stopped by the cops is a great idea."

"Road's full of idiots," said Brenda. "They think the fast lane is for Sunday cruising." But she slowed down a little.

Daniel said, "How many dates have you had with him? Three or four? How close—Um. Did you—"

"Yeah. On the last date he came up to my apartment. Yeah. We did. I liked him, dammit. I really did. How dumb of me, huh?"

"You didn't know."

"Well, now I know, and it's desperately important that I learn more, no matter how disgusting I may find him. Listen, you agree we can't let him know that we've found out who he is?"

"I agree with that. And we have to find out what he's up to. I understand, Brenda. I know he's up to something horrible. I just don't think you have to do it this way."

"You just agreed that we can't let him know I know."

"Yes, but—"

"So I have to keep seeing him."

"No, you don't. Tell him you're sick."

"He's invited me to his place in Washington tomorrow. I have a chance to find out more about him. Maybe if he falls asleep I can search his desk or his computer. Maybe I could drug him."

"Oh, shit, Brenda! No! That's hideously dangerous."

"So we let him get away with it? Whatever he's up

to, it's got something to do with the election, and the election is in three days!"

"You can't be wanting to actually let him touch you, knowing what you know about him now."

"Look, Daniel. Suppose somebody said to you, sleep with this horrible person or I'll kill Nate."

"I wouldn't believe him. I'd find another way."

"Don't argue my premise! Assume it's true. What would you do?"

"God, I don't really know. Can't you go into Cooper's place and get sick there and just spend the night?"

"No. It's either real or it's suspicious. We're playing in the very big leagues here. Maybe as big as they get."

Daniel was silent.

"Listen, Daniel. There were real, living people on that plane that crashed. People with lives, with hopes and futures. Berlesconi was a sweetheart and a very honest man, I think. And there were other people on that plane. Including six children. Think about it. You want me to take any chance of letting this killer get away?"

"We don't know for sure he's a killer."

Brenda took a deep breath. "True. We've been making a bunch of assumptions. Maybe it's time to take a look at what we really do know." Also time to change the subject, she thought.

"We know somebody's trying to kill us," said Daniel. "Trying to kill me anyway. And Nate."

Brenda nodded. "And damn near succeeded with both of you. They underestimated you, always a bad mistake."

"Daniel Bond, double-oh eight, that's me." He sounded morose.

"And they did kill a bunch of our people," Brenda

said. "And I'm prepared to bet they killed Sarah
Swettenham, even though I couldn't prove it. And for
sure they killed Hector Berlesconi and all those people
on that plane. So that leads us to . . . what?"

"A homicidal maniac you're prepared to take to
bed."

"Will you turn off that record? It got stuck miles
back. No, we don't know—I said *know*—that Coop
has anything to do with all this. All we know is that
he and Alexander Cabot are the same person. Damn,
I wish we could get back to the office and check out
some more stuff. This traffic—"

"Gives us longer to talk. Because there's something
else we know—that we've got somebody spying on
us, somebody who knows a hell of a lot about programming. Has to be somebody in the office. Has to
be. Better to talk here."

"Nobody's at the office. I told you . . . I made them
all go home."

"Somebody might have wanted to finish up something. Or thought you were overreacting. Or just
wanted to stick around and spy on us."

"You're right." Brenda sounded tired. "Well, is that
all we know?"

"No." Daniel's voice was hard. "We know that Sarah
created the vote-tallying program and was worried
about it. And Berlesconi was worried about it. And
they both died."

"Yes, but . . ." Brenda slammed her hand against
the wheel. The car swerved slightly. More horns
blared.

"Bren—"

"Okay, I know. I'll be careful. But see, Dan, that's
the part I still don't understand. It looks like this whole

godawful mess is centered around the election program. But Coop works for the NSAA, and he asked us
to vet the program! Why would he do that if there's
something wrong with it?"

"I've been thinking about that," said Daniel. "If
Cooper *is* Cabot, then he's the richest man in the
world. Why would he hold down a bureaucrat's job?"

"But . . . but he took me to the office . . . the guard
let me in . . ." She was spluttering.

"Look, you're the old movie buff. Did you ever see
a movie—I forget the name, but it had Walter Mat-
thau in it? He was supposed to be a bureaucrat, and
he had Audrey Hepburn up to his office, only it turned
out it was the lunch hour and he just used somebody
else's office to con her."

"*Charade*," said Brenda. There was a long pause.
"It could be that way. It really could. Cabot's a man
with a lot of power in Washington. He could probably get in that building, and get me in too. But, Dan,
why? Why would he do all this—all the pretense, the
elaborate second identity? What's this all about, anyway?"

Daniel shook his head. "There's still a lot we don't
know."

Brenda changed lanes, heading for her exit. "And
that, my friend, is why I'm going on that date with
Coop."

CHAPTER 33

"Nobody here. Looks like they took you seriously about going home." Daniel looked at the reception area, unlit and deserted. Both Helen's monitors were dark. No lights shone from the offices down the hall; no small sounds indicated human presence.

"That's just as well," said Brenda. "We don't need anybody supervising while we check out Cabot." She sounded grim. "Though we could actually have used Helen's help. She's the best we've got when it comes to low-down and dirty data mining."

Daniel said nothing. Brenda gave him a look. "What?"

"I didn't say anything."

"I know. You said it awfully loud."

"It's just . . . no, forget it."

"Dan." She crossed her arms. "Out with it. We've got work to do."

"Okay, but you're not going to like it. Has it ever occurred to you that Helen's been putting in an awful lot of extra time lately? Been here a lot when the office was closed, when nobody else was here? And don't forget she was the one who gave us all that info about Cooper—who doesn't actually exist."

Brenda looked at him hard. "I hope you're not saying what I think you're saying. Of course Coop would have given himself a background. And almost everybody here puts in extra time. Our employees are loyal and very, very hardworking. Besides, Helen's had more work than usual."

"More than anybody else? Enough to keep her here nights and weekends? Look, I know you like Helen. So do I. And I know she's good at her job. She's damn good at her job. Is she *too* good?"

"You are saying it. You're saying Helen is a spy." Brenda's voice was level, but her arms tensed more tightly around her body.

"I'm saying we have to consider the possibility, that's all."

Brenda said, "What about the CIA guys we hired early on?"

"Don't be silly. They don't have the computer expertise."

"Well, then, if we have a spy, the last hire is more likely," Brenda said.

"Malcolm Dudley? If you mean Cooper planted him, he was hired before we even met Cooper. And before you went to AllTech. Cooper could just as well have paid Helen megabucks to spy for him. Better than Malcolm because she knows more about us."

"I trust Helen as much as I trust you."

"You trusted Cooper too."

Brenda stood very still. When she spoke, her voice trembled, despite her efforts to keep it steady. "Let's not go there, Daniel. We've got enough to deal with. Let's forget this conversation happened and get down to the digging." She tried to smile.

"We have to face it eventually. Somebody here is giving information to the enemy. We have to find out who."

"Yes. Eventually. But Dan . . . the election is three days away. If something awful's going to happen that day, our priority is finding out what. And the first step is finding out as much as we can about Cabot."

Daniel shrugged. "Anything we do here at the office could be sabotaged by our mole."

"So we wipe out every trace of what we've done. Log onto the Net with some of our alternative IDs. Rip out the hard drives when we're done and dump them in the Hudson. Whatever. Let's just hurry up and do it!"

Daniel looked at Brenda. He saw in his mind some of the scenes of destruction he had encountered in Egypt, Turkey, and Italy, the dead bodies, the mangled computers. He saw television images of a smoking plane with over a hundred people dead. And he saw in Brenda's face her understanding of most of the danger, the urgency. "Right. Full steam ahead, with all reasonable precautions. Let's have at it."

"Cancel the order to kill." The suave Westerner sipped from his snifter of brandy.

"Why?" asked the man in eastern dress. He lifted

his glass of orange juice, then put it down to hide his shaking hand.

"Because you have failed."

"We chased him around the world and back here to New York." The Easterner dared to sound just a little angry. "We lost many men. In any case, if he knew something, he would have made it known. He has said nothing. Therefore he knows nothing. No one in Egypt knew anything of importance. The computers in Istanbul had important data but they were all destroyed."

"You lost your men, not mine. Your orders were to kill, to destroy a possible threat. You failed. However, I agree, he has demonstrated that he is not a threat. If he knew something, he'd have told. I still want to know where he is, what he's doing, but there's nothing he can do now to stop me." The Westerner smiled to himself. He would win, as he always did, and then . . .

His flight was announced.

All afternoon Brenda and Daniel plied their computers. They used every trick they knew, every hacking technique they had learned in training. They entered illegally into databases authorized only to law enforcement agencies. They got into bank records, credit card records, phone records, delved into every electronic transaction and communication Alexander Cabot had ever made.

Cabot, or his minions, had protected Cabot well. His businesses had operated under a score of different identities, as holding companies, at addresses all over the world. As she gradually learned tidbits about him—he'd been active in Hasty Pudding at Harvard, his holdings seemed to be concentrated in energy-related endeavors—Brenda knew it would take days, even weeks, to get a complete picture of the man's activities. More than once, Brenda wished Helen were there. Helen could find out things no one else could. Brenda didn't voice her frustrations. Daniel had a point about Helen, though all of Brenda's instincts wanted him to be wrong.

He'd been right about Coop.

Brenda thought for an anguished few moments about the ordeal coming up tomorrow, and then decided not to think about it.

Meanwhile, Daniel reviewed the entire jump drive he'd downloaded in Istanbul. He found nothing about Cabot. He exhausted all the esoteric data sources and decided to go to the obvious: Google. Deep into the forty-second page of hits, he found references to an obscure article in the *San Francisco News* written by a reporter named Vincent Dombrowski. After he chased it a little further, he called to Brenda in the adjoining office. "Hey, Brenda, I think I've got something."

"I'll be right there."

She hurried into his office.

Daniel said, "See, this is a little odd. This guy wrote an article about Cabot. Then, look." Brenda peered over his shoulder. The site Daniel had found said the reporter had been fired the day after his article on Cabot had appeared.

"Do you believe that's a coincidence?" asked Daniel.

"Not given what we know about Cabot and the way he operates. Let's find the article."

Daniel Googled and scrolled and switched screens. Brenda sat at the computer next to him. They spent an hour trying to find the actual article.

"This is way frustrating," said Brenda, stretching. "I know papers don't archive everything, but you'd think that somewhere—"

Daniel tapped her shoulder. "I've got something." Brenda rolled her chair over. Daniel pointed. "It's an obscure 'hate Kierkstra' site, and it alludes to all kinds of possible chicanery by Alexander Cabot and says that the article we're looking for revealed it."

"Well, at this point I'd believe almost anything about Mr. Bigbucks," Brenda said, "but to be fair— and I hate being the slightest bit fair about this— anyone remotely famous has sites put up by the envious, angry, demented, or jealous. Nobody edits the Net. Hard to tell what's truth and what's pure fiction. But if this reporter really knows something, he would be an excellent source."

Daniel said, "While you're bearding the lion in his den tomorrow, I can be tracking him down. If he's got the real story, I'd like to hear it."

"And if it's not the real story?" Brenda said.

"Then I've wasted some time. It's no real risk. But if Cabot catches on to you—"

"I could be dead." Brenda tried to keep her voice light, but she shuddered despite herself.

Daniel raised his hands in a frustrated gesture. "God, I wish you didn't have to see that sleaze ever again. But we need as much information as we can get." He kicked the wastebasket. "I wish he'd hit on me instead of you. Then I could deal with him."

Brenda managed a grin. "That's just because he has such a pretty face. Look, I know just as much as you do about how to take care of myself. And you said it yourself. We've got to try everything."

CHAPTER **34**

Sunday, November 2
Washington, D.C.
Two Days before the Presidential Election

Brenda toyed with her wineglass.

"You don't care for the wine?" asked Coop, the hint of a frown in his voice.

"It's wonderful. Warm, full-bodied but subtle. I love it."

"You're not drinking it," he pointed out.

"It's just . . . well, red wine makes me sleepy, and I don't want . . ." She let the sentence trail off and looked away. She hoped he would think she was being coy, or shy, or whatever. The general idea was that she was avidly anticipating the culmination of the evening, and didn't want anything to interfere with her enjoyment.

He smiled. Did she imagine his smugness?

No. He'd bought it, bought her miserable, simpering attitude. Another conquest! Another female so utterly in the thrall of the magnificent, the incomparable Coop that she just couldn't wait to get to his apartment.

In fact it was true, though not for the reasons he supposed.

She wanted to get to his place, find what she needed, and get out. If only it would be that easy.

She and Daniel had continued to argue about whether this dangerous venture was necessary. Daniel just wouldn't give it up. "Look what happened to Nate," he kept saying. "And he's just an innocent bystander."

Ultimately it was another old movie that had persuaded him. Brenda had said, "*All the President's Men*, Dan. When Woodward and Bernstein pull Ben Bradlee out of his house at night and tell him the scary things Woodward has learned from Deep Throat. And Ben says—"

"Jason Robards. He was great in that part, wasn't he? He tells them to go ahead and follow the story as far as it takes them, and then says something like 'There's nothing much riding on this. Except the Constitution of the United States and the future of the free world.' Words to that effect." He looked at Brenda for a long moment.

"That's why I have to do it," she had said quietly. "It scares me half to death and disgusts me even more, but I have to do it. For what this country stands for, or used to. For all the people who believe in it and for all the people who have been killed by the creeps who want to destroy it. For Jeremy."

"You're telling me," Dan had said, "that you're planning to go to bed with another guy, and you're doing it for Jeremy? Talk about kinky!"

And they had laughed a little hysterically. Brenda giggled now, remembering.

Coop raised his eyebrows. "You're in a peculiar mood this evening, my dear. I've never seen you quite so . . . fey, I think is the word."

Brenda was prepared for that one. "It's Washington. It always does something to me. Intoxicates me a little, I think. So much power all in one place. That's another reason I don't need much wine. Power. It's the ultimate aphrodisiac, don't you think?"

He looked amused. "Thank you, Henry Kissinger. That's not a sentiment I'd expect to hear from a woman."

"Oh, but a woman has power, if she chooses to use it." She picked up her wineglass and took a tiny sip. She wished she dared drain it. Her nerves were stretched to breaking point. But she had to play this exactly right, or the disaster that would follow would be not only her own, but . . . she'd better not think about that.

She put the wineglass down and shook her head. "I'd really better lay off. I'm beginning to talk like a B movie. Tell me about your day."

He laughed. "Have we segued into a 50s sitcom? I think you can't quite make up your mind whether you're Marlene Dietrich or Donna Reed."

"Oh, Dietrich every time, only I don't have that incredibly sexy accent. Or those legs. I always thought Donna Reed was a bit insipid actually. But I really meant the question. This must be a crazy time in Washington, with the election in two days."

"Damn. I would have been very happy to talk about your legs—which are quite nice, as you know perfectly well. However . . . yes, everyone's going bananas. In this town, with absolutely everything revolving around politics, every election is a major upheaval, but presidential elections are the worst."

"Especially in this world of terrorist threats. I imagine the security people aren't getting much sleep."

"Well, of course, I don't work directly with security forces. My job, NSAA's job, is the analysis of potential trouble. But you're right. This is a rare night off for me, and I intend to enjoy every minute of it not talking politics." His grin was almost a leer.

Brenda smiled in return and ate another bite of the sawdust on her plate. She hoped she wasn't going to be sick.

Cooper turned down the waiter's offer of coffee before Brenda had a chance to order some, and suggested after-dinner drinks at his place. She had little choice but to accept with apparent good grace.

He lived in Georgetown in a small but exquisite house on a narrow street. Brenda's nerves tightened even more when she saw it. She had counted on an apartment. Easier to search, no creaky stairs to negotiate, neighbors within shouting distance if worse came to worst. This was going to make things much harder.

"So what do you think?" he asked.

She adjusted her face to an expression, she hoped, of awestruck delight. "It's perfect! I love old houses, and I'll bet this one has a history."

"I'll bet it does, too, but I haven't lived here long enough to check it out. It also has a ghost, or so I'm informed by the neighbors."

"Of course. Like every proper house of this vintage."

"So you believe in ghosts?"

Well, believe in them or not, this one might prove a godsend if it offered her an excuse to be out of bed in the middle of the night. Brenda smiled brilliantly. "I keep an open mind," she said.

Coop took her coat, seated her in front of a gas fire in the book-lined living room, and brought out a cognac in a lovely bottle. Brenda had heard of it, but had never actually seen any up close and personal. It went, as she recalled, for well over a thousand dollars. A mistake, she thought exultantly. A little one, but a mistake. He shouldn't have let me see he can afford that kind of brandy. I have no doubt the real head of NSAA makes a good salary, but not that good. He isn't perfect after all.

She bit back a comment about how well paid public servants must be in Washington. Instead she swirled the cognac around in the snifter, inhaled its heady aroma, and took a tiny sip.

"Mmm. Heaven in a bottle. What is it? I'm sure it's not Christian Brothers."

That smug smile again. How could she have ever thought he was attractive?

"A rather nice old Rémy Martin. I'm partial to it. I thought you'd like it. You have excellent taste in everything."

"Well, I could get used to this stuff without any trouble. Even if it isn't American." The trouble was, she truly did love it and wanted to finish it. But with its high alcohol content, she didn't dare. And how on earth was she going to get out of it?

She stretched out her toes to the fire. Just like him, she thought, to have a gas fire. A wood fire was messy. And real. "I love this room," she lied. "Books make a room so warm and cozy." Bought by the yard, probably. "Is the rest of the house this nice?"

"Would you like a tour, or are you too comfortable where you are?"

"I'd love a tour. A quick one," she added, smiling at him in what she hoped was a seductive way. I'm disgusting, she thought bitterly. The cognac suddenly burned in her stomach.

She had to go through with it. Smiling again, she brought her glass with her as he began taking her around the house. Surely there would be a few potted plants along the way. She couldn't dump it all in one—too obvious.

This is, she thought, about a hundred bucks' worth of his booze I'm trying to get rid of. The thought made her smile, a genuine smile for the first time that evening.

Coop caught it and smiled back, that smug smile she had learned to detest in the past couple of hours. A true Cabot smile. She banished that thought. She had to go on thinking of him as Coop, if she could manage it.

There were potted plants. Unfortunately they were all silk. Never mind. When Coop's back was turned she watered first one, then another, with a few drops of distilled gold.

The tour was useful for another reason too. Brenda noted carefully the rooms he didn't show her. There were only two, one downstairs off the kitchen and one upstairs next to the master bedroom. The downstairs one might well be a maid's room or a pantry. The house had been built, she guessed, in the 1800s when there would have been servants—or slaves. Most of them would have slept in separate quarters, but one, at least, might have lived in that downstairs room in the main house. The room upstairs though—that one was promising. Standing with her back to the door as Coop explained something about a painting on the wall, she tried the knob.

Locked. Aha!

The tour ended, inevitably, in the bedroom. This was the acid test. Brenda staved off the moment by excusing herself to run down and get her purse. Let him think she was taking a birth-control pill. She was really after her library card.

In the bathroom, as she drank a little water to re-inforce the pill idea, she tried to relax. This was going to be the worst thing she'd ever had to do. Prostitutes do it all the time, she told herself. Let men they de-spise screw them. They do it for money. I'm doing it for . . . for love really. So get on with it, girl.

She took a deep breath and stepped into the bed-room.

She lay next to him as he slept. His arm was flung across her chest, which she hated. Not only was his touch now repugnant to her, but he would know if she tried to get out of bed.

It had been every bit as bad as she had feared. She had acted her head off, because he had to be con-vinced she was loving every moment. She'd sum-moned up her favorite fantasy, the one involving the deserted beach and the unexpected return of a lover. It got her through it, but as she lay there she felt filthy, despoiled, debased. She wanted a very long, very hot shower, a scrub with a rough brush. She wasn't going to get it any time soon.

It seemed like hours before he finally moved, rolled away from her. She waited until he was breathing evenly again, and then she got out of bed. He didn't stir. She picked up her skirt from the floor and found the library card in the pocket.

Moving quietly, as if not to disturb a beloved sleeper, she left the room and closed the door behind her.

Thank god the locked room was just beyond the bathroom. She stole toward it, grateful that the hall carpet was thick and that the old boards, remarkably, didn't creak. She wished she had a robe. The house was chilly—and a robe had pockets. Well, she'd have to make do.

She went into the bathroom, turned on the light, then left, closing the door behind her, and moved to the next room.

She wielded the library card—thinner, more flexible than a credit card—with the expertise learned in her training, and as she had expected, the simple lock yielded easily. With a quick glance back at the bedroom, she slipped inside and laid the library card carefully on a small table.

She dared not turn on a light, but a streetlight outside the house provided a dim glow. As she had hoped, the room was an office.

Allen Cooper's office or Alexander Cabot's?

Brenda looked longingly at the computer monitor, but it was dark, as was the tower beneath the desk.

No lights glowed to indicate the machine was turned on. She couldn't activate it. It would make unmistakable noises, and Coop would be there in a heartbeat.

Her own heart was beating fast and hard. Time. How much time did she have? She'd been away from the bedroom for about two minutes. A digital clock on the desk showed 2:17. She would give herself five minutes, no more.

A file cabinet stood against one wall. An elegant one, wood-paneled. Praying that the drawers moved quietly, she inched open the top one.

The files were labeled in neat printing. Well, thank god for that, anyway.

ACCT PRTS. Account printouts, probably. They'd be fascinating to study, but she didn't have time. AUTO INS. She wasn't interested in his insurance. BACKUPS. She opened that one, a fat accordion folder, but it proved to be only original software disks.

She glanced at the clock. 2:19.

Nothing else of interest in the top drawer. She opened the second.

CLPGS caught her eye. Another big folder. She pulled it out to take it to the window.

Her foot caught on something. She stumbled; a few papers fell from the folder to the floor.

She froze.

No sound from the bedroom.

She let herself breathe again and looked at the clock. 2:21.

She tiptoed to the window, clutching the file.

There was a draft, cold against her naked skin. Or perhaps only fear made her cold.

The file was full of newspaper clippings. She could read only the headlines in the dim light. They all seemed to concern disasters. She pulled one out. "OIL FIELD FIRE IN DUBAI." Another. "EXPLOSION IN KUWAIT KILLS 57." She was about to put the file back when she noticed some handwriting at the bottom of one clipping.

A date and "50K."

She heard the creak of bedsprings. "Brenda?"

Oh, god!

She didn't have time to get into and out of the bathroom, but she had to get out of here anyway. She'd left the file drawer open. She put the file back, closed the drawer silently, and heard the bedroom door open.

She was caught.

Looking around like a caged animal, she saw the door. A closet? Or . . . ?

It was locked. She spent a few precious seconds looking for her library card, found it, realized the door locked from her side, unlocked it, and found herself in the bathroom.

She locked the door and closed it behind her. But that left the office door unlocked!

"Brenda?"

Footsteps padded toward her.

"Coming," she said, trying to keep her voice steady as she flushed the toilet, then slipped her library card into the tank.

"A touch of indigestion," she said, as she opened the bathroom door to find him in the hall. "Must have been that rich food last night." She hadn't needed the I-got-scared-by-the-ghost excuse after all.

"Sorry," he said, and pulled her to him. He was naked and aroused. "We'll have to figure out something to take your mind off that."

She wrapped her arms around him for a long kiss.

He was the scum of the earth, but she was using him and she was going to bring him down. A black widow, that's me, she thought, and the thought lent passion to her kiss.

S he didn't sleep at all, but when he nudged her in the morning, she was lying with her eyes closed and her breathing even. "My dear, you can't imagine how sorry I am to say this, but we have to get moving. I'm needed at the office soon. Do you want to shower first, or shall I?"

She was hugely relieved. She had feared he might suggest showering together. "How about me first?" she said, and yawned. "Then I can get some coffee going while you get dressed."

"I'm not sure I have any. But there's a great coffee-house just down the street."

"Sounds good."

She took her clothes with her to the bathroom, and when she came out, both doors to the office—from the hall and from the bathroom—were locked, and her library card was safely tucked inside her bra.

"Coop, do you have a computer here? I didn't see one yesterday, and I really need to check my e-mail. I get nervous when I'm out of touch for more than a couple of hours."

It was a gamble, but if he said he didn't have one, she hadn't lost anything, and if he said yes, she wouldn't have to sneak around.

He hesitated only a moment before saying, "Sure. I keep the door locked so the cleaning people won't screw up the computer."

"Could you access the Internet for me before you

shower? Then we won't lose any time when you're ready to go."

"Of course. Although I'm sure you could figure out my password in a heartbeat."

She laughed. "It would take a little longer than that. And I wouldn't do it to a friend. In fact I'm not even going to stay in the room while you key it in. I need my lipstick and it's downstairs in my purse."

When she got back, he'd opened the office and turned on the computer. The MSN screen was showing on the monitor. "All set?" he said. "I really need to get moving."

"Scoot. I'm fine." She was too. She'd secreted another little tool in her bra, a jump drive. About half the size of a matchbox, it could store more data than a CD and could capture it much quicker. Now all she had to do was find the data.

She called up her e-mail. She didn't even glance at it. It was there so she could slip back to that screen at an instant's warning. Coop could walk in on her at any moment.

She waited until she heard the shower running and then went directly into an exploration of his files. She couldn't take the time to read any of them, only to copy a few that looked promising. She downloaded his Excel accounts—there might be any number of interesting things there. A folder in Word was labeled RK. Roger Kierkstra? Possibly. Onto the jump drive it went. She was just about to delve into his old e-mail files when the shower stopped. She coughed to cover the little pinging pop as she removed the jump drive. It was back in her bra and she was reading an innocuous e-mail—her own—when the door opened and Coop poked his head around it.

"You okay in there? I'm gonna be ready to hit the road in about ten minutes."

"I'll be ready. I just have to answer this one. Shall I shut down when I'm done?"

"Please. I'm paranoid about leaving it running."

"As you should be." She went back to the keyboard. As soon as she heard him pad down the hall to the bedroom, she erased all her e-mails and cleaned out the recycle bin, just in case. She got the computer ready for the final click that would turn it off, and turned her chair around to survey the room.

Did she dare look again in the file cabinet? She had no conceivable excuse if she were caught. But she had, in the long hours of the night, had an idea about those clippings.

She thought Coop might be able to hear the deafening beat of her heart as she opened the second drawer, reached into the folder, and pulled out a piece of paper from somewhere in the middle.

He was coming! In a panic, she folded the paper, thrust it into her pocket, and turned off the computer just as he entered the room.

"I'm sorry I can't take you to the airport," he said, as they hastily finished their breakfast at the coffeehouse, "but I'm running a bit late for a meeting, and with the election tomorrow, things are pretty chaotic. You won't forget about the party tomorrow night to watch the returns, will you? I've booked rooms for you and Daniel at the Willard."

"Right. I'm really excited about that. It's not often I get to hobnob with the president of the United States."

Who is a complete and total jerk, she thought, and deserves to have his victory celebration ruined.

"Well, I'll see you then. Okay if I put you into a cab?" He glanced at his watch.

"Fine. I understand. And Coop . . ."—she reached up to run her hand over his hair—"it was a lovely evening."

CHAPTER 35

Sunday, November 2
Charleston, West Virginia
Two Days before the Presidential Election

Before Daniel left New York on Sunday morning, he hunted once more through all their databases and the Internet and read all the other articles he could find about Cabot. All of them were puff pieces, short on facts and long on speculation.

Daniel did discover a little about Vincent Dombrowski, the reporter who had broken the story on Cabot. He was older than Daniel and had attended college in the late 1980s but never graduated. He'd worked for a while for a newspaper in Charleston, West Virginia, and was then hired by the *San Francisco News*. After being fired from the *News* he'd gone back to the Charleston *Sentinel*. The last records Daniel could find for him indicated he was still in Charleston. Daniel caught the next plane.

He rented a car at the Charleston airport, picked up a city map, and drove to the address he'd found for Dombrowski, three blocks from the Kanawha River on the western fringes of the city. The address was now an empty lot, surrounded by modest sixty- and seventy-year-old houses.

The only neighbor who was at home late on a Sunday morning was a woman who looked to be in her mid-twenties. Daniel introduced himself as an old friend of Vincent's from college and asked what had become of the house where the reporter had lived.

The woman said, "The fire happened before we moved in two years ago. The whole place burned down in the middle of the night. All I heard is that Mr. Dombrowski almost died. The only thing he saved was his laptop computer. Firemen had to keep him from going back in to save more things. It was sad. Someone died in the fire."

"Do you know who?"

"No. I've heard stories it was a wife or a mistress. I've never found out for sure." She had never met Dombrowski and had no idea where he was living now.

The newspaper office was next. It was in a decaying building scarred with graffiti, paint peeling in sheets and bricks crumbling to dust. Daniel had read that it was scheduled for demolition in the Riverfront Revival. On its Web site the city was bragging about what the revival would do for the town. Daniel thought the downtown could certainly use a few good solid bulldozers. The blocks around the newspaper office looked like a lot of river towns: two- or three-story buildings close together, boarded-up storefronts, dirt on the streets that would take a nuclear explosion to clear.

Daniel left his rental car in a parking lot dotted with potholes. He got out, straightened his tie, hitched up his new blue jeans, and strode to the front desk of the *Sentinel*, hoping he looked as if he knew what he was doing. The receptionist referred him to the newsroom. There, a few reporters told him they'd known Dombrowski, but didn't know where he was.

Finally, one older woman, a motherly type in her early sixties, took pity on him. "He's gone," she said. "He was fired. Nobody wants to talk about him. You can find Vincent in the Tip-Top Tap Room down the street. He drinks his lunch there."

"On a Sunday?" Daniel asked.

"On every day." She looked Daniel up and down, took in his white shirt, his tie, and nice sport coat. "You won't quite fit in at that dive. But give it a try."

Daniel hustled down the street. He hoped he'd find Dombrowski sober enough to talk. So far he hadn't learned a lot.

On this early November day, a fine mist was falling in downtown Charleston. Daniel's shoulders were damp when he got to the Tip-Top Tap Room.

The neighborhood bar had darkened windows you couldn't see through, even on a good day. The front façade had moldering stonework up to the windows. Inside, the atmosphere was dank. The bar was old wood, ancient, but not a valuable antique. The bartender was even older, but he had his value—as purveyor of liquid nourishment.

The lone patron was in the back booth. Daniel nodded to the bartender and strolled to the back. "Vincent Dombrowski?"

The man nodded. Bleary eyes fixed a stare at a

place about nine inches to the right of Daniel's nose. "May I join you?" Daniel asked.

"You'll be the first. Probably the last." Dombrowski lit a nonfilter cigarette from the butt of another one. He mashed the burning ember from the old one into a half-full glass ashtray.

Daniel sat. A strong odor of sweat and alcohol emanated from the reporter across from him. Daniel introduced himself. Dombrowski shrugged. Daniel wondered how much he could have put away in the hour or so since the bar had opened.

The bartender came over. Daniel ordered a beer.

"Paper tell you I was here?" Dombrowski asked.

"A woman in her sixties said you drank your lunch here."

"And breakfast and dinner." He took a sip from a dark mug. "Woman with light golden hair?"

"Yeah."

"Matilda. Dear old soul. I started at the *Sentinel* years ago, before I left this shit-hole of a town with sneer and jeers. Ha! Conceited. Naïve. Arrogant. I was all of them. When I got back to the paper here, Matilda's the only one even tried to be friendly. Most of them considered me a failure. A loser, back from the big city. The editor was an old college friend. Took pity on me." He drank from his coffee cup, which reeked of cheap rotgut. Daniel didn't bother to speculate on the psychological implications of taking your booze in a coffee cup. The bartender brought Daniel his beer and then went away.

Daniel said. "I'm interested in the articles you wrote about Alexander Cabot for the *San Francisco News*."

"Article. One," Dombrowski said, then coughed. He

grabbed his coffee cup, took a gulp, then banged it back on the table. "I've been looking for another fool wanting to commit career suicide. You'll be drinking more than beer soon." Another swallow. "People died because of me. I might just as well have been holding a gun. I killed them."

"People died because you wrote an article about a famous rich guy?"

"I found out things you're not supposed to find out about rich people. I hunted through everything. I got one article published. One. The rest got yanked. All copies destroyed. I got canned. I came back home to lick my wounds, and they burned my house. But I got out with my laptop and everything on it. I've got copies of the articles hidden everywhere. They can kill me, but they can't get every single one of those articles." He gave a ghastly smile. Daniel saw yellowed teeth. Dombrowski lit another cigarette as he had done the last. Daniel noted that his fingers were stained yellow.

"How do you know I'm not one of them?"

Ash fell from the cigarette and just missed falling in Dombrowski's drink. He didn't seem to notice. He coughed again. "Don't care if you are. Anyway, if you were, I'd probably already be dead. And if you are, you'll never find every copy. Someday it will all come out. All of it. Are you here to kill me?"

"If I denied it, would you believe me?"

"You look like a young FBI agent except for the clothes. Nice, but they never used to wear jeans. Maybe they've loosened up." The reporter's laugh turned into a dry hacking cough.

Daniel waited. When the coughing stopped, he said, "People know you wrote the article. Why not tell me what you know? I might be able to put it to good use."

Dombrowski said, "I told another reporter. I told him everything. Brand-new reporter. Just out of college. A good man. Sort of like you. They killed him as a warning to me."

"Why not just kill you?"

"Living in pain and torture can be harder than dying. I smoke now. Never used to, but I don't have the guts to kill myself with a quick shot to the head. At least this way I can have my guilt and feel like I'm killing myself at the same time. I take my comfort where I can get it."

Daniel didn't know if he could ease the man's despair in the time he had. Or if there was enough healing time in eternity to assuage the reporter's guilt. "Can I help you in some way?" he asked.

"No. No one can help me. Why are you here?"

Daniel doubted Dombrowski's extreme take on what had happened to him and those around him. Then again, somebody had been trying to kill Daniel from Cairo to Rome.

Daniel knew a few of the secrets of interviewing. One was the simple "How interesting, tell me more." The goal was to keep the person talking.

He felt sorry for this wreck of a man. Was Dombrowski a poor demented fool, or did he have real facts? Daniel would have to sift through what he was told.

"How'd you happen to be doing the article?" Daniel asked.

"I love politics. I grew up in South Dakota, where Kierkstra's from. I did huge amounts of research on him. He's a crook; he's always been a crook. Through all my digging, I kept running into this Cabot guy's name, but there was never a lot about him, and never a picture. I began to wonder why someone who seems to be around the president so much never had his picture taken. I couldn't find a reason. I Googled Cabot images. Nothing. I looked through the first three thousand hits for him. Nothing. But I got the goods eventually."

"How?"

"There are other ways besides Google to find stuff on the Internet, if you know what you're doing."

I know a lot more about it than you do, thought Daniel. But what he said was, "You believe everything you find on the Net?"

"I believe in my ability to ask questions. I sat down with everybody who put out blogs or rumors or anything on Alexander Cabot. Most of them were raving loonies. A few of them had snippets of facts. Finding out which were the facts took months."

"And the facts were?" Daniel realized he was holding his breath. He deliberately relaxed and took a tiny sip of his beer.

Dombrowski lit another cigarette and took another swig of booze. "Cabot had two kids, one in high school and one in college. Two years ago the oldest boy died at Harvard. It's not real unusual for a college kid to commit suicide and that's how it was reported. I found his roommate. He was drinking and doing more drugs than I am today, and that's hard to do. The roommate had been set up in cars and cash and women for the rest of his life. Trouble was, the poor kid had an honest streak. Happens to the best of us, I guess. He told me the truth. He was dead the day after the article came out. Another suicide. Two roommates committing suicide. Imagine that."

"He was your proof."

"He was my proof. And he's dead."

"What did he tell you?"

"Cabot's kid, Alexander Junior, had been doing drugs and booze since he was in sixth grade. He'd been expelled from every boarding school he ever attended. He got into Harvard because his daddy donated a building."

"A whole building?"

"A whole fifty-million-dollar building. But Daddy regretted it because the kid was turning into a major embarrassment. He was going to make headlines. Rumor was the kid killed his mother."

Daniel looked skeptical.

"You asked," Dombrowski said. "I didn't say you'd like the information. It wasn't like the kid had a smoking gun or anything. Supposedly he supplied the drugs for her overdose. Cabot put a stop to any investigations. With his money he can start and stop a lot.

"Alexander Junior had taken to even more drinking. In his cups, he would blab. Everything. The roommate said he heard the story at least a dozen times. Said Junior hated his dad. Probably true. Who wouldn't? The younger son is in school in Switzerland. That's all I know." Dombrowski signaled the bartender for a refill.

After the ex-reporter was resupplied, Daniel asked, "Why'd your editor stop publishing the articles?"

"The day after the first one appeared, my editor called me in. He wouldn't give me an explanation, just said that the stories were to stop, I was to turn in all my files on the story, and I was fired." Another sip of the booze.

"Maybe the editor was worried for you."

"Maybe he was worried for his own skin."

"Aren't you worried for your own skin?"

Dombrowski fixed his bleary eyes on Daniel's. "Look at me. I'm a drunk. I ingest as many recreational chemicals as a freelance writer can afford. You know how many that is?"

"How many?"

"Not enough. If I can get 'em, I use 'em. After I got fired from the *News*, I moved back here. A buddy gave me a break. He was kind of interested in the articles. Then one day I was out. Somebody got to him too. Eventually I lost my job, my lover, and my home. When they burned the house, I got out with my computer. My lover didn't. I thought he was right behind me. That's why I wanted to go back in. But the firemen were there. They wouldn't let me." Tears started down his cheeks. He wiped at them furiously with the sleeve of his shabby elbow-patched sport coat. "My lover was killed as a warning."

Daniel found this a little hard to swallow. He didn't remember reading in the gay newspapers about the lover of a gay reporter dying. Certainly there had been nothing in the *Times*. He was sure he'd have remembered that. "But wouldn't you both have been more likely to die in the fire? Maybe it wasn't just a warning. Maybe it was simply an attempt to kill you or both of you."

Dombrowski nodded. "I'll never know. What I do know is that he's dead." He took another sip from the cup. "Why are you so interested in Cabot?"

"I'm going to try to bring him down. Why don't you give me one of those copies of your articles?"

"They'll kill you and the ones you love. He is powerful and ruthless. You will die. I don't need more deaths on my conscience."

"My actions are the results of my choices, not yours. I'd really like to have what you have."

Dombrowski reached for his pack of cigarettes. He fished inside, came up empty. "You wouldn't happen to have a smoke?"

"Sorry," Daniel said.

Dombrowski shook his head, finished his drink, and signaled the bartender. Then he reached into his pocket and pulled out a square envelope the size of a CD. "Here're all my notes. Keep one copy on me, always. Figured, when they finally got me, somebody honest might find this and do something with it." He handed the envelope to Daniel. "Try not to wind up dead, kid."

CHAPTER 36

Monday, November 3
Manhattan
One Day before the Presidential Election

"Brenda! Are you okay? Where are you calling from?"

"Yeah, I'm . . . reasonably okay. I'm calling from a pay phone at the airport. I thought it was a little safer than my cell. Except they can listen in on yours just as well as mine."

"Yeah, well, you can run but you can't hide." Daniel uttered the cliché lightly, but it was so true. It seemed all he had been doing lately was running and trying to hide. "Which airport?"

"JFK. I just got back to town. Where are you?"

"The office. Meet you here?"

"As soon as I can get there."

* * *

S he made it to the office a little after ten. Helen greeted her with an anxious "How's Nate? How are you? What's going on?"

Brenda had already decided what it was safe to say. "Nate's okay. There was a burglary at their place, and Nate got shot, but it wasn't serious." She hated being dishonest with Helen, but she couldn't entirely dismiss Daniel's suspicions. Of course, it was impossible that Helen was their spy, but . . .

Helen frowned. "How about you? I hate to say it, but you look like something the cat dragged in. Through the cat door. Backward."

"I didn't get a whole lot of sleep last night, and I think I might be coming down with a cold," Brenda improvised. "Talk to you later. I've got a lot of work to do."

"But what about Cooper and Cabot? And what did Daniel find out in the Middle East?"

"I can't explain the whole thing right now. It's too complicated. And Helen, it's still dangerous here; you ought to go home."

In Daniel's office, Brenda was enveloped in a large hug before he held her out and looked at her. "Are you all right? You look like hell."

She grimaced. "Everybody's so flattering this morning. I'm okay. How about you? And have you checked on Nate?"

"As soon as I got back from Charleston. I took the red-eye. No point in trying to sleep at home. It's a disaster area. I called your farm from a pay phone in the airport. Nate's doing well."

"That's good. Has Jasper noticed anything going on? Like somebody spying on the place or anything?"

"All quiet, according to him. Maybe you're right

and the farm really is safe. I sure hope so, but I'm not sure any place is safe these days." Daniel's voice wasn't quite steady. He lowered it and changed the subject. "Listen, I talked to that reporter and found out some interesting things about Cabot."

"Me too. And I've got some data from his computer." She held out the jump drive.

"Outstanding! I can't believe he let you get near his computer!"

"Hubris, Daniel. The fatal flaw. He figures he's so damn charming he can hypnotize any woman. I don't think it ever even entered his mind that I wasn't totally bewitched by his beauty, brains, and brandy."

Daniel made an extremely rude noise. "What have you got?"

"I don't know yet. Haven't had time to look at it. I haven't even been back to my apartment. I wanted to check in with you first. Here."

Daniel looked at the jump drive she handed him, then at his computer, and said, "Well, I've got some info from that reporter. On disk. But I don't think we'd better—" At the same time Brenda said, "This isn't the place to—"

Daniel started again. "Your place? We can't go to mine."

"Mine might not be secure either. Besides . . ." She looked down. How could she explain that she didn't want to go to her apartment maybe ever again? That it was contaminated, that space that she had so loved, by the very fact of Coop's—of Cabot's—presence?

"I know," said Daniel quietly. Their relationship, which had been strained for a while, was back to normal. Whatever barriers had gone up between them in the past few days were down, washed away by the floods of disaster and fear and shared horror.

Brenda felt such huge relief that she nearly wept, but she recalled that she looked bad enough already. She didn't want reddened eyes to give Helen cause for any more speculation. She took a deep breath. "Okay, then, how about Brew-Ha-Ha? They're wireless."

"Not big enough to give us any privacy. I've got a better idea. How about the library?"

"Brilliant! Brilliant, Dan! Hundreds of people, hundreds of computers, dozens of guards. Hey, if we're safe anywhere on the planet, the New York Public Library has to be the place. How about I meet you by the uptown lion in, say, an hour? I guess I have to go to the apartment for a little while. I need a shower. Or two."

Again she didn't need to explain. Daniel said, "How about I come with you? I could use a shower myself."

Brenda managed a grin. "Also you think you need to protect me."

"That too."

She socked him gently on the arm. "Today I'll take all the protection I can get. Just don't make a habit of it."

Daniel took along the spare shirt and underwear he always kept at the office, and an hour later, their laptops in hand, jump drives in pockets, they were climbing past the lions to the doorway of the magnificent old New York Public Library.

Brenda paused and looked around before she went in. "If anything ever happened to this . . ."

"Yeah. One reason we do what we do."

They went in and found the computers on which they had reserved time. They could have only forty-five minutes; once that time was up, they'd have to cede their places to someone else and use their slower laptops. Daniel loaded the disk Dombrowski had given him and started reading. Meanwhile Brenda took a deep breath, inserted the jump drive, and began to dig through the secrets of Alexander Cabot, most powerful man in the world.

She opened the RK file first. It was written in a kind of shorthand, with lots of initials and cryptic references. To the ordinary reader it wouldn't have meant much, but to Brenda, experienced in reading complex computer code, it was a piece of cake. After a few minutes she was able to read it with ease, and what she read made her eyebrows rise higher and higher.

"Dan," she said at last. She kept her voice to a low rumble, far less penetrating than a whisper. "Hey. Come out of your trance and look at this."

Daniel was immersed in a similar exercise, decoding the reporter's notes. He'd had a harder time than Brenda. Alexander Cabot, Brenda had discovered, was a fanatically organized man whose abbreviations and shortcuts made sense once you figured out his system. Vincent Dombrowski was a drunken eccentric whose notes might not always have been clear even to him. Daniel turned with relief to Brenda's computer.

"What have you got?" he asked, looking at the cryptic entries.

Brenda smiled grimly. "Evidence that the president of the United States is a major-league crook. He's been taking rake-offs from government contracts for years, from back when he was a minor pol in South Dakota. And that's the least of it. If these notes are accurate, Cabot's got proof of contracts to shady operators, contracts for things like bridges and roads and railroad crossings. And when the bridges fell down and the roads washed out and the crossing arms didn't work, people died."

"Holy shit! Is this for real? How come we never heard any of this before?"

"Well, there've always been rumors about him, you know, but never anything that could be pinned down. Of course I haven't taken the time to check out any of this, but Cabot's got an awful lot of detail here. Dates, places, initials that I'm guessing are the names of the people involved."

Daniel frowned. "But if he—Cabot, I mean—if he's gone to all the trouble to collect this information, why hasn't he made it public? What's the point of collecting dirt about somebody . . . *oh*."

"Sure. Blackmail. Or at least it looks like that to me. Except what I can't figure out is why should Cabot want to blackmail anybody? It'd be like . . . like Bill Gates kidnapping somebody and holding the person for a couple of million in ransom, which would be petty cash to Gates. Except it's even more stupid than that, because Cabot's a lot richer than Gates. I'll bet he could buy Kierkstra a million times over. So what's the point?"

Daniel's expression changed, grew colder, darker. "I think you just said it, kid. He can buy Kierkstra. If Kierkstra knows Cabot has that information and is sitting on it, Kierkstra'll dance to any tune Cabot wants. What do you want to bet?"

Brenda looked slightly sick. "That's the way the game is played, isn't it? God, Dan, was there ever a time when politicians were honest?"

"There are still some that are a lot more honest than Kierkstra."

"I hope you're right. One thing I'm beginning to be sure about: almost anybody's more honest than Alexander Cabot/Allen Cooper. I'm going to dig some more."

They worked on. Brenda turned to Cabot/Cooper's spreadsheets; Daniel went on with the reporter's notes. Every few minutes they checked the room.

"Dan," said Brenda. Her voice was little more than a thread of sound. "There are a couple of guys over in the far corner. They're not reading or doing anything, just standing there looking around. Give it a minute, and then see if you can spot them."

Daniel's glance was casual. "Never seen them before," he breathed to Brenda. "They don't exactly look like they belong here, do they?"

"What do we do?"

"Wait and see if the guards deal with them. Loitering is supposed to be prohibited."

The next time they looked up, the men were gone.

When their time was up on the library computers, they switched to their laptops and continued working. Brenda wondered what they would do when the library closed. Where would they go then? What if the two men, or others, were waiting for them? In all of New York, what place was safe from the all-seeing eye of Alexander Cabot?

Half an hour before closing time, Brenda gasped.

"What?"

"I . . . Dan, let's get out of here."

They shut down their computers and left, lost—they hoped—in the crowds leaving the library, having backpacks checked, streaming out the doors.

It was after seven. The November evening was dark and cold. A thin rain was beginning to freeze. Daniel pulled Brenda into the shelter of one of the pillars and scanned the crowd.

"I don't see anybody," he muttered.

Hundreds of people hurried past, but Brenda knew what he meant. She huddled close to him. "Dan, I hate to admit it, but I'm scared."

"Me too. What I've learned about this man—"

"What do we do now?" She sounded forlorn.

"We go and get ourselves something to eat. I don't know about you, but half my trouble right now is hunger. And then we buy a couple of toothbrushes and find a couple of rooms in a big fancy hotel with a big impressive doorman out front and good security locks on the doors, and we work and we talk."

"Sounds like a plan." With a covert glance to left and right, she followed him down the steps and into the dismal night.

CHAPTER 37

Monday, November 3
New York City

They ate, ravenously, at a crowded deli near the library, talking about the weather when they talked at all. When they were finished they dropped into a big drugstore for toothbrushes, deodorant, combs, and a change of underwear. Brenda bought a big T-shirt to wear to bed, and Daniel a cheap white shirt to put on in the morning.

"Hey," said Daniel when they went out into the miserable night, "we'd better find an ATM. I don't think I want to use a credit card at the hotel."

"You're right," said Brenda. "But they can trace ATM transactions too, and anyway I can't get enough cash out of my account to pay for a luxury hotel. The bank limits ATM withdrawals to two hundred dollars a pop."

"Shit. Mine too. Then we'll just have to trust the hotel security."

They spent some time trying to find a cab, all of which had vanished, as usual in rainy New York. By the time they finally got one to stop, they were wet through and shivering.

"The Waldorf," Daniel told the driver. He settled back in the seat. "Might as well hide in style."

"Sheesh. I'm not sure the company treasury will stand it."

"For once the company treasury will have to lump it. Hell, we ARE the company."

"And Harlan," Brenda reminded him, referring to their partner and maintenance expert.

"Yeah, well, Harlan'll get his turn the next time somebody's trying to kill *him*."

The desk clerk at the Waldorf-Astoria was unruffled by their disheveled appearance, even their lack of luggage. Their rooms, as requested, were adjoining and on the highest floor available that night, the thirty-seventh. Brenda entered hers, looked around with appreciation, then knocked on the door that divided the two rooms. "If they come to kill me, I'll die happy," she said when Daniel opened the door.

"It's a pity we can't just revel in it," said Daniel. "Nate would love this. Especially the marble bathroom."

"Yes. Well. Are you ready to get to work?"

"Your place or mine?"

"Yours," said Brenda. "Your table doesn't look quite as fragile and antique as mine."

"You were scared just before we left the library," said Daniel. They were both seated, their laptops open and booted.

"Yes." She took a deep breath. "I found . . . well, I need to back up a little. While I was in his house, I had a minute or two to get into Cabot's files, and I actually stole something. It didn't make a whole lot of sense by itself. I tore it up and flushed it down the toilet on the plane after I'd read it. It was just a newspaper story about an explosion in the Middle East that destroyed most of a small oil field."

"But?"

"But it had a number penciled in on the bottom of the page: 50K. Now that could mean anything—or nothing—but I filed it away in my memory, along with the date on the article.

"So at the library I was going through his accounts. I thought they wouldn't be anything, just maybe his petty cash or little projects of some kind. I mean, a man like him, he's got lawyers and accountants and flunkies by the dozen to take care of his real money, so what would he keep on his home computer? Or one of his home computers."

"So tell me already!"

Brenda held up her hands. "I'm not trying to be dramatic or anything. I just wanted to explain why it hit me so hard. See, what I found on one spreadsheet was just a list of dates and place names and numbers. The place names all sounded foreign, Arabic mostly. And one of them—one of the entries—was dated the same as that newspaper story and was for fifty thousand dollars. And the place name was Abdali—the same as in the newspaper story. The place where the oil field was destroyed."

Daniel was intent now.

"So then I went to the Internet and checked out some of the other places and dates on the spreadsheet. And every one of them—every single one, Dan—was a place where some major terrorist activity had taken place. Most of them involved oil."

There was silence in the luxurious room, broken only by background noises. A siren wailed in the street far below. Somewhere a fan whirred gently, bringing warm air from a furnace in the bowels of the building. The computers made quiet noises from time to time.

"So you think—" said Dan, finally.

"I think Cabot is financing these terrorists. I think he's deliberately destroying oil capacity. And incidentally killing people left and right." Brenda paused. "You know, what I still can't figure out is why Cabot/Cooper asked us to help the NSAA look for terrorist activity. Wouldn't he be worried about what we'd find out?"

"He thought he was well protected," said Daniel. "And we'd be reporting to him anyway. What an irony—we'd report to Cooper about Cabot. Besides, he wanted to make us think that vetting the polling program was an afterthought when it was really his primary goal."

Silence again. Then Daniel turned to his computer. "Okay. This is what I've found out. This Dombrowski guy took notes like he was drunk and on six different kinds of drugs. Which he probably was. But what I've deciphered, plus what he told me, adds up to the ugliest picture I've seen in a long time."

Brenda waited.

"It's all rumor. None of it's provable, because Cabot made sure the witnesses didn't live to tell the tale. But the story is Cabot got rid of his wife by letting his son give her an overdose of something. Heroin, crack, meth—who knows? Then when the son got unreliable, he took an 'accidental' overdose himself. Same thing happened to the roommate who told Dombrowski all this."

Brenda nodded. She thought if she opened her mouth she'd throw up.

"And that isn't all. Dombrowski was a good reporter before he fried his head. Cabot's hidden his assets well, so well that almost nobody knows exactly how he made his money or what he did with it. The original mystery man—that's him. But Dombrowski found out—don't ask me how—that most of Cabot's capital these days is in energy concerns. It looks as though, through holding companies and dummy corporations and financial shenanigans I don't begin to understand, he controls almost all the world's oil."

"And he's systematically destroying pockets of it," said Brenda in a scared whisper, "to create a shortage so he can get whatever price he wants."

"He's cornering the market," said Daniel slowly. "He's gonna own all the oil in the world."

"Right. Maybe not instantly, but eventually."

"A monopoly."

"Right again! And to keep the nasty antitrust questions at bay—"

"—he has to have the president of the United States in his pocket. The president of the biggest energy-consuming nation on earth." Daniel paused. "Only, what's the point? Cabot's the richest man in the world already. He could spend a million dollars a day for the rest of his life and still not keep up with his earnings. Why does he want more?"

"That's where the crazy part comes in," said Brenda soberly. "It isn't money anymore. It's power. He wants to rule the world. Seriously. And if he gets a monopoly on oil, he will. Emperor Cabot." She shuddered. "That's the guy we're trying to stop. Think about it, Daniel. Honestly, I don't know why we're still alive. They killed Sarah, just because she developed the tabulation program. They killed a bunch of our people. They tried to kill Nate, just because he was in their way when they trashed your place. And Hector . . . and Dombrowski's lover . . . and who knows, maybe Jeremy and all the rest on 9/11 too. It could go that far back, Daniel. Think of it! Why are we left?"

"Because we certified the program," said Daniel slowly. "We're potential scapegoats. We have to stay alive, at least until after the election. Then if something goes wrong, if somebody tries to prove the election's been stolen, they can point to us and say, 'Well, the best firm in the business passed it. They must be the ones who screwed up.' Oh, they've set us up but good."

"But we did pass it. And it is okay. We put it through every possible test."

"No, we didn't. We missed something. I don't know what, but something. Something worth killing for. And as sure as Cabot is the world's greatest bastard, he's gonna steal the election tomorrow, and he's gonna own the world, and I don't think I want to live in it anymore!"

Brenda crashed her fist down on the table in frustration. "It's actually worse than that, you know. If they pulled this off, it would be the end of America. Not just because Kierkstra is an idiot, not just because he's in Cabot's pocket. We've had stupid presidents before, corrupt ones before. But they were elected legitimately. They could be impeached. The system mostly worked.

"If elections can be rigged though on a nationwide scale, then we're not a republic anymore, we're a dictatorship. We're the USSR. That's why we have to find the bug. This disaster isn't gonna happen, because we're not going to let it. We passed that program. Now we have to unpass it. Find the flaw and let the whole world know."

"And if we don't . . . god, Brenda, the man could be there for eight more years! He's only served two years of Miller's term, so now he can be elected to two full terms."

"Yeah, well, he's not going to be. We've missed something. We're going to have to go over it again. And again, until we find whatever it is."

"The polls open in"—Daniel looked at his watch—"in eight hours."

"I know. So we have to do it now. Right now."

"I'll bring up the program on the Net while you order coffee." She typed in the code. "Lots of it, very strong. We neither of us got much sleep last night, and if I ever needed to be alert, it's now."

They drank the coffee, quarts of it. Sometime in the middle of the night they ordered sandwiches. They sat at their laptops reading back through the program which the municipalities had downloaded to the polling machines. They worked until their eyes were red and gritty, their shoulders tense and sore, their right hands cramped over the mouse.

"There is nothing," Daniel said, as the elegant little clock on the mantel chimed four. "Nothing, nothing, damn nothing at all! It's beautiful, this code. Elegant."

"Sarah was good," said Brenda with a sigh. "More coffee? Personally, I'm going to check out the mini-

bar for some scotch. If I have any more caffeine I'll
fly into little pieces."

"Damn it all, there's no point! Yeah, fine, coffee or
scotch or whatever, but I mean no point in going on.
We've been over it and over it and over it. There's
nothing wrong with this program!"

"There is though. We know there is. They're going
to steal this election, and they're going to do it with
this program. There's a glitch here somewhere."

"Maybe they're just gonna shoot the election officials," said Daniel. "Or blow up the polls. Or Kierkstra is going to declare himself God."

"It's here, Daniel. We've just missed it. It's here. We
have to find it." Brenda was inexorable.

"And then what?" Daniel asked.

"I don't know. Find it first."

They drank a little excellent scotch in strained silence, not knowing what they were tasting. Then they
went back to work, Daniel accessing the Internet program, and Brenda backgrounding Cabot again.

Daniel said, "There's a patch to the program coming in. Apparently there's a bug that would slow the
counting and they're fixing it."

"Was the bug real?" Brenda said.

"Yeah. Perfectly innocent," Daniel said.

It was nearly six when Brenda stretched, stood up,
and said, "Dan, I've had it. I'm so tired I can't even see
the screen, and there's nothing here to find. It's officially Election Day, and whatever's going to happen
will happen. I'm going to bed."

"Wait!"

"What?"

"Have you got that code I found in Istanbul?"

CHAPTER 38

Tuesday, November 4
Washington, D.C.
Election Day

"How do I look?"
They had left the Waldorf that morning and gone to their apartments to pack party clothes and overnight necessities. After they'd both cast their votes at their respective polling places, they had met at Penn Station for the train to Washington and the Willard Hotel.

Now Brenda, rested and dressed, turned for Daniel's inspection.

Daniel cocked his head. "You look beautiful. You always look beautiful."

Her hair was chestnut tonight. She wanted to look attractive but respectable, and neither platinum blond nor Goth black would be right. "I'm usually not nervous," she said.

"Well, you don't usually bring down a president."

"God, Dan! Don't say it."

He shrugged. She added, "You look pretty spiffy in your dinner jacket too."

There were five celebration parties for the president in Washington. Harkinnon was holding his celebration parties in his home state. Of course, a few hours from now only one of the two candidates would be celebrating. The other set of parties would be wakes.

Daniel and Brenda left Brenda's room at the Willard and found their limo waiting for them at the front door.

"Every limo in D.C. must be out tonight," she said to the driver.

"Oh, we've brought in cars and drivers from Virginia and Maryland. And we're still running back and forth. Usually we can wait for people at an event, but not tonight. You'll have to call us."

"Of course, and we don't know what time we'll leave anyway."

"Well, when you call, be patient."

Courtesy of Allen Cooper, Daniel and Brenda were going to the most important of the five D.C. parties, the one at the Watergate. The president and his top aides were staying in suites there, as were the party chairman and major donors.

Alexander Cabot stood casually leaning against the wall of the presidential suite in the Watergate. Kierkstra was dithering around somewhere back in the dressing room. The president's makeup consultant was in there with him. Wouldn't want to pull a Richard Nixon, would he?

Cabot studied the closed-circuit television that showed the celebration ballroom from a camera situated about seven and a half feet above the floor on the wall behind the dais. This way the president and Secret Service could see everybody in the room without the distortion of a ceiling mount, and they could see the room all the time, regardless of what the networks were showing. Cabot knew who most of the people in the room were, even though most of them would not have known him by sight. Seven huge television screens were mounted high up around the ballroom, so that CBS, NBC, ABC, CNN, Fox, a D.C. channel, and one that rotated among other networks could all play at once and be seen by the partygoers. The cable feed was displayed on seven smaller TVs in the president's suite.

When he saw Daniel and Brenda enter, Cabot smiled. Wouldn't it be fun to walk out with Kierkstra and be introduced as Alexander Cabot, bosom buddy of the president? Just to watch her face as awareness swept over it, to see her realize that she had been thoroughly deceived. Security specialist! Such a smart girl!

There was no reason why he couldn't do it. By then the election would be over, and anyway DB had not found any problems with the voting program. She could snarl and spit and complain, but it wouldn't change anything.

And really, she couldn't even complain, could she? It would make her look stupid. If anything, she should hope nobody ever found out. She would just suffer a slow burn of shame. For years.

Maybe he would go out there.

Or maybe he wouldn't.

It was such fun to think about.

* * *

"I'm not usually nervous," Brenda said.

"You already said that," Daniel said. "Anyway, you don't look nervous."

"Well, duh. I'm not going to blow the whole thing. Hey! Isn't that John McCain?"

"Sure. What did you expect?"

"Wow! Is that Bruce Willis?"

"Shhh. You're embarrassing me."

"I'm trying to distract myself. That's Donald Rumsfeld."

The huge room buzzed. To look at it, it was a party, a ball in a regular ballroom, but nobody's mind was on dancing. Politics called the tune and paid the pipers in this city.

Daniel carried a thin leather folder, which had been thoroughly searched by the Secret Service, as he and Brenda made their way into the party area. When the agents found nothing but paper, not even pens, and just one pencil, Daniel was permitted through. He wasn't the only person with writing material. Print-media reporters were everywhere, taking notes for stories, some on paper, some with necklace recorders. Some photographers had been allowed in with still cameras. And of course, TV reporters and their cameramen were as thick as black flies in Wisconsin.

A small orchestra was playing on the far side of the very large room. The volume of the music was modest so as to allow conversation. If politics was the business of Washington, gossip was the gasoline the business ran on.

The music was low enough to allow the voices of the newscasters to be heard. The huge screens were mounted far enough apart that a person could stand near any one of them and listen to the audio. Brenda moved close to the screen that showed CBS, where she heard Bob Schieffer saying to Russ Mitchell, "Delaware, with eleven percent of the precincts reporting, has gone strongly for Harkinnon."

"Yes, Bob, and the polls are now closed in Maryland."

"With ten electoral votes, Maryland went strongly for Kerry in 2004. Exit polls in the state show voters favoring Harkinnon at a rate of about four to three."

Brenda and Daniel strolled to a different screen, where NBC's David Gregory was saying, "A state that went into the 2004 election leaning weakly Republican. In addition to Florida, states that could go either way are the same as in the last election: Oregon, Nevada, New Mexico, Iowa, Wisconsin, Minnesota, Michigan, Ohio, New Hampshire, and Pennsylvania."

"Of those, David," said Brian Williams, "which are the biggies?"

"Ohio has twenty electoral votes. Michigan has seventeen, and Pennsylvania twenty-one. They are certainly swing states this time around too."

"As you know, David, the total votes in the electoral college are five hundred and thirty-eight. Two hundred and seventy are needed to elect a president."

"At the present moment, if we relied on exit polls, we would call ninety-five for Governor Harkinnon and eighty-two for President Kierkstra."

"We're going to cut away for our affiliates to bring you the results in local and gubernatorial races—"

Brenda said, "I guess we'd better cut away, too."

"Yeah. You up to it?"

"Ready as I'll ever be."

* * *

"My name is Brenda Grant and this is Daniel Henderson. I am CEO and Mr. Henderson is president of DB Security. Our head office is in New York and we have twelve offices abroad and here in—"

"Well-known company," said Fredrick Cogdill of StreamingNews, a small network said to be baying at the heels of the biggies. StreamingNews was taping Brenda and Daniel, but hadn't decided whether they were legit enough or their news was big enough to go live. People tried to get on national TV all the time with puffed-up or completely fabricated stories, so Cogdill was wary. Brenda figured that in about ten minutes the StreamingNews research people back in New York would have located photos of Daniel and her and would know that they were who they said they were. There was the validation too of Daniel and Brenda being invited to the most important ball of the incumbent president. But right now she and Daniel had to sell their story.

"Thank you," Brenda said. "We were hired quite recently to vet the program for vote counting that would run on a 21st Century Polling machine. We were approached indirectly but hired by 21st Century Polling. The idea was to double-check that the data management program would work correctly, this being an era of doubts about vote tallies."

Cogdill's cameraman chuckled, then quickly shut up.

"We found nothing wrong until just this morning. We discovered a hidden problem that allows the vote tally code to throw a percentage of votes to President Kierkstra."

Cogdill turned to Daniel, following the TV news habit of switching from one face to another as often as possible.

"Can you prove this? These are very serious allegations."

"We have e-mailed copies of our analysis to all the major media outlets in the country. In addition, we have information here explaining in greater detail exactly what the program does, how it does it, and where it has been used. But the easiest way to access the data is to go on our Web site. Here's the info. We have large chunks of the program, including the patch, posted. With explanations."

Cogdill said, "If that's proprietary material, you could be sued."

Brenda said, "Ri-i-i-i-ight."

Daniel said, "Let 'em try."

Daniel gave his leather folder to Brenda, who opened it and handed a three-page printout to Cogdill.

While Cogdill continued talking to Daniel, Brenda seized the opportunity to glance at the tallies NBC was posting. Massachusetts, with twelve electoral votes, was being called for Governor Harkinnon. David Gregory gave the camera his profile as he studied his tally board. "As of now, with twenty-one electoral votes," he said, "the pivotal state of Pennsylvania is balanced on a razor's edge. Sixty percent of the precincts have reported in, and it's as close as close can be, fifty and a half percent for Kierkstra, forty-nine and a half for Harkinnon . . ."

StreamingNews was not important enough to rate its own TV monitor on the wall of the ballroom. One of its staff carried a handheld monitor of what the network was showing. Brenda was able to sneak a sidelong glance at it. Their anchor pointed at tallies on a giant map of the United States. She couldn't hear anything he said, but suddenly they cut away to a wide shot of the presidential ballroom, and then she saw herself, five minutes earlier, speaking with Cogdill.

They've decided we're the real deal, she thought, gloating. We've done it. Or at least we've started to.

Brenda watched, chills and waves of heat rushing across her skin, as CBS picked up on the Streaming News interview. Not able to use the competitor's video, Bob Schieffer reported it as an unconfirmed rumor.

Blond Christi Paul from CNN'S *Headline News* pushed through a crowd of onlookers and said to Brenda, "I want to go live with you in three minutes. Ready?"

"Ready," Brenda said.

The NBC screen across the room showed a view of Daniel talking with Cogdill. Then her own face popped up on CBS. It was a still from a magazine article, angled slightly away from a pundit who was probably explaining who she was.

Christi Paul's cameraman placed his feet, as her assistant said, "On my three . . . two . . . one . . ."

"I'm live at the Watergate, where President Kierkstra waits to hear the results of today's elections. With me is Brenda Grant, CEO of DB Security Consultants, who claims that DB was given a prototype of a vote-counting program that was used today in several states across the country. Ms. Grant and her company's president, Daniel Henderson, claim that just today they uncovered a glitch intentionally planted in this program that can alter the vote tallies. Ms. Grant, why should anyone believe you?"

Brenda drew a breath, hoping she would be convincing. She explained the program. She added that any municipality that had bought the 21st Century system could have its code checked. "However, on the chance that a self-destruct is being sent to the programs, several municipalities have disconnected from the Internet on the LANs, so that no destruct signal can reach them."

Christi Paul said, "Our staff is just now reviewing the explanatory materials on DB's website. I am told it will take some time to review. Now to our analyst in Atlanta. Christi Paul, *Headline News*."

Brenda glanced at the dais, empty so far of VIPs. Two Secret Service men stood on it, hands clasped behind their backs. The larger guy looked familiar— tall, round head. Oh, jeez! Mr. Tomato Head! Proof of Cabot's involvement if she ever needed any. Shit! To make himself look like a hero to her. To get up to her apartment. And it worked.

Brenda sank back against the wall, then realized that about twenty cameras were trained on her. She pretended to cough, straightened up, and gazed around the room expressionlessly, as four reporters elbowed each other to get to her.

Trying to appear calm, she casually studied Morgan Phillips, usually an anchorman but live at this scene tonight. Phillips scowled at something he was hearing on his cell phone. Then he turned to face the wall a few yards away from Brenda. He edged toward a corner, where he was secluded on two sides, and his cameraman came over and stood behind him, facing the room, his back to Phillips. With that set-up, nothing Phillips said would be heard by the guests.

Brenda wished she knew what he was saying.

Phillips was talking to, or rather snarling at, his station manager. About Brenda and Daniel.

"No, they are not loons," he hissed into his cell. "*Business Week* had an article on them a few months back. Look it up! DB has offices in a dozen countries and L.A., Chicago, and New York!"

The man on the other end of the conversation spoke a few words.

"Look at NBC! Now look at CBS! They're replaying their . . . ," Phillips shouted. Then lowering his voice, he said, "You want to make the call for me to miss the scoop of the year? Just because you're chickenshit?"

A few seconds passed while he listened.

"If we don't go with it, we'll be the only network that doesn't, and I'll be standing here looking like a fucking incompetent asshole!"

He listened.

"I'm going to be standing here with my bare face hanging out! What do you want? I'll be going, 'And exit polls in Halfass, Arkansas, are running close.' Meanwhile Geraldo Rivera's gonna be crowing about the scandal of the century."

Long known for his gentlemanly manner and courtesy to interviewees, Phillips interrupted. "Any century, you moron! I know this one is still young! No, they're really Grant and Henderson! Look in our obit file!

Why do we have you? Haven't you ever done any research? Take a look at CNN now. What did I tell you? I'm gonna have Mickey's camera on me now, going up to them and asking them for five minutes, and you better go live with it or my resignation is gonna be on Hopper's desk by sunrise!"

Bob Schieffer asked from the studio in Manhattan, "You had the program at DB for what? Several weeks? Why didn't you find the problem?"

"I blame myself for not figuring it out sooner," Daniel said. "But let me explain how it worked. You know how companies like Microsoft occasionally find glitches in their software and have to send out patches?" Every major network was going to want them to repeat this for their own live video.

"Yes."

Stifling a sigh, Daniel continued. "You also know that some programs have an expiration date, after which they no longer work? We thought that the 21st Century program might have a timing device, if it was booby-trapped in any way. We advanced the date so the program thought it was November fourth and nothing happened."

"So how could it work?" Schieffer asked.

"21st Century Polling claimed to find a glitch that slowed the counting, and they sent out a patch early this morning. The glitch was real. But when we looked closely, we found that there was a hook already in place for the patch. That seemed peculiar. Then in looking at the patch—mind you it was too late to break it down and study what it did—we realized it was identical to some code we had discovered several days earlier in the Middle East. And it had been written well before that. Weeks before the patch was needed."

"So what did it do?"

"We dummied up a polling place, entered a hundred votes, and ran the program with the patch in place. It changed one out of every ten Harkinnon votes to a Kierkstra vote. A small enough change so as not to raise serious suspicion, but a large enough change in razor-edge districts to elect Kierkstra."

In the president's suite, Cabot gave half a minute's thought to sending the Secret Service down to grab Daniel Henderson and Brenda Grant and get them both out of here. Kierkstra could have them held at least twenty-four hours if he claimed they had threatened him.

But that was obviously no good. Every major network in the country had a camera crew here. The whole world was watching. Live video of the two being arrested would be a political disaster.

There was no point getting help from the moron in the other room. Even now, he could be heard complaining about the yellow base the makeup person had used on his skin.

Cabot knew he'd have to take care of this catastrophe himself.

The huge flatscreen in the southwest corner of the room cut out from Brenda's last comments to

Katie Couric, CBS anchor in New York. "Professor Harold Firman from MIT is an expert in the analysis of polls and more recently in the use of various voting machine methods. Thank you for coming to help us out, Professor Firman."

Firman appeared on a flatscreen next to Couric. She had spoken to him as if he were in the same room, and he now answered in kind.

"Thanks for inviting me, Katie."

"Let me start with the basics, Professor. This is quite a bombshell from Grant and Henderson, the founders of DB Security." Playing straight man, she asked, "But is it really possible for just a few votes in just a few key precincts to change the outcome of the election?"

"Well, Katie, I think we've seen that happen in two recent presidential elections, 2000 and 2004. Florida tipped the balance in 2000, and Ohio essentially did the same thing in 2004. It's the effect of our winner-take-all electoral college system."

"Would you explain that briefly, Professor?"

"In 2000, if all the votes in the United States had simply been added up, Al Gore would have won. But if a candidate wins by a slim margin in a state with a large number of electoral votes, all those votes are cast for him in the electoral college. In Florida, even if the actual ballots were all correctly counted, there were 2,912,790 votes for Bush versus 2,912,253 for Gore. Bush defeated Gore by 537 votes. He therefore received all of Florida's twenty-five electoral votes and won the election. But if there had been no electoral college, just a nationwide popular vote, Al Gore would have won. Al Gore had more total votes than George Bush."

* * *

D aniel leaned toward Brenda's ear. "Look at CBS."

The CBS tally board was evenly split, and the analyst said, "Colorado and New Mexico have only fourteen electoral college votes between them, but in an election that proves to be as close as this, they are certainly swing states."

"Yes, Bill, and New Mexico has gone for every winning presidential candidate since 1912, except in the 1976 election."

The two were crosshatched blue and red, signifying an even balance. It could go either way.

C NN said, "All bets are off in Nevada—"

One by one, the majors picked up the story.

"Take the state of Michigan, for example," said Robert Morris Finnery, the expert brought on by CNN's *Headline News*. "Like most states, it's a hodge-podge."

Christi Paul said, "Tell us about that, if you will."

"Michigan has over five thousand precincts and they use a bewildering array of different voting systems. Just to give you an example, ninety-eight use paper ballots. Four hundred and fifty use the old lever-style machines. Three hundred and twenty use punch cards that are tabulated in the precinct. Eight hundred and seventy use punch cards tabulated centrally. Three thousand and five hundred use optical scans. A hundred use direct electronic recording. The accuracy of all these systems is vitally important. Michigan has been a battleground state in the past three elections. In the 2004 campaign, Miller visited Michigan twenty times."

NBC said: "We spoke with Margaret Innis in Dade County, Florida, who tells us that thirty percent of the precincts there use the 21st Century system."

ABC said: "Repeated attempts to reach a spokesperson at 21st Century Polling have been unsuccessful."

CBS said, "We would have predicted that West Virginia, with a large population of veterans, would go for President Kierkstra. And we would project Kierkstra the winner. But this bombshell has thrown all of our predictions into a cocked hat."

"Get down there, you dumb son of a bitch!" the president bellowed. "Get down there and fix this."

Bret Culligan looked in disgust at the man he'd come to loathe like no other. "Fix it how?" Culligan asked.

The president banged his hand on the top of the television. "Bullshit how. You're in charge of *how*. Fix it. They told me there wouldn't be any problems. Who are those two assholes? I bet they're a threat to national security. We should have them arrested."

Culligan walked out.

* * *

To Greta Van Susteren, Daniel said, "Look, this is easily verified. You don't have to spend two months counting hanging chads. And you don't have to take my word for it. Get one of the machines. Plug in a hundred votes for Harkinnon and a hundred votes for Kierkstra. You'll come up with about ninety votes for Harkinnon and a hundred and ten for Kierkstra."

Bret Culligan walked into the ballroom. Immediately reporters rushed to him, jammed microphones in his face, and shouted questions at him. Culligan looked around at them and said, "I don't have the slightest clue what you're talking about." Then he turned and walked away. After putting some distance between himself and the chaos, he decided to keep walking. Maybe he'd walk all the way to South Dakota.

At midnight Katie Couric said, "With eighty-one percent of the precincts reporting, it looks like the decision in Ohio will be a thin margin for President Kierkstra. In the other battleground states—Michigan, Wisconsin, and Florida—the situation is similar. All of them are close, but not too close to call. All have gone for Kierkstra by a narrow margin. We could declare President Kierkstra the winner."

"Yes, Katie," said her expert, Firman. "But if Grant and Henderson are correct, these are the very states where investigation would show fraud."

"That's true."

"In other words, if the vote tallies are recounted, it is perfectly possible that Governor Harkinnon will be our next president."

Couric said, "This is an election that will not be decided tonight."

"Absolutely right, Katie."

B renda turned, sensing someone standing near her.

"Coop!" she said.

Cabot wore a perfectly cut dinner jacket. His eye color was different from Coop's, his carriage less casual, and the hair was combed differently. She wondered whether she would have recognized him at first glance, if she hadn't been prepared. She might have thought he was Coop's brother.

"Well, Cabot, actually," he said.

"I know."

She detected a slight downturn motion of his mouth, suggesting that he was disappointed not to have surprised her. His cold eyes gave nothing away. Very conscious that the media all around might be watching them, even getting them on video, she kept smiling, even though her knees trembled and she felt waves of nausea.

"As a matter of fact," she said, "I've known for some time."

"Oh," he said.

Brenda expected him to be angry that she had deceived him. But his face was smooth and worry-free. He cocked his head. "So that's why you came on to me," he said.

I came on to him? Brenda felt the breath leave her

body. How divorced from reality was he? She studied his face, keeping a slight smile on her lips so that any photographer who was filming them would have a boring shot. Inside she was raging.

He said, "I'm willing to forgive this move you've made tonight. You just need to tell them you attacked the voting program for personal reasons."

He's mad, she thought. No, he isn't. Not really. He's insanely arrogant. He really thinks he can turn all this around just by turning me around.

"They'll believe you."

"It's too late, Cabot. Way too late."

"And you know what? You know what I'll do for you?"

Brenda couldn't speak.

"You know," Cabot said, smiling benignly, "if you do, I would even be willing to marry you."

A single voice rose above the crowd noise. His angry shouts grew to bellows. The crowd roar diminished to a hum, to the near silence of apprehension.

The pandemonium was behind the scenes somewhere, but it suddenly erupted onto the platform. The curtained backdrop parted and the President of the United States appeared in front of the lectern and its microphones. His face was red, his tuxedo disheveled. He shook off the entourage of nervous Secret Service men and worried campaign workers. The television reporters swung their cameras around to him.

"Where is he?" screamed the president. "Where is that shit Cabot? He promised me. He promised me!"

A stunned silence followed, pierced by another

scream from the platform. The president was close to the microphones. They picked up his too loud, too high voice and turned it to an agonizing electronic squeal, but not before the crowd saw him turn to the corner where Brenda and Cabot stood. They heard the president shriek, "There you are, you—"

The amplified feedback masked the noise as the one man in the country who was never subjected to a security search pulled a gun out of his pocket. In front of a dozen TV cameras, before the stunned Secret Service could react, the President of the United States fired on his dear friend Alexander Cabot.

CHAPTER 39

Thanksgiving Day
New York City

Brenda pulled up and parked in front of Nate and Daniel's brownstone. She got out of the car and reached back in for the big dome-covered pie pan. By then, Daniel had seen her and was opening the door.

Nate, standing behind him, said, "What's the dessert?"

"Black bottom pie with chocolate ganache filling and cocoa whipped cream drizzled with dark chocolate."

"Brenda, I think you win the chocolate prize."

Brenda entered the hall. "No! I don't want to win."

"Why not?"

"I want the competition to go on forever."

Taking the dessert, Daniel said, "Come on in."

"Wow. Things certainly look better than the last time I was here."

"Yeah, I'll say." A young guy came from the kitchen down the hall.

"Brenda, this is my nephew, Drew. I don't remember whether you've met."

"Hi, Drew." Brenda held out her hand. "I've heard a lot about you." She hoped she sounded upbeat. Almost everything she had heard was bad.

Nate asked Drew, "You saw the place before we cleaned it up?"

"Yeah. I came by and everything was all torn up."

"How did you get in?"

"Door wasn't locked. That guy was cleaning up for you."

"What guy?"

"Just a guy."

"Drew," Daniel said firmly. "Pay attention. Please describe him for us."

"Like maybe my height. Twenty-five maybe."

"Hair color?" Daniel asked.

"Red. Like blond. Skinny guy. Wore round glasses. Like pictures of John Lennon."

"Malcolm Dudley!" Brenda said.

"Malcolm Dudley, and he was here looking for something," Daniel said.

He and Brenda looked at each other.

"So he's the spy," Brenda said. "Not Helen."

"Thank god," Daniel said.

"But he applied and interviewed before we ever met Cabot."

"It was before you visited Sarah's office. Right?"

Daniel said. "But her PDA probably showed she had an appointment with you, right?"

"Oh. Yes."

"Drew is helping me make Thanksgiving dinner," Nate said, as they sat in the living room drinking a cocktail Nate had invented. It involved rum, sparkling water, and raspberries.

"Are you living here now, Drew?" Brenda asked.

"No," said Drew.

"No," said Daniel.

"No," said Nate. They were like a chorus.

"I'm going back to Mom's place tomorrow."

"To get a job," Daniel said.

"Maybe," said Drew.

"Weren't you living in a . . . um . . . commune, Drew?" Brenda asked.

"Yeah, but they wanted me to do dishes."

"When is the Andrews news conference?" Brenda asked.

"Six," Daniel said.

"Who's Andrews?" asked Drew.

"The vice president of your country, Drew," Daniel said. "And President Kierkstra's running mate. And maybe even our next president, since Kierkstra is under indictment."

"Oh. I would have voted for him."

"For Kierkstra? You would, but you couldn't. You're sixteen."

"Well, I would've if I could've," Drew said.

Brenda and Daniel took their cocktails over to the window to watch the snow. Daniel put his arm around

Brenda, who said, "Danny, I just don't see Sarah writing that patch. She wasn't a crook."

"My guess is she wrote in the glitch and the hook under orders and then started to get suspicious."

"She was bright. She would have flagged that."

Nate got up.

"Okay. You two get to the table. Drew and I are going to serve the dinner."

They brought in mashed potatoes, gravy, freshly made cranberry sauce, sweet potatoes, peas cooked with mint leaves, and a big, well-browned turkey.

"I basted it with melted butter," Drew said.

"I made the side dishes," Nate said, "but Drew cooked the turkey all by himself."

Daniel picked up the carving knife and fork. Nate said, "I saw the stuffing in the refrigerator, Drew. Didn't you want to use it?"

"Didn't need it."

"Why not?"

"The turkey wasn't empty."

After several beats of silence, Daniel said, "Well, I'm sure all the outside parts will be perfectly delicious."

They grouped around the TV at six. On-screen were the flags, the paneled walls, the massed microphones, the backs of reporters. A scene very familiar, but this time unique.

Portentously, an announcer said, "The vice president of the United States."

Conrad Andrews entered somberly. He was a strikingly handsome man, white-haired and of upright bearing.

"My fellow Americans," he said, "I will not keep you long from your Thanksgiving dinners.

"Since the sad emotional breakdown of our beloved President Kierkstra, we have all known that it would not be possible for him to hold office, no matter what the results of the balloting.

"The counting of the ballots has gone forward, however, and I come here today to make an announcement. Even though there are still some disputed precincts across the nation, the result is clear. I am here today to concede the election.

"Your next president will be Governor Evan Harkinnon. God bless America."

We were very fortunate in the recent presidential election not to have serious questions raised about the validity of the vote count. In past decades, voting fraud was local and on a small scale—interfering with people getting to the polls, miscounting, filing votes from the deceased. Now, with the increased use of computer-based vote counting, we are at risk for election fraud on a huge scale.

Forge

*Award-winning authors
Compelling stories*

. . . .

Please join us at the website
below for more information
about this author and other great
Forge selections, and to sign up for
our monthly newsletter!

. . . . www.tor-forge.com . . . .